Sandpipers

RAVEN'S MARK

JADE ARCHER

Raven's Mark
ISBN # 978-0-85715-977-9
©Copyright Jade Archer 2012
Cover Art by Lyn Taylor ©Copyright January 2012
Interior text design by Claire Siemaszkiewicz
Total-E-Bound Publishing

Published in 2012 by Total-E-Bound Publishing, Think Tank, Ruston Way, Lincoln, LN6 7FL, United Kingdom.

Total-E-Bound Publishing is an imprint of Total-E-Ntwined Limited.

RAVEN'S MARK

Dedication

For Ian and for all the 'Ravens' out there. May you find strength and peace in the people that love you.

Prologue

With a tired sigh, Raven pulled into a vacant parking space and stared up at the stark white facade of the optimistically named 'Oceanview Apartments' building. A dozen blocks back from the sea there wasn't much chance of an ocean view, but right now Raven couldn't have cared less. After weeks of aimlessly wandering and purposely backtracking, doing battle with a geriatric hatchback and more unpleasant rest-stops than he ever wanted to recall, he was exhausted. He just wanted somewhere safe and secure to settle and start again. He sincerely hoped apartment twenty-one of the building in front of him would be that place.

Admittedly, it had looked more impressive on the website. In real life, the structure wasn't anywhere near as stately or pristine as the images suggested. Here and there small signs of wear and tear marred the weathered exterior, and from front on, instead of the more flattering side angle the apartment rental site had used, the whole thing looked rather squat and dated. But then that was usually how these things worked in his experience—reality was always just a little less bright and sparkling than advertised.

Seconds later, Raven had to amend his cynical thoughts. Above the faded red roof tiles, the sky was a perfect blue. No amount of Internet research prior to making the gruelling drive from Chicago had prepared him for the Southern California sky. Today there wasn't a cloud to break the pale blue expanse that seemed to go on forever. It was breathtaking.

Finally dragging his eyes away, Raven continued to check out the building and surrounds. While definitely older, it looked solid enough. Along the front, the tall, thin trunks of a row of palm trees were lined up like soldiers guarding the entrance. Their rough, shaggy crowns towering high above cast splotches of shade across the front of the building. Even at ten in the morning, the summer sun was strong and bright. It would be interesting to see what the temperature was like inside. Raven noticed the grass was a vibrant green against the white of the sidewalk. The grounds were obviously well-tended. That was a good sign.

"Is this where we're going to live now, Daddy?" Ryan, his four-year-old son and reason for making it out of bed each day, asked from the backseat.

"M-maybe."

"Is there a swimming pool?"

"N-no. Sorry, buddy."

"Okay."

The lack of emotion in Ryan's voice bothered Raven. He suspected most kids would have whined, or commented, or...or something. But Ryan just stared out the window.

The caregiver at the last day care centre Ryan attended up until recently had expressed 'concerns' regarding Ryan's social skills and lack of engagement with others. They'd left Chicago not long after, but the comments troubled Raven more and more. They really needed to make friends or people might start asking questions. Worse still, they might find answers and decide he was an unfit parent and take Ryan away from him and…

"So w-what do you think? Do you l-like it?" he asked, desperately fighting down the spiralling panic attack closing in on him.

"Uh huh."

"You w-want to see inside?"

As he looked up into the rear-view mirror he saw Ryan nod, but his son's expression remained unreadable. Swallowing down the lump forming in his throat, Raven struggled against the inner voice that told him once again he sucked as a father.

"Okay. We're just w-waiting for the property m-manager and we can go have a l-look."

A fresh wave of fear washed over Raven at the mere thought. His heart began to pound, there was the familiar white-noise-like rush of blood in his ears and his palms started to sweat. He really wasn't looking forward to the meeting. In fact, he'd give just about anything to get out of it. But it was a necessary evil if he wanted to rent an apartment.

He took a deep breath and tried to calm his runaway nerves. Fortunately, with the help of the Internet, he'd narrowed it down to two possibilities — two places they could pretty much move into straightaway. Which was a good thing — they couldn't afford to waste any more of their money on motels, and two appointments like this were about his limit.

"There's a playground," Ryan said.

"M-Maybe there are kids your age h-here."

He studied Ryan in the mirror, hoping to get more of a response, or at least some idea of what was going on in his son's head as the little boy continued to stare at the swings, slides, and bright red climbing frame just visible, tucked in against the side of the building. The opportunities to get out and about in Chicago had been few and far between for various reasons. His own fears and difficulties in dealing with other people certainly hadn't helped. But here in sunny California things would be different. He'd make sure they were. If nothing else, it was a relief to see Ryan taking an interest.

"Do you think you'd like to l-live here?"

"Uh huh."

It would have been nice to hear more of what Ryan thought of the place, but a vehicle pulling up a few spaces away instantly caught Raven's attention. A slim woman with blonde hair pulled back in a tight bun got out. Her short black skirt, black tailored jacket and crisp white blouse contrasted painfully with the promise of another beautiful, hot summer day.

She tucked a portfolio under one arm, locked her car with the push of a button and stepped up onto the sidewalk, looking left and right before turning to face the street. Every instinct told Raven this was the property manager he'd been waiting for and he should get out and meet her. But his muscles were locked tight, pinning him in place.

He watched her glance down at her wrist and check her watch. Her expression grew pinched with exasperation before she looked back up and scanned the street again. She looked out of place in the neighbourhood that, while quiet and reasonably neat, was a million miles away from suit-and-tie. It only served to make her look even more intimidating.

Raven gripped the steering wheel until his knuckles blanched white. He knew he had to get out of the car. If he didn't meet the woman and jump through the final hoops, he wasn't going to secure a place for them to live. But he couldn't seem to move.

"Daddy, can we get out?"

With every ounce of courage and determination he possessed, Raven unbuckled his seatbelt. He had the feeling, as long as there were no rats, meth labs or gaping holes in the floor, they'd take this one. He couldn't face doing this again.

"Sure th-thing, b-buddy. I think that's the l-lady we're supposed to m-meet."

Raven bit back another sigh. It was going to be a really long morning.

Chapter One

Eight months later

Mark wiped his hands on a clean dishcloth and cast a professional eye around the kitchen of Sandpipers Restaurant. Dave put the finishing touches to the fruit salad, Andy whisked batter for pancakes, and Brody had already started on the clean-up. Everyone looked busy, but their movements were organised and controlled. The heat from the ovens, the clatter of pans and the sound of fast, efficient mixing filled the space. Yet it was an industrious, productive cacophony that soothed something deep inside Mark—a need for order and direction.

Unfortunately, he couldn't relax and lose himself in the rhythm of the kitchen. Not yet.

"Did you get the prawns shelled and deveined, Brody?"

They'd added prawn omelette to the brunch menu this week. It would be a disaster if they were somehow forgotten in the rush.

"Yep."

"The pastries all ready to go, Dave?"

"Uh-huh."

As Mark turned his head, Andy fixed him with a dark look and continued to whisk the pancake batter vigorously—as if daring Mark to even ask if he'd forgotten anything.

Mark knew he was probably coming across as an overbearing asshole...again. But he needed to check everything was ready. As the executive chef, it was his head if things went wrong.

Allowing a small nod of approval, Mark started towards the doors that separated the kitchen from the dining area. Experience had taught him good preparation now meant less chance of things descending into chaos later. If he came across as a fussy prick while making sure everything was done right, so be it.

Fortunately, everything in the kitchen looked tight and ready to go for another busy Sunday morning brunch. But Mark knew he wouldn't be able to relax until he'd done the rounds.

"I'm going to check out front. Finish up and take a break before the rush, guys."

"Will do," Brody called as he dumped another dirty bowl in the clean-up area.

Dave raised his knife in mock salute. "Aye, aye, Captain!"

A snort of laughter at Dave's antics was Andy's only acknowledgement. Which was fine—Andy was taciturn, but a damn hard worker. And that was all that counted in Mark's book.

As he pushed his way through the doors, Mark had to admit they were a good team. He'd caught a lucky break picking up the head chef's position here six weeks ago. No prima donnas. No bullies or egotistical assholes making everybody's life a misery. They all just got on with the job. It was a nice change from some of the kitchens he'd worked in.

Entering the dining room, Mark took a moment to check everything out on the 'elegant' side of the kitchen doors. The wait staff were all bustling about in a last minute rush to put the finishing touches to the room, but no one appeared flustered or distressed. There was just the steady dull clunk of cutlery and glassware being laid on crisp white linen and a low babble of chatter punctuated by the occasional burst of laughter. Everything seemed to be under control and on schedule out here too.

A band of tension he hadn't realised he'd been carrying around eased across his shoulders and the tight, wound up feeling at his core loosened slightly. Wandering through the room—continuing to examine the last minute preparations with a critical eye as he went—Mark finally allowed himself to relax. It looked like they were ready.

Settling on one of the bar stools to take a break while he could, Mark swiped the soft cotton bandana from his head. He scrubbed his hand through the short strands of his hair, then hunched his shoulders and rolled his head from side to side to ease the muscles in his neck.

Last night had been a fairly standard Saturday night—busy, in other words. He barely felt as though he'd crawled into bed before he was getting right back up to do it all again. Shifts like that made even thirty-three feel ancient. But then, mornings really weren't his thing either.

Gazing out through the long panels of glass on the far side of the room, Mark could already see small knots of people out and about enjoying a lazy stroll along the esplanade. While technically still winter, it was so late in the season and such a mild morning on the cusp of an early spring, the crowds were building early. Soon they'd be looking for a place to 'do brunch' and the fun would really start.

Mark rubbed at his tired eyes. At least the restaurant was closed tomorrow. They could all enjoy a day off and get some much needed rest. Still, one day it would be nice if *his* Sunday mornings were about sleeping in and long lazy walks with a lover and afternoon naps and—

"Coffee?"

Glancing back over his shoulder, Mark came face to face with Jaime's smiling face. But it was the coffee pot in her hand that really got his attention.

"Please," he groaned pitifully, only partly in jest.

Jaime's lips twitched and her blue-grey eyes sparkled as she poured the strong, black liquid pick-me-up into a mug. "Not a morning person?"

"It's showing, huh?"

"Just a bit." Jaime set the mug down and pushed a sugar bowl and milk jug towards him.

"Thanks."

"Welcome. You all ready to go back there?"

"Yep. How about you?"

"I was born ready, honey," Jaime quipped with a little toss of her head that sent her ponytail dancing.

Jaime was unofficially in charge of the wait staff. A kind of second-in-command over the front of house to Lark—one of the owner-managers. She'd proven herself on more than one occasion to be cool, calm and capable in a crisis. Mark liked her a lot.

He smiled at her saucy reply. She really was quite beautiful—with long blonde hair pulled back neatly from the pale oval of her face and soft pink lips. It was just a pity he didn't swing that way. Then, of course, there was the little matter of—

"Hey, you got some sugar for me too, Jaime?" Dave called as he stepped out of the kitchen and ambled towards them—all masculine confidence and loose-limbed, self-assured stride. But Mark didn't miss the narrow-eyed glare the sous chef shot his way.

"In your dreams," Jaime chuckled as she reached for more mugs.

Andy—a few inches taller and narrower than Dave—wasn't far behind his best friend. He smiled and winked as he retrieved his mug from Jaime. "Thank you, beautiful."

Jaime blushed very prettily, which Mark was sure was exactly what Andy had intended. But then she tilted her head, a little frown of concern furrowing her normally smooth brow. "You look tired, Andy. Are you okay?"

Now that Jaime had pointed it out, Mark could indeed see dark rings under Andy's eyes and a slightly pale cast to his skin.

"I'm fine," Andy mumbled, hiding in his mug by taking a sip of coffee.

Dave stared at Andy as if seeing his friend for the first time and scowled as he picked up his own coffee. "We've got to get some more people in that kitchen, Mark. This is getting ridiculous."

Dave continued to watch Andy over the rim of his mug as he drank. But Andy refused to meet his friend's eyes.

Interesting.

"Zak's interviewing for another chef as soon as he gets back from the conference in San Francisco." Mark hoped the promise of help being on the way soon would be enough to hold them. The last thing he needed was resentment in the kitchen ranks because they thought no one was listening to them. And he had to agree that an extra set of hands to lighten the load would be very welcome.

"When's he due back?" Jaime asked as she fixed herself a cup of coffee.

"The end of the week, I think."

With that, everyone settled back into various it's-too-early-in-the-morning-for-this   postures — leaning against the bar as they concentrated on their caffeine hit and the last moments of quiet before the storm of Sunday brunch.

Suddenly, Dave let out an irritated huff as he focused on something over Jaime's shoulder, drawing everyone's attention to the restaurant's front doors.

"Can't people read?" he grumbled as he lowered his head in disgust. "The sign says we're not open for another forty minutes."

Mark glanced up, expecting to see a gaggle of tourists trying their luck at getting in early, and ended up staring at one of the most striking men he'd ever laid eyes on. And he'd been looking for a good chunk of the last two decades.

The man's collar-length hair shone a glossy black in the sunlight. His short, slim figure, perfectly encased in a simple black T-shirt and jeans, highlighted sleek muscles and a trim waist. But it was his face that really caught Mark's eye. He had the kind of angular, high cheekboned features and full kissable lips that would make top models green with envy.

He definitely deserved a 'wow' and a second look, and probably got them all the time. But instead of the easy, self-assured air Mark expected to see from such a stunning guy, the man looked almost nervous as he hovered indecisively on the other side of the glass. It was an intriguing dichotomy that instantly got Mark's attention.

Then he noticed the small boy clutching the man's hand.

Typical. Contrary to popular belief, most good-looking guys were either taken or *straight*. Usually both. At least they were in Mark's experience.

Meanwhile, Jaime looked over her shoulder, following their collective gazes to the front door. "Oh, hey! They're here."

Hurrying around the bar, she rushed to open the door.

"Who's that?" Andy murmured in a voice that held a touch more than casual interest as he stared at the dark-haired stranger.

Mark raised an eyebrow. He hadn't realised Andy would notice the man in more than a why-is-he-interrupting-my-break way. He'd watched Andy and Dave angling after Jaime ever since he'd arrived. But now that he thought about it, the pair didn't seem to *compete* for her attention, more…tag team. Like a well-rehearsed and long-practiced dance.

Mark looked between Andy and Dave. There was probably a very interesting story there. The activity at the door, however, soon got his attention back on the fascinating stranger again.

"Hey, Raven. Hi, Ryan," Jaime enthused as she ushered the pair in and locked the door behind them.

"Hello, Miss Jaime," the little boy replied in a soft, polite voice.

The dark-haired man ducked his head, his pale cheeks turning bright red. "I'm s-sorry. Lark said to come to the f-front door."

"It's fine, honey. Come on in and I'll introduce you. I'm sure Lark will be right down. Guys, this is Raven. And this handsome young man is his son, Ryan." Jaime ruffled the little boy's dark hair playfully, then introduced each of them in turn. "This is Andy, Dave and Mark."

While the general chorus of hey, hi and how-ya-doing ensued, Mark discreetly checked for a wedding band. Nope. And no mark where one had been recently either. He was somewhat of an expert on long distance, covert wedding ring checks. If he had to guess, he'd say single dad. Not that it helped him in the grand scheme of things.

Then he caught Raven staring back—his glorious brown eyes so damn beautiful, framed by long dark lashes, but somehow managing to look rather sad and...evasive as they were quickly lowered away. The look did funny things to Mark's stomach. A fluttering, excited jitter. He wanted to make the sadness and apprehension in Raven's eyes go away and fan the tiny spark of interest he'd seen there instead. To see where things might go.

Mark sighed. He wasn't going to overanalyse the sudden spike of protectiveness he felt. He was too busy enjoying the fact his initial assessment might have been wrong and the churn of excitement that thought induced. If only he could get the obviously shy Raven to look at him again.

"You want me to go track down Lark for you, Jaime?" Andy asked.

"Thanks, Andy. I think he's upstairs in the apart—"

But before Jaime could finish the sentence, Lark bounced into the room, a laughing Wolf hot on his heels as they finished off some sort of impromptu dance out of the kitchen area.

"Hey, Raven! Hiya, Ryan!" Lark called as he spotted them and headed towards the bar. "It's good to see you."

"Ryan!" Wolf yelled as he raced ahead and grabbed Ryan by the hand to drag him away. "Come and see the fish tank."

After watching the boys wind their way through the tables to the huge aquarium with an indulgent smile, Lark turned to Raven. "Thank you so much for agreeing to look after Wolf today. Our regular sitter couldn't make it and with Zak away—"

"Lark! Can I show Ryan out on the deck?" Wolf called, still tenaciously clutching Ryan's hand as he pulled him towards the door leading outside.

"Sure buddy, just don't get in Eve and Drew's way." Once again Lark focused on Raven. "Are you still okay to take care of Wolf after preschool this week? Brody's supposed to start at the community college, but we forgot about Zak being away for this management conference thing."

Raven nodded, not meeting anyone's eyes. "Ryan likes p-playing with Wolf."

"Oh! You're a life saver. Brody wants to go to culinary school," Lark announced proudly, "but he's all stressed out about going back to get his high school equivalent so he can apply. The last thing he needs is an excuse not to go."

"Hey!" Brody said as he pushed through the kitchen doors, but his indignant tone was belied by the grin on his face and the affectionate way he wrapped an arm around Lark as soon as he was within reach. "I heard that."

"And?" Lark replied, raising an imperious blond eyebrow at his lover.

"I'm not stressed out."

"Yeah, right," Lark snorted, then smiled to soften the blow.

Brody bumped his hip in a playful reprimand.

Mark couldn't help staring. He wondered what it would be like to find that kind of comfortable intimacy with a lover. He'd never really had the time to devote to a relationship in the past—too busy with family and struggling his way up the kitchen food-chain. One-nighters and casual hook-ups had been the order of the day...when and if he could find the time for them. But now that he'd made head chef, had a place of his own and a nice little nest egg idling away in the bank, he found himself drawn to the idea of something more. Without conscious thought, his gaze settled back on Raven...who looked like he was trying to disappear into the large potted palm at the end of the bar.

Brody turned from smiling down at Lark to fix Raven with a serious expression. "I do want to say thank you though, Raven. I was always lousy at school. I need all the help I can get."

Raven stared at his feet as if he hoped the restaurant floor would open up and swallow him whole. His cheeks were stained a dark red now as everyone's eyes focused in on him and a thin sheen of perspiration formed at his temples, despite the room being pleasantly cooled by the ocean breeze. But nobody else seemed to notice Raven's distress—they were all too distracted by Lark's antics as he gave Brody a hard nudge with his hip and sent his partner stumbling a little to one side.

"You, Brody McAllister, are brilliant," Lark said with complete confidence and a firm no-nonsense tone as he pulled Brody back against his side. "You're going to blitz those exams."

"If you say so."

"I do. Now" — Lark made a show of scanning around the room—"where are those boys? We'll take you all up to the flat and get you settled in before we open."

"Wolf!" Brody called out across the restaurant to his brother, who was busy pointing out a flock of noisy gulls over the railing to his friend.

Only Mark saw Raven flinch at the sudden loud shout.

"You should find everything you need in the apartment, but if anything comes up or something happens just call down to the restaurant and one of us will come straight up," Lark said as he watched Wolf towing Ryan along in his wake through the sea of tables and chairs.

Raven nodded, but otherwise remained completely silent and still.

Mark couldn't help but wonder what the man's story was. There had to be one. He was so handsome and yet so very insecure and reticent. Was it a result of the mild stammer he'd detected earlier, or was there something more? What had happened to put the hesitant, nervous look in Raven's eye? Mark found he really wanted to know. But more than that, he really wanted to make it better. Even for him—a chronic fixer with a compulsive hero complex—the reaction was extreme and powerful. Something about Raven called to him.

"You ready to show Ryan upstairs?" Lark asked Wolf when the boys finally stopped in front of him.

"Yep!" Wolf grinned up at the adults, apparently supremely confident and comfortable with his audience. "Can we make a tent in the living room and have a picnic?"

"I don't know, you'll have to ask Raven. He's looking after you for the day."

Wolf immediately turned his attention to Raven. "Please! Please, please, please!"

Raven looked cornered as the boy bounced up and down on the spot enthusiastically. "S-sure," he finally stuttered.

Wolf crowed with excitement. "Yay! Come on, Ryan."

Lark chuckled as Wolf took off, heading for the back door and the flight of external stairs that led up to the apartment above the restaurant. "That kid is a force to be reckoned with when he sets his mind to something."

"Wait at the door!" Brody shouted after the boys.

"You guys sure are going to have your hands full with that one in a few years," Jaime laughed.

Dave snorted. "Looks like they've already got their hands full to me."

"Oh, yeah!" Brody agreed, but with a smile that suggested he loved every energetic inch of his little brother.

"Don't worry about the mess they make, Raven," Lark said. "We've got tomorrow to get everything back in order. Just as long as there's no bloodstains on the carpet, we're cool."

Raven blanched.

"He's kidding." Brody elbowed Lark. "Don't scare our sucker...I mean sitter...off."

The wan smile on Raven's face spoke volumes. It was obvious he was floundering. Mark wished Lark and Brody would stop cracking jokes. Unfortunately, it wasn't his place to step in, and even if he did, he wasn't sure it wouldn't just make things worse for the obviously shy man.

"Oh! Such a bully!" Lark said as he rubbed at his ribs theatrically and stepped away from Brody.

"Yeah, yeah. You're so hard done by," Brody drawled, turning Lark around and giving him a gentle push in the right direction. "Come on. We better catch up to the boys before they get bored. Then we really would be in trouble!"

As Brody and Lark headed out after the passionate pre-schooler and his more reserved friend, Raven trailed along behind. Mark really wanted to reach out to Raven. To touch him, or at least introduce himself. But it didn't seem the time.

At least it looked like Raven was coming back again—he'd promised to bring Wolf home after preschool in the coming week. Mark would just have to make sure an opportunity arose to say hello. Getting Raven to talk back might be somewhat of a Herculean task, but he'd cross that bridge when he came to it.

Resigned to playing the waiting game, Mark was shocked when, at the last second before disappearing into the kitchen, Raven turned and looked directly at him with soft, dark brown eyes. Caught out, Raven blushed fiercely and hurried away.

Oh, yeah! He definitely needed to say hello.

Chapter Two

Two weeks later

Raven breathed in. Then he breathed out. Then he repeated the process and tried very hard not to think about what he was about to do.

Walking the final three steps to the front door of Brody, Lark and Zak's apartment had been hard, but he'd managed it. Ringing the bell was just an extension of that. Really.

It was just a kid's birthday party. Children and maybe a few parents and — *No! Don't think about it!* — the strangers and their questions and the looks as he struggled to get words out. The eyes that seemed to see right into his deepest, most shameful secrets.

All he had to do was walk to the door. Ring the bell. Wait for the door to open and say —

Okay, he was getting ahead of himself again. He could feel the panic rising up from his belly, squeezing his heart and making it hard to breathe.

Stop!

Breathe in. Breathe out.
Relax.

He'd come this far, he could make it the next few inches to the buzzer.

Beside him, Ryan gripped his hand a little tighter as they hovered at the threshold. It gave Raven the final push he needed to depress the innocuous little button that had almost defeated him. It also gave him something else to focus on as the muffled chime sounded on the other side of the door, drawing him away from the spiralling fear racing through his system and threatening to overwhelm him.

The little hand in his was all that mattered. He had to hold it together for Ryan's sake. With every breath in his body he was determined his son would grow up healthy, strong and...normal.

Raven shifted nervously in place. *Damn!* Talk about setting himself up for the task of the century. He didn't even know what normal looked like anymore. He wouldn't know it if it walked up to him, smacked him upside the head and started lecturing him on how far away from ever being normal he was.

Breathe in. Breathe out.

"Do you think Wolf will like my present, Daddy?"

Raven looked down at the serious little face tilted up to regard him with big brown eyes. The only indication Ryan was just as nervous about coming to Wolf's party as Raven was the way he clung to him fiercely, his hand white-knuckle tight around Raven's fingers. Other than that, Ryan's expression was completely blank and bland. He was already so good at hiding everything deep inside.

And Raven absolutely hated it.

Leaning over, Raven made sure he looked the little boy right in the eye. "You worked very h-hard on Wolf's gift, Ryan. You did well."

Shit. That didn't sound right. Was that what a father said to ease his child's mind? Did it work?

Ryan studied him for a few seconds, before nodding his head—expression still serious, but accepting. Raven breathed a sigh of relief. Another test passed. For now. Maybe.

Suddenly, the door swung open and Zak's huge, broad-shouldered frame filled the doorway. Raven straightened and locked his knees—it was the only way he managed to hold his ground.

They'd met Zak a few times now—coming and going from preschool and when Ryan had been invited over to play—but the big man was still incredibly intimidating. Only his clear, light green eyes and gentle expression helped to stave off Raven's descent into true, debilitating terror. He sensed that Zak would never hurt him. Hell, intellectually he knew most people wouldn't. Unfortunately the instinct and knowledge that told him to be calm was doing battle with years of experience. And the contradictory messages were messing him up completely.

Thankfully, Zak was focused on Ryan at the moment, giving Raven time to compose himself.

"Hello, Ryan. Come in, we're just getting started." Ryan held up the present he'd so very carefully chosen and wrapped to the big man. But Zak simply smiled and stepped back. "It's okay. Why don't you go in and give it to Wolf? He's in the living room."

Raven was so grateful the present hadn't been whisked away he almost sighed with relief. He really wanted Ryan to give the gift to Wolf himself. He was desperate for the boys to connect. Wolf was the only one Ryan had responded to with even a tentative attempt at friendship since they'd arrived in Riversands over eight months ago. So far things had been going well between the two of them, but it never hurt to reinforce the success with a little gift giving.

As he watched Ryan walk hesitantly down the hallway he held his breath—well aware this was the point at which it could go either way. The noisy, rambunctious sounds of young children playing seemed to stop Ryan for a moment, but finally he took the plunge and moved into the living room.

A swell of pride filled Raven as he watched his son disappear. He knew exactly how hard that had been for Ryan.

Glancing up, Raven noticed Zak watching him with a curious expression he couldn't quite read. It looked like it was his turn to be brave.

"Hi." He had to force the word out of his suddenly desert-dry mouth. And still it came out far too soft.

Raven winced deep inside. He hated when he sounded weak and pathetic. Unfortunately, it happened all too frequently. He just couldn't make his vocal cords work like he wanted them to when he talked to other people.

"It's nice to see you again, Raven." Zak held out his hand to shake and Raven managed to return the gesture, albeit somewhat awkwardly.

Damn! He needed something to say. Something to fill the gap. He remembered the relief he'd felt that nobody was hurt when an intruder had broken into the family's apartment a few weeks earlier. The details were vague, but apparently he'd been some fanatic with an axe to grind when Zak and Lark had added

Brody to their relationship and formed a ménage á trois.

"I...umm...I h-heard what happened...in the paper...with the guy that tried to... I just wanted to say...glad you're okay."

Well that hadn't gone too well. Raven felt his cheeks heat with shame.

Why can't you get even one simple sentence right?

Even as the thought occurred, he felt his muscles tighten. Blast! The voice he'd heard in his head sounded hauntingly familiar—the sharp, claw-like hooks of criticism still raking him, every bit as capable of leaving him bruised and battered as the physical abuse ever had. And after he'd been so determined to put it all behind him, to not let the past control him anymore.

"Thanks," Zak said. "It could have been a lot worse. I'm just glad it didn't seem to have any long-term effects on Wolf."

Raven nodded, lowering his eyes. Yeah, no long-term effect on Wolf was good. He wanted to hope the same thing for Ryan, but he wasn't sure he had the right to. The guilt of how long it had taken him to get his act together, to be even half the man Ryan needed as a father, ate away at him every day.

Suddenly, Lark appeared—a bright, flamboyant distraction that was more than welcome, heading down the hallway towards them. It was strange, but Raven actually found himself relaxing a little as Lark approached. Normally, he'd be on tenterhooks waiting for something bad to happen at this point, but nothing about Lark was in any way threatening or frightening. Quite the opposite, in fact. Over the last couple of weeks of bringing Ryan over to play with Wolf, he'd actually found himself looking forward to seeing Lark. And Brody, too. He hoped—once he got to know him better—he'd be able to relax around Zak as well.

He wasn't exactly sure how it had happened. It had literally been years since he'd had a friend. Years since he'd been *able* to have one. But everything about Lark and Brody screamed...happy. It attracted Raven like nothing else could have. Not in a sexual way, although Brody and Lark were certainly handsome enough for him to notice. It was more something deep inside him that gravitated towards them—perhaps hoping some of their natural ease and contentment might rub off.

The really incredible thing was, Lark and Brody never treated him differently. They never looked at him like he was a moron when he stammered, or glanced away with pity or disgust when he got nervous or embarrassed. They just treated him...normally. It was wonderful.

"Hi, Raven. I'm so glad you could come," Lark announced with a dazzling smile Raven found himself returning, if somewhat tentatively. "Would you mind helping Mark in the kitchen for a second? I really think he could use a hand, but Zak and I need to get the games organised before the revellers revolt."

There was an ear-splitting squeal from the living room and Raven felt his heart race at the sound. He half expected Ryan to come flying out to him, but apparently his son was made of stronger stuff. Several loud thumps and another bout of high-pitched laughter, however, convinced Raven he needed to head straight to the kitchen. He didn't even feel like a coward as he hurried away, having seen the pained look on Zak's face. He was just damn grateful Lark had given him an out.

Moving down the hall, Raven let the delicious smell of food draw him along. He hadn't been up to eating before they'd left for the party, too nervous to force down more than a slice of dry toast all day. Now his stomach was telling him in no uncertain terms he was starving. His head felt thick and slow, like molasses on a cold day. The rich smell of tomato, herbs and the mouth-watering scent of bacon, fried onion and garlic called to him.

It wasn't until he'd stepped through the doorway that Lark's words finally registered. *Help Mark*…a stranger. Well, sort of a stranger. He knew Mark—had caught glimpses of him that were both unnerving and thrilling. The very notion of coming face to face with and actually *talking* to him, however, should have made him feel physically ill. Instead, all he could focus on as he stepped into the kitchen was the tight pair of faded blue jeans stretched across a deliciously firm ass bent over at the oven.

Raven felt a little flutter of excitement as he stared at the hard globes. Then the man turned around and the flutter turned into a vicious stab of lust that buried itself deep in his gut.

Short blond hair, piercing summer sky blue eyes, solid muscles packed under golden tanned skin that seemed to glow against the stark white of his T-shirt. Mark was…

No!

No, this couldn't happen.

Damn! Damn! Damn! Damn!

There were so many reasons he shouldn't be attracted to Mark—or indeed anyone—not the least of which was the fact he should be concentrating on raising Ryan. But apparently his body was bypassing all higher brain functions in favour of drooling and panting after the hottest guy he'd seen in a very long time.

* * * *

Mark bustled about putting the finishing touches to the party food. It wasn't exactly a challenge. In fact, he could have done it in his sleep. But he prided himself on perfect presentation and service every time, even for a five-year-old's birthday party. So he happily lost himself in the work. Besides, it helped keep his mind off why he was really here.

Raven. Beautiful, mysterious, devil's-own-job-to-pin-down Raven.

And he *had* tried.

Several times over the last couple of weeks, in fact, he'd tried to instigate a conversation with the man. But Raven always ducked away, completely focused and preoccupied with either bringing Wolf home from preschool or dropping off his son to play.

It didn't take a huge leap to figure out Raven was avoiding him. But his elusive behaviour only made Mark more determined to get to know the man behind the big brown eyes and timid attitude. Manipulating his way into helping out today had been a final desperate attempt to catch more than a fleeting glimpse of a dark head of hair as it vanished out the door again. And Lark had been only too happy to have an extra pair of hands. In fact, he'd seemed downright ecstatic.

Mark frowned. Maybe a little too ecstatic...which could be a worry. He hadn't known Lark long, but already he'd picked up on the fact Lark liked to be in the thick of things. Or put less politely, he was a meddler. Perhaps with the best of intentions — Lark

The warmth that he could feel radiating off Raven's skin.

If he leaned ever so slightly to the side they'd brush shoulders. Which was odd. He'd thought Raven was shorter.

Glancing down, he noticed the abnormally thick-soled boots on Raven's feet. They easily added a good inch or so to his height. Which meant Raven *would* be shorter than him by a few inches if he ever managed to get him naked. It was a decidedly caveman-like notion, but he couldn't help liking the idea. A lot.

Even as the salacious thought ran away with his imagination, Mark watched Raven follow his gaze down. Instantly, all the colour drained from Raven's face. He looked back up and the only description Mark could come up with was pure terror.

"I f-f-forgot," Raven whispered in horror. "I f-forgot to take my b-boots off."

"It's okay—"

"I'm s-sorry. I'm s-sorry."

Raven stumbled back, and Mark reached out to support him. But Raven only cringed away farther, ducking his head and raising his hands to protect himself.

With Raven struggling and panting for breath, Mark took a small step back, making sure to stay close enough to intervene if Raven started to fall, but not crowding him. "It's okay, Raven. Breathe. Just breathe."

"I didn't m-mean to," Raven said in a small, shaky voice that somehow managed to sound far away.

"You're okay, Raven. Look...I've got my boots on too. You shouldn't work in a kitchen without good shoes. Just breathe. Slow and easy. You're okay."

Raven looked white now, shaking and still struggling for breath. One hand clutched the front of his shirt over his heart, while the other reached out to steady himself against the counter.

Mark swallowed down his own anxiety and continued to talk, repeatedly reassuring Raven he was all right as he waited for it to be true.

Suddenly, Lark burst into the room. His usual energetic bounce disappeared in an instant when he spotted Raven. "Are you alright?"

"Raven's fine," Mark hurried to interject, shooting Lark a look over Raven's bowed head, hoping to cut the barrage of questions off. The last thing Raven needed to think about in the middle of a panic attack was whether or not he was all right. "He just needs somewhere quiet for a few minutes."

"Oh! Ah…sure. I…the study. Come down to the study, Raven."

Mark didn't want to leave Raven's side. Not like this. He tried not to hover, but at the same time he didn't want Lark to take Raven away either.

"The food's all ready to go. Do you think you could get it out to the kids while I sit with Raven for a bit?" he suggested quickly.

Lark eyed Raven for a second, then nodded. "Um…sure. I mean as long as Raven's okay with that."

Mark held his breath, desperately hoping Raven wouldn't send him away. It seemed to take forever, but finally Raven nodded—slightly erratically but a definite yes to letting him stay. It was enough of an answer for a firm punch of relief—infused with a little hope—to hit Mark in the solar plexus and for Lark to back away slightly.

"Okay then. Do you need anything?" Lark asked, still watching Raven closely and sounding reluctant to let him out of his sight.

"Not right now," Mark replied.

Zak's study was a quiet, restful room—a good choice for somewhere Raven could collect himself. But not if Lark was fussing and fretting over him.

Guiding Raven away without crowding him was tricky, but soon they were heading down the hall in the right direction.

"S-sorry," Raven whispered.

"Nothing to be sorry for. You back?" Mark asked.

"Yeah."

But Mark noticed Raven looked pale and clammy. And he was still struggling a little for breath, his hand still clenched in a fist over his heart. Mark had enough experience with his mother's panic attacks to recognise the symptoms and know that Raven wasn't quite out of the woods yet.

"You're doing fine," he continued to murmur.

After settling Raven on the couch, Mark sat beside him. And for a moment he wasn't sure what to do. He knew what he wanted to do. He wanted to reach out and take Raven's hand, to hold on until he was sure Raven really was going to be okay. It was a strong, slightly disconcerting compulsion, and he was pretty sure it would freak Raven right out if he followed through with it. Then, of course, there was the little voice that reminded him over and over again, *you really don't know jack about this guy.*

So instead he quietly talked nonsense—words and sentences he knew he'd never remember later—and tried not to think about how much he wanted to touch Raven right then. He couldn't help enjoying having Raven sitting beside him, however—so close and finally not running away. That was a pretty big deal in itself.

Finally, Raven seemed to calm. The trembling stopped. His breathing settled into a steady, slower rhythm.

"This happen often?" Mark asked quietly.

"No." Raven flushed with embarrassment and went to shift away. "S-s-sometimes."

"Hey. It's okay," Mark rushed to reassure, reluctant to let Raven go too far and even more reluctant to let him retreat in on himself again. Raven stared at him, his eyes wide and uncertain.

It was Mark's turn to feel the creeping heat of a blush rising up into his cheeks. He'd heard the little hint of desperation in his voice too, but he refused to look away. Not now that Raven was actually looking him in the eye.

"So what do you do? For a living, I mean," Mark blurted, hoping to get Raven talking and keep him where he was for just a little longer.

"I'm a freelance t-t-technical writer."

"Sounds interesting." Mark didn't have a clue what a freelance technical writer was, but at least Raven was talking. It was a big step forward, but he didn't want to push too hard.

Raven shrugged and looked away. "It can be. I m-mostly do software and data m-management work."

"So you work with computers?"

"Yeah. Sort of. I h-help people understand their way through the techno b-babble. Write manuals and reports. That sort of th-thing."

Which meant Raven was smart. Much smarter than he was—he'd barely made it through high school. Mark studied Raven. Even with his good looks and obvious intelligence, there was no air of superiority about him. Mark had the feeling Raven simply wasn't the type. And he liked that. It was unusual in his experience. Most of the smart, good looking guys he'd met knew it and had their heads firmly up their asses.

But just when he was working himself up to asking Raven what sort of things he liked to do when he *wasn't* busy being a technical writer—edging slowly towards finding a way to ask the shy man out—a small dark-haired head poked around the study door.

Ryan.

"Daddy?"

Immediately, Raven's entire demeanour changed. He straightened in his seat and squared his shoulders, seeming to pull himself together in an instant by sheer force of will. And as he opened his arms, Ryan flew into the embrace.

"Hey, Ryan. How ya d-doing, buddy?" Raven asked softly.

"Good."

The pair hugged fiercely, Ryan studying Mark with big brown eyes so like Raven's the entire time.

"Hello, Ryan," Mark said, hoping to break the ice.

"Hello."

"This is Mr..." Raven shifted nervously. "I'm s-sorry. I d-don't know your last name."

"Mark Carter. But Mark is fine."

Raven and Ryan both nodded.

"How long are we staying, Daddy?"

"Until f-five o'clock."

Ryan looked expectantly at Raven. "What does that look like?"

"I...ah...I h-haven't got my watch fixed yet," Raven replied, rubbing anxiously at his bare left wrist.

Mark held out his arm so Ryan could see the face of his beat up old Seiko.

"It's when the big hand is on the twelve and the little hand is on the five."

Ryan stared at the little second hand marking time around the watch face for a while, then reverently reached out to touch the scratched glass cover.

"Lots of minutes," he observed.

"Yep. Plenty of time to enjoy the party and play with your friends," Mark replied with a smile.

Ryan peeked up at him from under the heavy black fall of his fringe.

"Are you my daddy's friend?" the little boy whispered after a few seconds of intense scrutiny.

Mark stared over at a self-conscious Raven. "I'd like to be."

"Wolf is my friend."

"Yeah, I see you guys playing together all the time."

Ryan nodded. "I'd like Daddy to have a friend like Wolf. Would you like to play with my daddy?"

Raven's eyes went anime-wide with horror and his whole face turned an instant, fiery red. "Ryan! I-I... I-it's—"

Mark couldn't keep the laugh in to save himself. Oh, Ryan was precious. He loved the little boy already! "Yeah. I'd really like to get to know your dad. If that's okay with you."

Looking over at Raven again, Mark tried to convey just how serious he was. He knew Raven and Ryan were a package deal. It didn't bother him at all. In fact, he kind of liked the idea. Family was important. He liked what he saw when Raven and Ryan were together. A lot of guys he'd met didn't get it—too busy partying and enjoying themselves to understand why he'd hung around to help raise his brother and sister. The fact Raven had a son certainly didn't scare him off. After the tearaway twins, not much could.

He watched as wide-eyed realisation slowly crept into Raven's expression.

Mark smiled. He couldn't have planned this better if he'd tried.

"You're not allowed to hurt him. Friends don't hurt each other," Ryan suddenly blurted.

What the…?

"Ryan!" Raven looked mortified at his son's outburst.

As a sick sense of dread filled Mark, he felt the smile slip away from his face. He could tell by the way Ryan watched him — and Raven didn't — that something deep and dark was festering beneath the little boy's statement. He wondered what had happened in their lives to provoke such a comment.

"You're right. You don't hurt friends."

"Promise."

Mark crossed his heart solemnly. "Promise."

And if it was the last thing he ever did, he would keep that promise. He would never hurt Raven or his son. In fact, he wanted to make sure no one got the chance to hurt either of them ever again.

Chapter Three

With Ryan safely dropped off and settled in at preschool, Raven headed towards the waterfront. Stretching and warming tight muscles as he went, gradually increasing his heart rate and letting the rhythm of his footfalls take over, he slowly lost himself in building up to a run. At least that was the theory.

He ran every morning. The temptation to bury himself away and hide inside the vast, anonymous depths of the internet was too strong. In fact, if it wasn't for Ryan he probably would have succumbed long ago. But he couldn't let that happen. Ryan needed him. He had to get out and about and, if not mingle comfortably with others, at least not trap himself at home.

So he ran, letting his feet take him away and his mind clear step by heart-pounding step. Unfortunately, hard as he tried, he couldn't find any peace in the endorphin release and physical exertion today. Over and over again his mind replayed the embarrassment of Wolf's birthday party…in vivid, excruciating details that just wouldn't let him go.

He couldn't believe, on top of his stupid, tongue-tied, can't-get-a-damn-sentence-out-right stuttering, he'd had a panic attack. And as if that wasn't bad enough, he'd had it right in front of Mark. He was horrified with himself. He wanted to crawl away and hide and never come out again. And it had all started over something as stupid as forgetting to take off his boots at the door.

Damn it! He knew better. Shoes in the house had always been a big no-no. Of course, it was by no means the only trigger that would have brought a world of hurt down on him, but it was certainly one he knew better than to tempt. When he'd looked down at his feet and seen the thick rubber soles against the tiles, something had flipped inside him. He'd been right back there—getting pummelled and screamed at for daring to mess up the floors. And panic had been hard and fast on the heels of the flashback.

He felt so pathetic. Guys that had been to war zones had flashbacks. Not wimps that didn't have the balls to just get over it and move on.

Stop it! Stop it! Stop it!

Finally arriving at the boardwalk, Raven gritted his teeth and balled his hands into fists as he ran. All he needed was a chance…an *opportunity* to get on with it and eventually—just maybe—be normal. But he'd never manage it if he gave in to the negative thoughts and images swirling around in his head.

Pouring on the speed, he tried to drown the thoughts out—to smother the doubts and fears riding him hard. But try as he might, he couldn't shut them down or silence the little voice that wondered if he would ever manage to be a good role model and father to Ryan. Someone that could actually string more than three words together in a conversation and not feel the urge to run away the whole time.

Finally admitting defeat, Raven slowed to a walk and started his cool down routine. It wasn't going to happen today. He'd only done about half his usual distance but he knew from experience the loop that had started up in his mind would just continue to play over and over again. The only way to break it now was to do something different. Which was appropriate—he'd needed to do something different his whole life.

And finally I am!

Like a lifeline he clung to the realisation. He *had* started to change things—to make things better, for Ryan and for himself. He had a way to go yet, but he'd come an incredibly long way already—both physically and mentally. The move to Riversands had been the best thing he'd ever done for them. It was a fresh start—a chance at a new life far away from the memories of torment and abuse and never being quite good enough.

A little calm he'd never have been able to achieve even twelve months ago settled inside him. No, it wasn't going to be easy, but he could do it. Of course, just as he was shaking his limbs out and starting to feel better about the day, he spotted the very last person he needed to see right now...

Mark—his light grey T-shirt stained around the collar and pits with sweat, suggesting he'd just finished a run himself. He'd set one long, bronzed leg up on a bench to stretch out his thigh and calf muscles. Reaching forward to touch the toe of his runners emphasised his strong forearms and solid biceps. He looked magnificent set against the backdrop of bright morning sun and dark blue sea, and Raven noticed more than one set of eyes following Mark's every move as he continued to bend and stretch.

Raven wanted to groan in frustration. Unfortunately, just as he realised he should be getting out of sight rather than ogling the man's hard body, Mark looked up.

"Raven!" A huge grin lit up Mark's face as he strode across the boardwalk towards him.

Watching the smooth, confident strides, the way his tight T-shirt pulled across firm pectoral muscles and the dazzling smile that graced his strong, square-jawed face, a thrill of excitement laced with an equal measure of dread raced through Raven's body.

Okay, so maybe Mark wasn't the very last person he *wanted* to see. But he certainly wasn't someone that was going to make Raven feel settled and centred anytime soon.

"Hey! Raven! Fancy meeting you here."

"Um…yeah! H-hi." *Damn!* Raven wanted to kick himself. Smooth was so *not* his middle name. And watching Mark's body as he continued to shift from foot to foot and shake out his limbs certainly didn't help.

"Do you run here often?" Mark asked, then let out an easy chuckle. "Oh, wow! That sounded so lame. I didn't mean it like some sort of cheesy pickup line."

Raven felt familiar heat climb up his neck and fill his cheeks. "I…ah… I t-try to run here every m-morning."

"Yeah? I've only just started running again. Been getting kind of lazy and flabby since I started at Sandpipers."

Yeah, right! There wasn't a flabby inch on the man!

"Hey, I was just about to get a drink." Mark pointed to a small refreshments stall displaying rows of drinks and fruit under the shade of a brightly coloured beach umbrella. "You want one?"

Raven froze. He had absolutely no idea what to say. Or more specifically, he had no idea why Mark would be asking. Especially after yesterday's little debacle.

"I...um... I d-don't know."

"Please?"

"I'm not... I mean I'm n-not sure."

"Just a drink." Mark locked eyes with him, but instead of feeling intimidated and trapped, Raven found the steady gaze reassuring somehow...which only added to his confusion. "Come on, it's too nice a day to be heading home yet."

"Just...a drink?" Raven asked, battling doubt and insecurity. Much as he wanted to relax, maybe even trust Mark, neither came easily to Raven.

Mark smiled again and Raven felt the heat right up to the tips of his ears. Embarrassment and an odd, unexpected wash of pleasure fought for dominance inside him.

"Promise." Mark used his finger to draw a cross over his heart...just the way he'd done the day before when he'd made his promise to Ryan. "We can sit in the park."

As Mark pointed out the park across the road with its huge shade trees and convenient picnic shelters, Raven studied his face, looking hard for any hint that Mark was making fun of him or had some malicious intent. But there was no mockery. No spiteful glint in his eyes. There was just Mark staring back at him — open, honest, hopeful and maybe just a touch anxious, as if worried he might be knocked back.

Oddly enough, the touch of uncertainty was what gave Raven the extra shot of courage he needed.

"I-I think I'd l-like that."

Mark's expression—a potent mix of relief and delight—filled Raven up with a strange, warm pleasure from deep inside right through to the tiny hairs that stood up on his arms in heightened awareness.

"What would you like? My treat."

"Um…just w-w-water, please."

After paying the woman behind the stall and collecting two bottles of water, Mark led them across to the park and one of the bench seats sheltered from the sun under the sprawling branches of the trees.

"So, have you lived in Riversands long?" Mark asked, handing across one of the clear plastic bottles before cracking the lid on his own.

Raven watched, mesmerised as Mark tipped his head back and swallowed the water in long pulls, his throat muscles working in fascinating waves.

"No," Raven finally managed, distracted by a bead of sweat that trickled down the strong column of Mark's neck. "We…ah… We m-moved here about eight months ago. From Ch-Ch-Chicago."

Even as the last word finally slipped out, Raven wanted to bite his own careless tongue off. He hadn't planned on telling anyone where he'd come from. Ever. Just because he didn't want to have anything to do with his old life, didn't mean it wouldn't try to track him down and drag them back.

"Wow. That's a big move. You like it here?"

"Yes."

"You don't miss the windy city?"

Raven shook his head, hiding the fact his throat was too tight to answer by taking a sip of water. Every bad memory he had started there. From the first time he could remember being teased for stuttering to the bitterly cold morning he'd sneaked out of the house he'd been sharing with his drug and alcohol dependant brother. He'd packed up his dilapidated old hatchback and started driving, determined never to look back.

And with any luck the whole sordid, messy past would stay there, far away from him and Ryan.

"So how long were you in Chicago?"

"I g-grew up there." Desperately wanting to change the subject, Raven cleared his throat. "Why are you d-doing this?"

"Doing what?"

"This." Raven indicated the two of them sitting together with a wave of his hand. "Asking me to j-join you for a drink. T-talking to me."

Mark studied him for a moment, as though wondering if Raven was ready for the answer. "Honestly?"

Raven nodded but he still wasn't really prepared for Mark's reply.

"I like you."

Raven blinked.

"But—" Really and truly it didn't make sense to him. Mark was the kind of good-looking, self-assured man who would never have to go home alone if he didn't want to. Why pick out someone so obviously messed up to hang around with? "You d-don't even know me."

"No, but I want to."

The memory of Ryan asking Mark if he wanted to be his daddy's playmate, then warning Mark off hurting him, instantly filled Raven's mind. His face heated to scorching and he looked away, thoroughly humiliated.

"The truth is…I'm attracted to you, Raven."

Panic started to muscle in on the embarrassment. Suddenly, their little spot under the trees felt isolated instead of sheltering. He didn't do well with people that were attracted to him. Never had, from the 'uncle' whose hands had tended to wander inappropriately when no one was looking to his ill-fated marriage. It never ended well.

"Breathe, Raven. Just breathe." Mark reached out, but Raven was on his feet in an instant, backing away before the hand made contact.

"I c-can't do this. I just c-c-can't."

"Raven! Wait! Please, hear me out."

"No. Really. It's just n-not a good idea. For either of us."

"Why not?"

"Trust me. I'm not a good…p-prospect."

"What makes you say that?"

Raven just stared at him. He couldn't believe Mark even had to ask. Once again, he wondered if he was being made fun of. But he couldn't find any evidence of ridicule in Mark's eyes. They just watched him patiently — unblinking and terrifyingly sincere.

"I'm m-m-messed up."

"Well we're all messed up a bit somehow. But I can be patient. All I want is a chance. Let's just take things slow and see where they go."

A chance. The words hit home with a resounding thud that reverberated right through him. A chance was all he'd been looking for when he moved to Riversands. It was all he'd ever been looking for, really. And now Mark was asking for one, with such earnest determination.

"Why?"

"Why what?"

"Why me? I mean… W-Why would you w-want to pick someone like me?"

"There's nothing wrong with you."

"Don't!" Raven snapped. Even as his teeth clicked together, he couldn't believe he'd spoken so sharply. But Mark's glib retort had stirred something dark and angry inside him. The words felt like a dismissal of everything that had happened to him. Everything he had struggled with and fought for to be at this point in his life. "Y-yesterday—"

"You had a panic attack. It's nothing to be ashamed of. Lots of people have them."

"It's not just the p-panic attacks. Or the s-s-stuttering. There are…things you don't know. Stuff you w-won't understand."

Mark was quiet for such a long time, Raven started to squirm.

"You're right," Mark finally said, and Raven's heart sank at the admission even though he'd been the one pushing him to finally come to his senses. "I didn't mean what I said to sound offhand. You're right when you say I don't understand. But I want to. That's what I'm asking for. A chance to get to know you and for you to get to know me."

Raven just stared at him for a moment. "But…w-why?"

Mark let out a frustrated sigh and ran a hand through his hair.

"I don't know. I can't really explain it. There's just…something about you." Mark turned his head and grinned at him. "And no, it's not your looks. Though I do think you're gorgeous."

Raven suspected the comment was supposed to lighten the mood, but all it did was make him more uncomfortable.

Mark's smile quickly faded. "Sorry. What I meant was...I've seen you for weeks now—coming to the restaurant, playing with the kids, talking to Lark and Brody and Zak and Jaime and...well, I like what I see." Mark shrugged, suddenly looking terribly self-conscious. "I'd like to get to know you better."

Raven couldn't help wondering when the other shoe would drop.

"What about R-Ryan?"

"What about him?" Mark asked, sounding genuinely confused.

"Doesn't he... I m-mean...doesn't the fact I have a ch-child put you off?"

"No. Why would it?"

"Most guys... I can't d-do a casual fling kind of th-thing."

"I know. That's not what I want. Never has been."

Raven stared at Mark. He couldn't seem to get himself to move or say anything either way. He was completely paralysed by past hurts and a very real fear of the unknown future. At the same time, he couldn't deny being attracted to Mark. He felt completely torn, not sure what to do or which way to turn.

"I'd really like to get to know Ryan eventually," Mark continued cautiously, as if he worried Raven would bolt at any second. "But...maybe you and I should see how we get on together first."

Raven couldn't deny he liked what Mark was saying. It demonstrated more than anything else that he was serious. That he knew Raven had to think about his son and that a casual fuck buddy wasn't in the cards. It also showed that Mark knew that if somehow something more should ever develop between them, Ryan would be part of the deal.

"Raven. I really like you. And I think... Well, I think maybe you like me too. Is there any reason why we can't explore this?"

Lots, thought Raven, but he didn't stop Mark reaching out to take his hand this time.

"Just think about it, huh? Please." The murmured request was made all the more intimate by the low hanging branches of the trees that surrounded them and the sound of the ocean that drowned out the rest of the world. There was just the two of them...and one giant leap of faith.

Raven found himself nodding without any conscious decision to do so. And the really crazy thing was that what he was agreeing to—to thinking about getting to know Mark and seeing where it might lead—didn't absolutely terrify him as he stared into Mark's earnest blue eyes.

* * * *

A little over twenty minutes later, Mark watched Raven walk away. While he wished he'd been able to convince Raven to stay, managing to keep him as long as he had was a huge step forward. And he couldn't deny he thoroughly enjoyed the view. Raven's tight, rounded ass was just something else.

With a sigh as Raven finally disappeared around a bend, Mark thought back through their morning together. Most of the time had been spent simply sitting together, watching the gulls squabble over scraps in the park. And Mark hadn't pressed for more. In fact, he'd actually enjoyed the quiet restfulness of just being with Raven under the trees and watching the birds. He'd never taken a lot of time to chill out in the past. It seemed like there was always something that needed doing—another crisis to manage at home, extra hours to put in at work. He was a little surprised how much he'd enjoyed doing nothing and how relaxed he felt right now.

Mark wondered idly if Raven liked fishing. It was something he'd always wanted to try, but could never spare the time for. He was going to have to remedy that. He didn't want to end up one of those guys who got so wrapped up in his work he neglected everything else. Life was too short.

He suspected he'd enjoy going fishing with Raven. A river, perhaps. Somewhere quiet and peaceful away from the hustle and bustle. But it would have to wait for now. At the moment it was a case of seizing whatever opportunities came his way to spend time with Raven and patiently convincing him he was not only serious, but worth the risk.

Of course, he didn't think for one second Lark casually mentioning Raven's habit of running each morning after dropping Ryan off at preschool had been an accident. The man was about as subtle as a kick in the head. But once again, he wasn't about to look a gift horse in the mouth—even if it did come in the form of a meddlesome, match-making twink.

He was still kind of stunned it had worked, though. Not only had he managed to drag his sorry ass out of bed at the crack of dawn, he'd actually spotted Raven on the boardwalk. Considering how long the running path was, it was something of a miracle to have bumped into him...something he hadn't considered until he was well into his run and finally awake.

Heading back towards the boardwalk and ultimately home, Mark reflected on their time together in the park. Reaching out and taking Raven's hand, even if it had only been for a few moments, had definitely been a risky move—one he didn't regret for a second, but he knew he'd taken a chance. He needed to take things slow and easy or he risked scaring Raven off. He knew that. But it was hard. Patience wasn't really one of his strong suits.

Still, while it wasn't much, at least it was a start. Now it was up to Raven.

Chapter Four

Settling himself on a chair at the kitchen table, Raven stared around the warm, comfortable room. The apartment above Sandpipers Restaurant was spacious and well appointed. But more than that, it felt like a home—lived in and loved in. Hearing the sound of Wolf and Ryan laughing happily in the background only reinforced the image. He'd never experienced anything even remotely like it when he was growing up, but this was exactly what he wanted for Ryan. A home. A loving family. A haven.

Without meaning to, his mind strayed to thoughts of Mark. What sort of family did Mark come from? Did he have a happy home growing up?

One of Raven's biggest fears had always been that, while he wanted to be a good father, he didn't really know how. He didn't have much personal experience to fall back on. He didn't know what one did or even looked like. Although, on that score, watching Brody, Lark and Zak with Wolf certainly helped.

What would Mark be like with kids?

Of course, gazing around the kitchen and thinking of Mark quickly led to the memory of him bent over at the oven the weekend before. Raven realised he'd probably never be able to walk into the room again and not remember that moment...or what had happened directly after.

Still, Mark really had been pretty incredible about the whole panic attack thing that day. Not many guys would have been so understanding and —

"Thanks for bringing Wolf home again today," Brody said as he pulled two cups out of an overhead cupboard.

Heat rushed into Raven's cheeks. Brody had invited him in for a cup of coffee. It was the same every afternoon he brought Wolf home from preschool — a gesture that had slowly made him feel welcome and almost at ease in their home. It had also relieved some of the loneliness that plagued him at times. And yet here he was, lost in his own head thinking about Mark...again! He'd never make friends — never mind keep them — if he kept zoning out on them.

Raven shifted self-consciously in his seat. "You're w-welcome."

Looking down at his hands, he tried to concentrate on the here and now and push all thoughts of Mark to the back of his mind.

The whole situation was getting completely out of hand. All he seemed to do at the moment was think about Mark. Well, Mark and the unexpected attraction that had sprung up between them. He was starting to fall behind in his work too — constantly slipping into daydreams and random deep thoughts. It —

"White with two sugars, right?" Brody asked, reaching for another cup.

Damn!

Raven cleared his throat. "Yes p-please."

"You want a cup of coffee, Lark?" Brody called out, although it looked like he'd already anticipated the answer as he pulled Lark's cup out.

"Yes, please!" a disembodied voice shouted back from somewhere in the direction of the living room. "I'll be there in a minute."

Several squeals and a barrage of high-pitched giggles followed as Lark let out a dramatic roar.

"Sounds like the children are all playing nicely." Brody grinned, setting down the third cup and turning to start working the fancy coffee machine in the corner.

With Brody occupied as the beans ground and the water heated, Raven found his thoughts drifting again. The scene in the park — a constant distraction — replayed in his mind.

"Just think about it."

And the real kicker…

"Please."

Raven stifled a snort. He'd been doing nothing *but* thinking about it for days. He heard the soft plea over and over. But it was crazy. He hadn't even considered…whatever it was he was supposed to be thinking about in years. Hell, he couldn't even *think* the word 'date'. So why couldn't he get Mark out of his head? And why did his cock start to stir and want to come out to play every time he even thought of the man, never mind set eyes on him? He hadn't had a libido in forever. Why now?

"Earth to Raven. Come in, Raven," Lark suddenly said, breaking into his heavy thoughts.

"Huh?" He hadn't even heard Lark enter the room.

Looking up, he caught the tail end of Brody scowling at Lark, before his expression cleared and he turned to face Raven, handing over a steaming mug. "Everything okay?"

"Yes." But Raven couldn't hold Brody's gaze long enough to make either of them believe it. Taking a deep breath, he knew he needed to do something. To take the plunge—if only to try and save what was left of his sanity. "I was wondering, w-would you... That is..."

"What?" Brody prompted gently when the silence stretched out too long.

"Would you guys maybe...l-look after Ryan for me one evening for a f-few hours."

"Sure. Anytime."

"Any date in particular?" Lark asked with a sly grin.

"Lark!" Brody admonished.

But Lark looked wholly unrepentant. "What?"

"I h-haven't decided yet."

"Well when you do, just let us know," Brody said, fixing Lark with a stern glare. "We'd love to have Ryan over."

"Thank you. I'm just th-thinking about it."

"Ryan would be fine if that's what you're worried about. He seems right at home here," Brody reassured in that gentle, quiet way of his.

Raven nodded. He knew and trusted Brody, Lark and Zak. He'd seen first-hand how they loved and treated Wolf. But more than that, Brody was right. Now that he stopped to think about it, while the party had been a challenge—a strange, noisy situation that Raven completely understood Ryan being nervous about—ordinarily his son was very comfortable here. "Thank you for h-having him over so often. It's nice to see him so...h-happy."

"Ryan's a great kid. And Wolf's completely taken with him." Brody blew gently across his coffee cup.

"Ms Gwen says they're virtually inseparable at preschool."

"And you know, we'd be more than happy to make it a sleepover," Lark suggested with an enthusiastic grin and a cheeky waggle of his eyebrows.

Raven felt himself flush to the tips of his ears.

"Lark, give the guy a break, huh?" Brody mumbled.

"I'm just saying he should go for it. A good looking guy like Mark...well, they don't come along every day. Present company excluded, of course."

How on earth did they...

Raven watched as Brody grinned and shook his head at Lark, but he didn't look at all shocked that Mark's name had been mentioned.

"I d-don't know what you're talking about," Raven finally managed to stammer.

Two sets of eyes swung around to stare at him. Neither looked like they believed him for a second.

"Yeah! Sure," Lark drawled.

Raven lowered his eyes and fiddled with the handle of his coffee cup. Apparently — somehow — they knew. Maybe Mark had said something. Maybe he just wasn't as inconspicuous about his attraction to Mark as he thought he was. Either way, it was obvious he wasn't fooling anyone, least of all himself. And in the end, Lark was probably right — Mark wouldn't hang around forever. He needed to make a decision —

No! On second thought, he just needed to do it. Life wasn't meant to be lived scared of your own shadow all the time. It was no example to set for Ryan.

"Is Mark w-working tonight?"

"No. It's his day off," Brody supplied quickly, eyeing Lark the whole time.

Raven slumped a little. This was hard enough. If he didn't do it right now, he'd probably chicken out. And funnily enough, deep down he didn't want to, and it had nothing to do with setting an example for Ryan, or any other flimsy excuse he might come up with. He didn't want to let the chance slip away. He didn't want to miss out on seeing what might happen. It was a quite liberating realisation.

"You don't have his phone number?" Lark asked, sharp blue eyes boring into him now.

"No."

"Mmm…tricky," Lark murmured, pulling out his mobile phone. "And we can't just give it to you. Staff confidentiality and all that." But even as he spoke, Lark's thumb was flying over the keypad. Within seconds he lay his phone down on the table beside Raven's hand, the screen lit and showing a number ready to be dialled. "Hey, how about we take the boys out for a walk along the esplanade before dinner, Brod?"

Brody chuckled and shook his head at Lark's antics. "You're such a pushy bastard sometimes."

"But you love me."

"Yeah," Brody said, letting out a long suffering sigh.

"Good boy," Lark said, moving to snuggle into Brody's side.

Brody smiled down at Lark, and Raven's heart contracted with longing. He wanted that sort of look directed at him one day. And he had a sneaky suspicion he knew just who his heart was craving it from.

"So is that okay with you, Raven? If we take Ryan for a walk with us?" Brody asked, breaking into his deep thoughts.

"Um…s-sure." He stared back down at the glowing LCD screen by his hand warily, hoping he could go through with it. And not just because he didn't want to disappoint them.

"Excellent!" Lark crowed, already heading for the door. "Wolf! Ryan! Who wants to go for a walk?"

Enthusiastic squeals greeted the question followed by the pounding of feet on floorboards.

Ryan flew through the door, barely missing Lark and skidding to a stop in front of Raven, a huge smile on his face. He was the most relaxed and lively Raven could remember seeing him in…well, ever. Which was both sad and wonderful at the same time. Wolf, Lark, Brody and Zak were good for both of them, apparently.

"Can I? Please," Ryan begged.

"Sure. But no r-running in the house." Raven brushed back a wayward lock of Ryan's black hair.

"Sorry."

"It's okay." Raven gave his son a reassuring smile and it warmed him right through when Ryan returned it easily. Maybe he could do this parenting thing after all. "Off you go. Make sure you m-mind what Lark and Brody say."

"I will." With that Ryan threw his arms around Raven's neck for a quick, brutal hug and disappeared out the door again, following Lark and Wolf in the hunt for shoes.

As he passed, Brody squeezed Raven's shoulder. "Do it. Really. You deserve to be happy too."

Yeah. Maybe I do, he realised.

Still it took him half a dozen attempts to finally let the call go through.

* * * *

Mark put the finishing touches to the vegetarian lasagne he was experimenting with, sprinkling crumbled feta cheese evenly over the pre-roasted vegetables before popping the pan into the oven. He knew most people would think he was crazy working on refining recipes and creating new menu items on his day off. But quite honestly he enjoyed the thrill of creating or improving something to be just that little bit better than it had been before. Plus it took his mind off waiting for Raven.

It had been three days since their talk in the park. Three days of watching and waiting. Sure, he'd seen Raven a couple of times, and the lingering looks suggested Raven was thinking hard about what he'd said, which was a huge relief. Raven had even managed a shy smile at him yesterday. Mark thought he'd end up going into cardiac arrest his heart had started pounding so hard.

Unfortunately, waiting wasn't really something he was naturally good at. He liked to jump in and get on with things. Only his promise to be patient kept him in check. He prided himself on never breaking a promise. And he suspected Raven's past included quite enough broken promises already.

Still, he should have given Raven his number. Or got Raven's. Or…something.

Fortunately, before he could really start to fret about should haves and could haves, his phone started vibrating and the sound of *Trouble* by Pink brought a smile to his lips.

Lark. He might be quirky and meddlesome at times, but he was still always guaranteed to distract and lighten the mood. Pulling his phone out of his pocket, Mark flipped it open and answered with a grin.

"Hey, Lark. To what do I owe the pleasure?"

"Um...hi... I m-mean...it's not Lark. It's—"

"Raven?"

"Yes?"

"Oh! I mean, wow. That's...wow, that's...great." Mark cleared his throat and tried to kick some brain cells into action. "It's good to hear from you."

Mark winced. That sounded lame even to his ears.

"It is?"

"Yes. Definitely," Mark rushed out. "I was just thinking about you. How'd you find my number?"

"I um... I b-borrowed Lark's phone."

Mark resisted the urge to smack himself in the forehead as a hot flush of embarrassment crept up his neck. His only defence was that he'd become so tied up in knots to find himself suddenly talking to Raven after spending days thinking about him, he'd completely forgotten about hearing the distinctive ring tone he'd assigned to Lark's mobile number. So much for engaging brain cells.

"I'm s-sorry," Raven murmured. "I shouldn't have—"

"No, it's cool. Really. I mean, it's just great to hear from you."

Mark closed his eyes and pinched the bridge of his nose. He hoped he could stop sounding like a complete moron sometime soon.

"R-really?"

Despite his embarrassing gaffe, a small smile tugged at Mark's lips. The innocent surprise in Raven's voice was both a relief and a turn on. "Yes, really." Mark swallowed against the sudden dry knot of nervousness lodged in his throat. "I've ah...yeah, I've been thinking about you a lot."

"Me t-too."

As suave and sophisticated conversations went, Mark wasn't sure he could have made a worse impression if he'd tried. Or a bigger fool of himself. And yet, Raven's soft admission still managed to make him feel like a king as his heart started to race wildly. He grinned, probably making him look like an even bigger idiot than he felt, but he didn't care. He felt so good right now he was surprised he wasn't floating.

"So, what's up?" he asked, hoping his voice didn't give his stupid expression away.

"Well... I was just w-wondering...if the offer's still there...if m-maybe you'd like t-to...you know. To m-maybe...go...out."

Raven suddenly growled in frustration—a soft adorable little sound that made Mark's cock instantly take notice. He wondered what other noises Raven might be capable of, given the right incentive.

"I'm m-m-messing this all up."

Mark managed to drag his mind back out of the gutter. "No. Honestly you're not. I'd love to go out. The offer's definitely still there."

"Oh!"

Mark smiled at the sweet sound of surprise again. He only wished he was there to see the expression on Raven's face right now. If he looked half as cute as he sounded...

Mark cleared his throat, trying to get back on track. "Would you like to come over to my place and I'll cook for you, or would you like to go out somewhere?"

Both ideas had merit. At Mark's house Raven wouldn't have to cope with a lot of extra people—something Mark had noticed Raven sometimes had trouble with. But at the same time, he might not be comfortable being alone with Mark on his home turf, so to speak, either. It might imply a whole different level of pressure. And he knew Raven wasn't ready for anything like that.

Mark could see a lot of cold showers in his future.

"I...ah... I think m-maybe going out somewhere. If that's ok-kay."

"Sounds wonderful. Do you want to pick where we go or can I surprise you?" Mark held his breath. As trust went, it was a minor, almost inconsequential testing of the waters, but he really hoped Raven would let him pick somewhere special for them. For him.

Baby steps, he told himself.

"I...ah... I don't know many p-places around here yet. Maybe you should p-pick."

"I'd love to." Mark let his very genuine pleasure at the idea fill his voice.

"Oh! I mean, that's...g-good. Um... Th-Thank you." Once again there was that surprised little sound Mark would have given anything to be able to see.

Mark swallowed down the impulsive urge to jump in and suggest they go out tonight—right now before Raven could change his mind. He wanted to, but it felt too pushy. Too desperate. And probably wouldn't be at all practical considering Raven would need to find a babysitter for Ryan.

"Does next Monday sound okay? It's my next night off," Mark suggested instead.

"Um...s-sure. At least I think so. I'll have to ask B-Brody and Lark. They said they'd look after Ryan for me."

"Okay. Let's make it Monday and if something changes you can let me know."

It seemed the safest way to go. He wanted to make sure they had a date fixed, even if it needed to change later. Ambiguous just wasn't going to work for him right now.

"That s-sounds...yeah. Ok-kay."

Mark didn't want to end the conversation, but it was rapidly coming to a natural close. "So, will you be at Sandpipers this weekend with Ryan?"

"Yes. I'm looking after the b-boys Sunday morning again. Just for a few hours."

"Hopefully I'll get to see you then."

There was a long pause, and for a worrisome moment Mark thought he might have pushed too far, too fast.

Then he heard Raven murmur, "I'd l-like that."

It was such a small admission, but Mark wanted to pump his fist in victory. Instead he contained his sense of triumph and offered a calm, "So, I guess I'll see you then."

"Uh huh."

It was a start. A good start, he promised himself. Considering only a week ago he would have been lucky to catch a glimpse of Raven before he disappeared out the door again, and now Raven was initiating phone calls and agreeing to a date. It was an incredible achievement, really.

Yeah, baby steps, but a good start.

"Bye, Raven."

"Bye, M-Mark."

As soon as Raven hung up, Mark set to work finding the perfect place for their first date. It had to be just right. He had a really good feeling about this. About Raven. He needed their first date together to go off without a hitch.

Chapter Five

By the time Raven made it to the small landing in front of Brody, Lark and Zak's apartment, he was a bundle of nerves. Holding Ryan's hand, he took a moment to gather his thoughts. Not to mention his courage.

Tonight was the night. Date night. Or 'D-day' as he'd started to think of it. He couldn't believe he was really here, ready to go through with it. Okay, so maybe not ready exactly, but he was still certainly standing on the edge of the precipice, preparing to jump.

He had to admit, somewhere deep inside—really, really deep—it felt kind of good. He was taking another step towards becoming stronger, more resilient and normal. But another part—a cynical, distrustful and definitely more vocal part—wondered if it was actually bravery or just plain stupidity to put himself in this position.

And on top of everything else, finding the guts to actually announce their arrival turned out to be a bit like raking water into a bucket—rather futile and wholly frustrating.

Really, it shouldn't have been that hard. After all, he'd been to the trio's apartment dozens of times now—bringing Wolf home or taking Ryan over to play. He liked the family, and had even found himself starting to relax in their home—children's birthday parties and random panic attacks aside. But then, he'd never arrived with a pillow tucked under one arm, Ryan clutching his teddy bear as if his life depended on it gripping his other hand, and the minutes fast ticking down to the first date he'd had in...well, forever.

Raven caught himself about to start shifting nervously from foot to foot and managed to stop just in time. The last thing he needed right now was to let Ryan know how nervous he was. But it was hard to stifle the restless movement.

Taking a deep breath, Raven tried to reason with his anxiety. It would just be a handful of hours—at most—face to face without any distractions, where he and Mark could get to know each other better. Enjoy a meal. Perhaps a little light conversation, but they'd end up talking about largely unimportant, non-controversial issues while they sized one another up. Then, if all went well and depending on where they ended up going for dinner, maybe they'd take a stroll along the waterfront. A normal, non-threatening, getting-to-know-you, first date, leisurely walk on neutral ground.

Raven felt like a nest of fire ants had taken up residence in his belly.

"Are you okay, Daddy?"

Raven looked down at Ryan—so small and yet so serious. "I'm f-fine. Are you looking forward to movie n-night with Wolf?"

Ryan nodded. "You could come too if you want. Wolf won't mind."

Raven was embarrassed by how tempted he was to accept the offer. "No. It's a special n-night just for you boys. But th-thank you."

The truth was, more than anything, Raven wanted to run away and hide right now. A wicked little part of him had even thought about pretending the date had somehow slipped his mind—that he'd been so busy with work and Ryan he'd clean forgotten what day it was. But he knew that would be the ultimate cowardice. Not to mention a truly despicable thing to do. Mark deserved better. He seemed to be a genuinely nice guy. He'd certainly been nothing but kind in the short time they'd known each other.

Deeply ashamed of himself for even entertaining the idea of standing Mark up, Raven took a deep breath and pressed the buzzer.

Almost instantly, Lark threw open the door.

"Raven! Come in! Come in! Hey, Ryan!" Lark ushered them into the foyer and gestured for their coats.

The man couldn't have been more than a few inches from the door when Raven had rung the bell. Somehow, it wasn't all that much of a surprise—Lark had been keyed up and excited about 'the date' ever since Raven had officially asked them to look after Ryan for the evening. And nothing Raven did or said seemed to dampen his enthusiasm.

In contrast, Raven felt like he could probably market his stomach acid as an industrial strength solvent. He desperately wished he'd remembered to bring along some antacids.

"Wow! You look good," Lark said with a low whistle as he hung their coats in the hall closet.

"Thanks," Raven managed to mutter as he eased off his shoes—he wasn't about to make that mistake again.

He *had* gone to quite a bit of effort to look his best tonight. And the only reason he could come up with for the shameful amount of time he'd spent getting ready and picking out just the right outfit was that he didn't want to disappoint Mark. Which was both confusing and a little uncomfortable to admit, even to himself.

"What do you think, Ryan? Don't you think your dad looks hot tonight?" Lark continued with a huge grin and a wink, obviously hoping to generate some support and enthusiasm for him.

Ryan nodded, but it was an extremely reluctant little movement. He really didn't look at all happy with the situation.

Raven's stomach twisted into a tight, guilty knot. This was starting to look like a bad idea all round. But at the same time, he didn't want to appear ungrateful. "Thank you for agreeing to l-look after R-Ryan tonight."

"How many times in the last couple of months have you helped us out?" Zak asked as he stepped into the hallway and walked towards them. "It's the least we could do."

Zak wrapped his arms around Lark from behind and Lark readily snuggled back into the embrace. Raven's stomach clenched at the display in something that, if he was forced to put a name to it, might have been jealousy. Only it wasn't Zak or Lark he was jealous of, but the deep comfort and affection they shared. He wanted that. Always had.

Having never received much in the way of care and attention growing up, Raven knew he was susceptible to wanting to soak up any and all warmth that happened to come his way, no matter how small. But it was an incredibly dangerous longing that could quite easily lead him to do all sorts of reckless, stupid things, and had in the past. He needed to keep his head on straight and be very careful he didn't let his hungry heart lead him blindly into a bad situation…again.

"How are you doing, Ryan?" Zak asked, breaking into Raven's dark thoughts.

"Good."

"All ready for movie night?"

Ryan nodded mechanically.

"Wolf's just finishing up his bath, then you guys can get started right away if you like."

As if summoned by his name, Wolf appeared in the hallway, wearing pyjamas and still a little damp around the edges. Brody followed in his wake, looking almost as wet as Wolf.

Spotting Ryan, Wolf ran up with his usual enthusiasm. But something happened along the way. Instead of the standard pounce and drag away routine he usually engaged in, Wolf slowed as he approached, as if sensing something different about his friend. When he was finally close enough, he threw his arms around Ryan for a hug, then stood quietly by his side with his arm still wrapped around Ryan's waist. It was kind of eerie actually. And made Raven feel even more anxious—it looked like even Wolf was worried now.

"So when's Mark picking you up?" Lark asked, eyeing the boys as they huddled together.

Raven swallowed. This just wasn't going to work. "Seven."

"He's coming here, right?" Lark continued.

"Yes. But I..." Raven stared between Brody, Lark and Zak, not sure what to say or do to make things right.

He did want to go out with Mark. At least in theory. But he wasn't sure he was ready. Hell, he wasn't sure he'd ever be. With the amount of baggage he had he could rival a jumbo jet's cargo hold. And Ryan's apprehension played on his mind too. What if it wasn't just that he was worried about his dad — which was bad enough? What if he wasn't ready for the whole daddy-has-a-date thing either?

"Just give it some time, Raven," Brody said, low and calm, like he thought everything would work out. Then he turned his attention to Ryan. "So who's your friend, Ryan?"

Brody pointed to the well-loved teddy bear currently in a fierce headlock against Ryan's chest.

"Chewy."

"*Star Wars* fan, huh?"

Ryan shook his head. "Daddy called him Chewy 'cause I used to chew his nose. I don't chew him now, 'cause I'm not a baby anymore."

"Yeah, I know. You guys are growing up so fast." Brody nodded.

"So, what are we going to watch tonight, anyway?" Lark asked, rubbing his hands together, apparently hoping to just ignore the tension in the room. "Should we head into the living room and have a look at the choices?"

Ryan clutched Raven's hand a little tighter.

"How about we all go into the living room?" Zak suggested, still watching Ryan closely.

Ryan clung to Raven the whole way and even in the living room refused to leave his side. Settling on one of the couches, Ryan almost sat on top of him in a bid to stay close. The situation looked completely hopeless. There was no way Raven would even think about leaving Ryan like this.

Undeterred, Lark laid out a few DVDs on the coffee table for the boys to choose from. "There you go, guys."

Then he settled into the corner of the large leather couch and started chatting casually—asking Wolf which he thought was the best choice, engaging Brody in a heated debate about which superhero was superior. Silly, inane topics. And gradually, miraculously, it seemed to work. Ryan eventually slid off the couch and joined Wolf on the floor to pore over the DVD selection and act out his favourite scenes with some of Wolf's action figures.

"How about some snacks, boys?" Zak asked as Wolf started spreading out his sleeping bag on the floor to build a city for them to rescue.

"Yeah!" Wolf cried enthusiastically, grinning and relaxed again.

Lark clicked his fingers. "Oh, hey! That reminds me. Did we invite you guys to the picnic next month yet, Raven?"

"Um...n-no."

"Huh, I was sure I'd already invited you. But Brody said we hadn't. Well, anyway, we're having the first official Annual Sandpipers Restaurant Family and Friends Picnic on the eighth," Lark announced grandly. "It's just the guys from the restaurant, a few friends. Nothing huge."

Zak snorted. "Lark planned it, just so you have some idea of 'nothing huge' there, Raven."

Lark glared at Zak. But before he could say anything, the doorbell rang.

Zak leapt up off the couch. "I'll get it."

"Coward," Lark muttered, then focused on Raven again. "You will come, won't you?"

"Ah—"

"Come on. We can't have a family and friends picnic without you guys."

"It's really not going to be that big," Brody added. "And it's on a Monday so everyone from the restaurant can come, which means it should be pretty quiet at the park too. We're organising for Wolf to have a day off preschool."

Just as Raven was trying to sort out a halfway decent, coherent reply—his brain already catapulting into overdrive as it registered who was most likely to be at the door—Zak and Mark walked into the room.

Raven leapt to his feet. Sitting just didn't feel right. He needed to be up and moving. At the same time, Ryan and Wolf stood up. Much as he wanted to stare at Mark—because yes, the man looked damn fine tonight—Raven couldn't tear his eyes away from the boys standing side by side, Wolf holding Ryan's hand and both watching the adults in the room with serious expressions on their little faces.

It was just too much. He couldn't do this.

Before he could suggest they call the whole thing off, however, Mark cleared his throat. "Hi everyone. What's up?"

It was a little startling how uneasy Mark sounded. Raven instantly felt guilty for what he was about to do to the poor man.

"Hey, Mark!" Brody said with the kind of false cheerfulness reserved for moments of high tension. "We were just talking about the Sandpipers' picnic."

"Oh, yeah?"

"Raven was just deciding if he and Ryan could make it or not."

"You're coming, right, Mark?" Lark asked quickly.

"Yeah, I thought I might come along for a while."

"Great. See, Raven? Everyone's going to be there. I hope you'll at least think about it."

Raven managed a nod. He would think about it, but right now Ryan and Mark and the whole date disaster looming on the horizon was taking up all his attention.

"So where are you guys going tonight?" Brody asked, still sounding too cheerful.

It seemed his friends were just as anxious right now about everything as he was. In a strange, twisted kind of way, it was...nice. Raven couldn't remember the last time he'd thought anyone would care.

"The Grapevine. If that's okay with Raven."

Zak nodded in approval. "You'll have to let us know what their menu's like."

At that, Lark gave Zak a little shove—one that hardly registered on the bigger man's broad frame. "No spying on the competition on a date, Zak. You know the rules."

"I thought those were just our house rules."

"They're in the house. Hell, they're practically family."

Mark focused in on Ryan, ignoring Zak and Lark's banter. "Are you okay with this, Ryan?"

Ryan paused, then shook his head. Raven's breath caught in his throat. That was it. He was putting a stop to the whole thing right now. But just as he opened his mouth to say something, Mark carefully went down on one knee in front of the boys.

Raven's heart seized in his chest before it started an erratic double-time.

"What's up?" Mark asked gently.

Wolf turned his head to look at Ryan, but neither boy said anything.

"You don't want your Dad to go, do you?" Mark prompted in a quiet voice that held no anger or resentment.

Something tight and scared Raven hadn't even realised had been wrapped around his heart loosened a little as he watched Mark—his voice soft, his expression kind and accepting—as Ryan shook his head again.

"I can understand that. He's pretty special, huh?"

Ryan nodded.

"Yeah, I think so too. How about I make you a deal?" As he spoke, Mark took off his watch and fitted it around Ryan's left wrist, adjusting it until it wouldn't slide off Ryan's thin arm, although there was nothing to be done about the fact it dangled upside down. It was just too big to do anything else. "You know, *my* dad gave this to me when I was a kid. I guess I must have been slightly older than you—it's a bit big. But how about you look after this for me and I promise to take care of your Dad and bring him back by the time the big hand's on the twelve and the little hand's on the ten."

Raven opened his mouth to intercede—the watch looked old, and obviously had a lot of sentimental value to Mark as well. But Ryan beat him to it.

"How long is that?" he asked in a small, but considering voice.

"Three hours."

For a long time, Ryan simply stared at Mark. And Mark held his gaze patiently the whole time, waiting for Ryan's verdict.

"You promise to look after him?"

"Promise," Mark replied, crossing his heart.

Chapter Six

Mark pulled out of the Sandpipers Restaurant parking lot and pointed his SUV in the direction of the pier and the restaurant he'd so very carefully picked out for both its reported quality and expansive view of the ocean.

The Grapevine was a relatively new place, but one that had nevertheless been getting some pretty good reviews. And being right on the pier the atmosphere at night should be a little bit romantic — with the lights and the moon playing on the water — without being too over the top.

But right now, the only thing Mark could really focus on was the gorgeous man sitting next to him.

He couldn't believe he'd actually pulled it off. He was on a date with Raven. No matter what else happened tonight, the mere fact they'd made it this far gave him a huge boost of hope.

And he needed that. He wanted Raven with a hollow ache of longing that was rather embarrassing, actually.

Raven was special. He could feel it in his bones. If he could just get Raven to let him in.

Mark stifled a self-deprecating snort. His mother always did say he was hard-headed and stubborn once he got his mind set on something. And Raven was most definitely on his mind. Nearly constantly at the moment, in fact.

"Thank you," Raven suddenly said, breaking into Mark's musings.

He glanced across to see Raven studying him with a strange, almost wondering expression.

"You're welcome," Mark replied with a smile, although he wasn't sure what Raven was thanking him for. There were a few options, really — some better than others. "Um...what for, exactly?"

"For w-what you did for Ryan. That was... You were incredible." Raven ducked his head away as if embarrassed as he blurted the words.

"Oh!" Mark felt his cheeks getting hotter too. "Um...thanks."

It *had* been a pretty intense moment — walking in and feeling the tension in the room, seeing the way Ryan eyed him as if he was a circling shark. He would have understood completely if Raven had called the whole thing off. But he was very glad he hadn't.

By the time they'd left, Ryan was looking...maybe not happy, but at least secure enough to release his father after a quick hug and watch him walk out the door...albeit clutching Wolf's hand in a death grip.

"How did you d-do that?"

Mark shrugged. He wasn't really sure. It had just sort of...happened. "I don't know. I thought it might help. I have a little brother and sister fourteen years younger than me. I remember when they were little... I don't know... Sometimes they just needed something real and solid to hang onto, you know? And I thought it might help to reassure him we'd be back."

Out of the corner of his eye, he saw Raven nod as he stared down at his fingers, twisting them together nervously in his lap.

"Ryan has a real thing about t-time at the m-moment."

"Yeah, I saw that the other day at the party."

Damn! Mark cursed silently. *Way to kill the mood.*

A heavy silence settled over them as Mark was forced to concentrate on the road while he negotiated his way through a tricky intersection. To be honest, he wasn't exactly sure what to do about it even if he didn't have to keep his mind on the road. He wasn't going to put pressure on Raven to talk if he didn't want to. But at the same time it was going to be a very long night if Raven shut down and wouldn't talk to him at all.

Of course, it might help if you could keep your big fat foot out of your mouth, Mark admonished silently.

"I was g-going to cancel," Raven finally confessed.

Mark nodded. He'd seen that quite clearly. "I would have understood if you had. But I'm glad you didn't."

"Yeah," Raven murmured. "M-me too."

Man. How did he do that? With just three little words Raven made him feel better. It was ridiculous. And yet so wonderful he just couldn't bring himself to care how much of a sap it might make him.

Raven settled back into silence, and Mark let him. It was an okay, peaceful kind of quiet that wrapped around them this time. There was just the hum of the road, the low white noise of early evening traffic and a small, calm thankfulness that things were all right between them again. At least so far.

The next ten minutes passed without comment or conversation, but it didn't feel strained. Not until they entered the restaurant and the waiter led them to their table.

Mark could feel the stress radiating off Raven as they were shown to their seats. The way he focused straight ahead and pointedly didn't look around at anyone else. The set of his shoulders. The pale thin line of his normally full lips. Raven looked brittle enough to crack right open at any moment.

Of course, Mark knew saying anything about it would be the worst thing he could possibly do right now. He just had to hope Raven would relax once they were settled at their table — at least enough to enjoy the food and, with any luck, ultimately the date. It would put a real dampener on things if he didn't.

"May I take your drink orders?" the waiter asked as he offered them both menus.

Mark saw Raven stiffen at the question. And it was hard to miss the look of apprehension as their eyes met across the table.

"Just a glass of water for me, thank you," Mark replied.

"W-water, please," Raven added in a low voice, looking distinctly uncomfortable and turning bright red.

As the waiter inclined his head and stepped away, Mark laid his menu down then reached out to lightly touch Raven's hand. "You okay?"

"S-sorry."

"What for?"

Raven shrugged and looked away.

Mark frowned. He didn't know for sure what had upset Raven, but he was going to take a guess. He could at least make one thing clear up front anyway.

Mark took a deep breath and hoped he wasn't making a mistake. "I don't drink alcohol."

"You d-don't?"

Raven looked shocked, and Mark guessed that was fair enough. He hadn't met a lot of people who didn't drink alcohol either. He'd been the odd man out whenever he'd gone anywhere for as long as he could remember.

"I never really acquired the taste. I don't like the way it makes me feel."

Raven's brow furrowed slightly in confusion.

Mark shrugged, feeling a little self-conscious. "You know, kind of spacey and out of control. I don't...yeah, I don't like the way it makes me feel."

"Oh!" Raven studied him carefully, then quickly looked away when he seemed to realise he was staring. "That's...um... I'm... I'm g-glad."

Mark nodded.

Raven had a story, that much was obvious. And it was more than likely a pretty sad, painful one. Mark had no intention of trying to pry it out of him before he was ready to tell it, though. But he had to admit he wanted to know what was going on in Raven's head right now.

When the waiter returned with their drinks and took their orders, Mark thought it was probably time to change the subject. He watched Raven take a small sip of water from his glass. There was one thing that had started to intrigue him—mainly because the more he thought about it the more he realised he just didn't know...and couldn't tell.

"How old are you?"

"Um...t-twenty-four."

Mark considered Raven carefully. He had to admit he was a little shocked. Raven seemed older somehow. More...mature. Maybe it had something to do with the fact he'd seen Raven with Ryan at his side so often. Or perhaps it was in his eyes—that look that said Raven had seen a lot in those twenty-four years.

"You must have been pretty young when Ryan came along then."

"Not quite n-nineteen," Raven said as he looked away again.

Another story. The more he found out about Raven the less he knew, apparently. But he tried not to let it worry him. He'd promised to be patient.

Still, he hadn't realised just how young Raven was. It presented an interesting and potentially troublesome little side issue he hadn't thought much about before. Was nine years—well, nearly ten really—considered a big age gap? Would it bother Raven?

"I'm thirty-three. Thirty-four at the end of the year."

Raven nodded.

"Not too old for you?" Mark asked, trying to sound light-hearted, but somehow it came out a little strained even to his ears.

When the hell had he become the older man? Wow, life really had sort of got away from him.

Raven looked startled. "No."

"Well, that's a relief," Mark chuckled.

The tightness in his chest eased a little. Still, it was a bit of a jolt to realise he'd somehow got older while he wasn't paying attention. He'd never resent the time he'd given to his brother and sister, but it definitely brought home the fact that life really was too short. And it made him even more determined not to muck things up with Raven. Because something deep inside told him Raven could be 'the one'. And he didn't want to waste a second of the opportunity to find out.

Unfortunately, Raven didn't look like he was anywhere near relaxed yet, despite the fact they'd been settled at their table a good ten minutes.

"I-I n-need to..." Raven glanced around, stress and tension bleeding out of every pore now.

"What do you need?"

"I n-need to call and ch-check on Ryan."

"Oh! Right. Yeah, I should have thought of that." Mark started scrabbling in his jacket. "Do you need to borrow my phone?"

But Raven shook his head, pulling one from his pocket as he stood up. "N-no. I'm fine. I'll..."

Raven gestured vaguely towards the front of the restaurant.

"Yeah! Sure. I'll...um...I'll just wait here. Take your time."

Mark clamped his mouth shut before he could add anything even more inane to his ramblings. Raven looked like he needed a moment to himself as well as wanting to check in on his son. What Mark couldn't work out was why it made him feel so nauseated.

He really liked Raven. As in *really* liked. But their date just wasn't turning out the way he'd planned. Mark felt his muscles growing tight across his shoulders and up the back of his neck into the base of his skull.

Shit!

He needed to relax. Being tense and edgy around Raven would not be a good idea.

Mark tried not to fiddle too much with the silverware—instead occupying himself with taking small sips of water at regular intervals and concentrating on setting the glass back in exactly the same spot every time.

When their meals arrived and Raven wasn't back, Mark waited. A few minutes later he spotted Raven heading towards the table. Unfortunately, as he took in the meal set out waiting, he paled quite noticeably.

"I'm s-s-sorry."

"Hey, it's fine. They haven't been here that long. How's Ryan?"

"F-F-Fine."

Damn! Raven's stammer was getting worse—a sure sign he was stressed. Mark hunted around for something to keep him talking, hoping they could muscle their way through the awkwardness.

"So…um…Raven. That's a pretty unusual name. How'd you come by that one anyway?"

"R-Ryan."

Mark frowned in confusion. "Ryan started calling you Raven?"

Raven squirmed in his seat. "My real n-name is…I mean, w-was Raymond. But when Ryan first started to talk he couldn't p-pronounce it. It came out mangled and eventually sort of morphed into R-Raven." Raven shrugged self-consciously and looked away. "I liked it. So I k-kept it."

Mark thought it was kind of strange that Ryan would have called his father by his first name when he first started learning to talk. He'd only ever heard Ryan refer to Raven as Dad or Daddy since meeting them. And he remembered Raven trying to introduce him to Ryan as Mr Carter not so long ago. It seemed a little…odd and inconsistent.

Raven shifted in his seat again, as if aware of Mark's scrutiny.

Damn! I didn't even have to open my mouth to mess things up this time!

"You…ah…you said you have a b-brother and a sister?" Raven said.

"Yeah. Twins," Mark replied eagerly, relieved they hadn't fallen back into an uncomfortable silence. "They're unholy terrors when the mood strikes them, believe me. And don't let anybody tell you it gets easier when they reach eighteen. They're more of a worry now at nineteen than they were as toddlers!"

Raven considered him carefully for a few seconds — or perhaps more accurately, considered the sentiment behind his words. "It sounds like you really l-love them."

Mark was a little startled by Raven's frank observation. But it was only the truth. And sharing that honesty with Raven…actually felt pretty good. "Yeah, I do. I figure that's what it's all about in the end. Family."

"Y-yeah."

Unfortunately, Mark wasn't sure if that was a good yeah or a bad yeah. He had absolutely no idea what was going on in Raven's head at the moment. So he ploughed on, hoping for the best. He could hardly expect Raven to open up if he didn't do it himself anyway. "Our dad was killed in a car accident so I sort of ended up helping to raise them."

"I'm s-sorry," Raven whispered.

Mark nodded, his throat suddenly tight. He hadn't talked about the accident in years. Hadn't even thought about it in a long time, really. It was always there, but pushed back and quiet…like quicksand. He couldn't believe how painful the memories of that time still were.

"Mom…well, she was pretty messed up in the accident too. And she never really got over him being gone like that. Right in front of her. She tried, but…yeah, she sort of fell apart."

"Is she…?"

"She died five years ago of breast cancer."

As if she hadn't been through enough.

Mark couldn't help the bitter, acidic bite to the thought. It all seemed so unfair. He remembered how happy his parents had been. How warm and perfect his family had always felt growing up. They'd been one of those lucky, fairy tale kind of families you heard about or saw on television but never thought were real. And then, in one twisted, wicked moment everything had changed, and nothing he or anyone else did could make it right again.

He absolutely hated that last part. No matter what he did, he could never make it better.

Suddenly, Raven reached out and lay his hand gently over Mark's, offering a little squeeze of support and sympathy. It was the first touch Raven had ever initiated between them and Mark clung to it, turning his hand over to hold on to Raven. It felt so good.

"I'm so s-sorry."

Mark nodded. Memories of his mother's final years settled heavily over him—the blank, hollow looks, the panic attacks and the endless medication that never seemed to make any difference. "I don't know…sometimes when I look back on it, I think…I think it was almost a relief to her in the end. It was pretty quick. The cancer. She didn't fight it at all. I think… Sometimes I think she wished she'd died in the accident with Dad."

Raven's eyes were suspiciously bright, and Mark couldn't hold his gaze. It was way too dangerous.

After a few moments, Raven pulled away and Mark felt the loss of contact keenly. The connection that had slowly been starting to form between them seemed in danger of slipping away again. And he was desperate to hold on to it.

"What about you? Any brothers or sisters?"

The question was out before Mark had a chance to really consider what he was asking. And it was met with complete silence. Raven didn't even look like he was breathing.

Panic rode Mark hard. He couldn't believe he'd asked such a stupid question. It was obvious the story wasn't going to be a good one. Hell, he'd figured out a long time ago that Raven's family story was probably a bad one. Yet, he'd still opened his big mouth.

Shit! So much for not prying!

But just as he was frantically trying to think of some way to salvage things, Raven cleared his throat.

"I've got an older b-brother. Well, half-b-brother. Dad was m-married before he met my Mom. But...Sam and I d-don't get on."

"I'm sorry."

"Sam's into d-drugs in a big way. He's a small time d-dealer back home, but...he can't stay away from the stuff himself. It's...not p-pretty."

Mark didn't know what to say. He reached out and squeezed Raven's hand, trying to make it clear how sincerely sorry he was—both for bringing the subject up and for the pain he saw in Raven face.

Raven stared at the tablecloth for a long time, as if struggling to regain his composure. Mark didn't interrupt.

When Raven started to speak again it was barely a whisper. "Our p-parents were...are...they're both engineers. Working for the same f-firm. I think it's where they m-met. But...well, they definitely weren't soul m-mates. And they never should have had k-kids. They were always fighting and…"

Raven took a deep breath and Mark felt sick. It was a telling pause—one that said everything and nothing. Poor Raven! What must it have been like growing up like that?

"Dad drank too m-much and Mom… I think she ended up resenting being t-tied down to us. Once I was old enough to g-get out, I did."

"What about Ryan's mother?"

"She's"—Raven swallowed hard, like the memory hurt him—"g-gone."

"Shit! I'm sorry." Again. Damn it. They really needed to change the record.

Guilt ate away at him for asking as Raven refused to look at him and picked up his glass to take a sip of water with a hand that trembled faintly.

"Ryan and I ended up living with my b-brother for a while, but it got…ugly when he figured out I was starting to earn good m-money with my writing. I was saving to m-move away."

Mark didn't need pictograms to see exactly what would have happened next. "He stole it."

"N-not all of it. I had a good bit hidden away under a different n-name. He wasn't very happy though. He guessed I was h-holding out on him."

"What did you do?"

Raven shrugged. "Grabbed what he hadn't taken, p-packed up and got out when he wasn't around to stop us."

"Bastard," Mark murmured, incensed Raven had been forced to sneak away like that. Family should look after one another.

"Ryan and I g-got out. That's all that m-matters."

The way Raven said it made it sound almost easy. Mark figured it had probably been anything but. He didn't know too many drug addicts that liked to lose a free ride.

Mark noticed Raven looked horribly tense and uncomfortable again—his eyes lowered as he smoothed his thumb over non-existent wrinkles in the tablecloth and steadfastly avoided eye contact. After a few minutes of strained silence between courses, Mark knew he needed to say something, but he wasn't quite sure where to start. Saying something like 'So, how about those Lakers?' just wasn't going to cut it right now. The last thing he wanted to do was sound flip and dismissive. Part of him wished he'd thought about some easy, first date topics ahead of time. He was rather clueless about dating, really. But he knew better than to do *anything* without good prep. He wanted to kick himself for forgetting that golden rule.

Mark cleared his throat and hoped for the best—flying by the seat of his pants.

"So how did you end up becoming a technical writer?"

Raven blushed. "I was l-lucky enough to get a scholarship to do English Literature."

Mark was pretty sure luck had nothing to do with it. "And the computers?"

"I took some C-computer Science electives. It seemed like a good idea at the time. I'm glad I did. I've p-picked up a lot of work because of it."

"You must read a lot?"

"Yeah. I mean... I really l-love books. When I was a kid I'd spend hours holed up in my r-room reading. I always w-wanted to—"

Raven's cheeks turned dark red as he cut the sentence off and ducked his head.

"What?" Mark prompted.

"Well… I always w-wanted to write young adult fiction when I was growing up. I thought that would be really…c-cool."

"Yeah. That would be cool." Mark considered Raven for a moment. "So do you write? I mean stuff like that, not just the technical writing."

"Yeah. A l-little."

"I always wished I was better with words," Mark admitted.

"Do you read?" Raven asked.

Mark squirmed. "Not a lot. No."

Raven looked away.

Damn! And just when Raven was starting to open up.

"Maybe you could suggest some things."

Raven simply studied him for a while. He did that a lot, Mark noticed. It was harder to keep still under the scrutiny this time for some reason. Perhaps because reading and writing had never really been his thing at school. He was more a hands-on, jock kind of guy.

"Really?" Raven finally asked.

"Yeah. I mean, I just haven't had a lot of time before. But now…well, Evan and Lucy, my brother and sister, went away to college last year and…yeah…I want to try new things. Stuff I haven't had the time to do before."

Things felt a little more relaxed as they finished their meals and discussed books. But as the meal drew to a close and the conversation dwindled, Mark noticed Raven getting uptight again. Now and then he saw Raven steal furtive, nervous glances at the people around them. But he'd quickly catch himself and focus back on the table. It was unlikely the floral centrepieces had ever been so closely inspected. A change of scenery seemed to be in order.

Once their plates had been collected and coffee refused, Mark cleared his throat. "Would you like to go for a walk along the pier before our curfew?"

Raven glanced away. "I'm r-really sorry about that. The c-curfew thing."

"Hey, don't be," Mark said, reaching out to touch Raven's hand and let him know how sincere he was. Raven's head snapped up to stare at him and Mark felt the heat crawling up his neck. "Really, it's fine. More than, actually. I want you *and* Ryan to know you can trust me."

Eventually, after watching Mark closely for several endless seconds, Raven nodded. "I'd l-like that. I m-mean...the walk, that is."

Mark allowed a small smile and stifled a sigh of relief. After the rocky, awkward moments of the evening he was obscenely grateful Raven was still willing to hang in there with their date and join him on the pier. He certainly wasn't going to take anything for granted right now.

"Come on then. Let's get out of here," Mark said, standing up and allowing Raven to walk ahead of him.

After paying the bill and stepping out to head along the pier, Mark tried to let the ocean breeze carry away the last of his own pent up tension. It was a beautiful night. A few couples were out and about—some hand in hand, others just walking alongside each other companionably like he and Raven were doing.

"I still don't g-get, why me?" Raven suddenly said.

"Haven't we covered this already?"

"But why p-pick out someone like me?"

Mark hated that Raven had such a low opinion of himself. And he loathed thinking about what Raven must have been through to have it so ingrained he couldn't see past it to what Mark saw — a quiet, caring and intelligent man who had so much to offer.

"If you're trying to get me riled, you're going the right way about it," Mark replied in a calm drawl that belied the tight knot of emotion building up inside him. "I like you. Just the way you are."

Raven looked away.

"Don't do that." He couldn't stand seeing the beaten down slump of Raven's shoulders.

But the words made Raven flinch.

Shit! He hadn't meant to...

"I'm sorry." Mark let out a sigh and ran his hand over his head in frustration. "That seems to be this evening's theme song, doesn't it?"

Raven wasn't looking at him, but Mark saw the shadow of confusion on his face clearly enough, illuminated by the pier lights.

"Sorry," he elaborated. "We've been saying it over and over again to each other tonight."

Raven looked out of the corner of his eye...searching. Mark wasn't exactly sure what Raven found, but something eased in his expression. It was Mark's turn to glance away, feeling suddenly exposed and vulnerable. Raven — quiet and intense — seemed to see so much. More than Mark was entirely comfortable with.

He concentrated on his shoes and putting one foot in front of the other as they continued down the pier. Before he knew it, they were standing together side-by-side at the end rail, close enough to brush against each other occasionally as they watched the water — although he suspected it was the last thing either of them was focusing on—yet somehow feeling miles apart at the same time. Mark certainly felt a long way from gaining Raven's trust and getting to really know him right now.

Damn! Nothing about the evening had gone the way he'd planned.

And it was getting late.

"We should probably start heading back. I don't want us to be late dropping you off."

Raven nodded and turned to head back down the pier to where they'd parked the car.

Unable to help himself, Mark reached out and touched Raven's hand—not holding, but still managing to halt him for a moment.

"Thank you for this evening."

Raven nodded. "Th-thank you too," he replied, somewhat awkwardly. "It was…nice."

Maybe he was being fatalistic, but that sounded suspiciously like a death knell to Mark.

Chapter Seven

The Tuesday night bookings at Sandpipers Restaurant were fairly light. They usually were, but Mark was inordinately grateful for the fact this evening. While they could expect a few drop-ins, he didn't anticipate it being terribly busy — the usual slow start to their working week. Which was just as well, because Mark wasn't sure he could handle any more than that.

He felt tight and agitated tonight. His gut was all tied up in knots. His neck and shoulder muscles were stiff and sore. And last, but certainly not least, the base of his skull ached with the dull throbbing of a stress headache. It was going to be a really, really long night in the heat, noise and activity of the kitchen. Thank goodness it wasn't Saturday.

Although, if it was Saturday, yesterday wouldn't have been Monday and there might still be a chance to get his date with Raven right.

Damn it!

Mark absently sampled the clam chowder being kept warm on one of the burners. Happy with it, he plated it up, sprinkled the surface with a light garnish of parsley and sent it on its way before moving on to the next order.

The date hadn't turned out anything like the way he'd imagined. Mark had to suppress a cynical snort. He'd pictured something *very* different, in fact— candlelight, smiles, light conversation, a romantic walk on the pier. He'd even fantasised about a kiss, although he'd at least acknowledged that wasn't very likely to happen. But it had been a nice dream. Now it looked like that's all it would ever be. A dream. Why would Raven want to inflict last night's disaster on himself again? Even if Raven *had* said it had been 'nice'.

Mark cringed at the remembered word.

He straightened his shoulders and tried to shut down his pessimistic thoughts. They weren't helping and there wasn't a whole lot he could do about it right now in the middle of a shift anyway. No matter how quiet it was.

Still, while sautéing garlic prawns for the next entrée, he couldn't help wondered if he should have done more at the time to try and end the night on a high note. Maybe if he'd tried harder to engage Raven in different conversations—more books, sports, politics...hell, even the damn weather. Maybe it would have distracted them from the heavier, tenser moments of the evening. Maybe he should have...

Oh, who knew what he should have done to make things better?

What was really worrying him was whether or not they'd be back to square one after last night's little fiasco, with Raven avoiding him—refusing to even

look him in the eye. He just didn't know.
Unfortunately, it was a case of the old wait-and-see
game. Again.

What a mess! It was at times like this he almost
wished he was a smoker.

"You okay, Mark?"

Startled out of his deep thoughts, Mark turned to see
Brody standing beside him with a rather concerned
frown on his face.

Damn! He'd been caught wool-gathering. And what
a depressing fleece it was turning out to be.

"I'm fine," Mark replied, probably too quickly
judging by the expression of disbelief on Brody's face.
He rescued the prawns and plated them up, ready to
go out. "You got the mains started?"

"Yep, all ready to go."

"Okay. Good." Mark took a cursory glance over the
entrée order and nodded his approval for it to leave
the kitchen, but he wasn't really concentrating on
what he saw. He needed to get his head together.
"Looks like everything's under control for a second.
I'm going to take a quick break. You be okay for a few
minutes?"

If Brody thought it was odd Mark wasn't his normal
obsessive-compulsive self running the kitchen tonight,
he didn't say.

"Sure. See you soon."

Mark stripped off his apron and walked out the door
to the back steps—the ones that led up to the
apartment above the restaurant. It was a good spot to
sit and cogitate. Or brood, if the mood struck him. He
hadn't decided which it would be tonight yet.

He sank down onto a cold, hard tread and ran a
hand back through his hair, stripping away his
bandanna as he went. The dark and relative quiet of

the evening was a welcome relief, but it felt kind of...lonely too. He'd been feeling that a lot lately — lonely. Like something was missing, or needed or...something.

Resting his forearms on his knees, Mark fondled the soft black folds of his bandana and absentmindedly undid the knot that had held it in place on his head, readying to re-tie it when his break was over. He gazed out across the back dock area. The orange wash of the security light was strangely soothing. He watched the insects buzzing around the soft glow. Listened to the dull rumble of cars and the ocean in the distance. Breathing in through his nose, he thought he might have been able to imagine the faint hint of a storm on the way, carried in on the vaguely salty breeze.

Rubbing at his temples, Mark tried not to think about anything for a moment, allowing the tension to bleed away into the oblivion. It helped sometimes when he could feel himself getting all worked up about something — kind of like meditating, he guessed, but nothing so formal as to require true navel contemplation.

The sound of movement behind him — someone coming down the steps — snapped him back to reality. He glanced over his shoulder, only to stare up into the face of the very man he'd been thinking about all day.

"Raven!"

Mark jumped up in surprise — glad he managed to end up landing on the deck outside the kitchen's back door where he had plenty of room to stumble about rather than on one of the narrow steps he'd been sitting on where he was sure he'd have fallen flat on his ass.

"H-hi," Raven said, staring down at him from several steps above.

At least Raven was still talking to him. That was a plus. And looking him in the eye, too. Definitely a good sign. But this late at night Raven should have been long gone, even if he had dropped Wolf off from preschool and stayed to let the kids play for a while. Mark felt a little flutter of unease.

"What are you doing here?"

Raven continued carefully down the steps until he was standing on the small landing outside the kitchen as well. "I'm b-babysitting."

"What happened to Cindy?"

"She quit."

"Really?" Cindy — Wolf's regular sitter — was a really nice girl. Young, but she'd seemed to love looking after Wolf. Mark certainly couldn't imagine her up and leaving Brody, Lark and Zak in the lurch. "What happened? Is she all right?"

"She's p-pregnant and has bad m-morning sickness. Like all day m-morning sickness. She couldn't keep working, so Brody asked me if I'd be interested in the j-job."

"Oh! Um...wow." Mark considered Raven — standing in front of him, talking to him, looking back at him. "So, I guess that means you'll be around here even more from now on, huh?"

"Y-yeah."

Raven blushed and looked away shyly. But the tentative smile that tugged at his lips at the same time made Mark's heart pound.

"Ryan really loves the idea. And the extra m-money won't hurt."

Mark sobered instantly. "Are you and Ryan okay?"

He felt a definite twinge of guilt for asking—money being one of *those* subjects—but he had to make sure the two of them were all right.

"Oh, yeah. But you know...k-kids are expensive."

"Yeah," Mark replied with a wash of relief. "I remember that part well." They shared a smile and Mark felt instantly, pathetically better for it. Even his head wasn't throbbing so badly anymore. "So...um...what are you doing? I mean now. Out here."

Smooth. Mark fought against the urge to roll his eyes at himself. What was it about Raven that turned him into the village idiot? And it seemed to be getting worse, he realised, as he finally noticed the garbage bag Raven was holding up.

"I was c-cleaning the kitchen upstairs. Just trying to help out a b-bit. I thought I'd take the g-garbage out."

It took Mark several seconds to realise Raven was looking at him expectantly, and then several more seconds to figure out he was blocking the way to the dumpster.

"Oh! Um...sorry. I'll just..."

Mark stepped aside to allow Raven to dump the bag he was carrying. But when Raven finished and turned back to face him, he didn't rush to hurry away as Mark had expected. Instead, they stood staring at one another in silence. Mark's tension now had more to do with a quivering anticipation and the need building inside him. And he desperately wanted to know if he was the only one feeling it. Judging by the look on Raven's face—part wonder, part desire and part panic—he didn't think he was alone.

"I...ah...I really enjoyed last night," Mark finally managed.

In the dim light, Mark could see Raven's blush, but it looked more like shy pleasure than embarrassment.

"Me t-too."

His heart rate really picking up the pace now, Mark decided to push his luck...just a little. "I was wondering, are you going running tomorrow?"

"Y-yes."

"Would you like some company?"

As usual, Raven took his time studying Mark and carefully considered the question. Which made the answer all the more heady when it finally came. "I think...I'd l-like that."

It was like he'd been sucker punched, but in a completely wow-do-it-to-me-again kind of way. Mark just knew he'd have a goofy grin on his face for the rest of the night.

Raven watched the hope and pleasure light up Mark's eyes and felt an answering jolt of happiness.

It was all sorts of crazy, but seeing the obvious relief on Mark's face made all the difference. It certainly made Raven feel better about his decision to continue getting to know Mark.

He'd seen something last night. Something he came back to over and over again that made him think Mark just might be worth the risk. That he should take a chance and explore the connection that pulled at him whenever they were together. There was a vulnerability about Mark he hadn't appreciated when they'd first met.

The fact he had never been a foregone conclusion to Mark also reassured him into thinking he might just be making the right decision. Mark hadn't assumed Raven would agree to more dates without question. He hadn't acted as if Raven didn't have any options, or should be so grateful for the attention he would simply fall into line. Knowing Mark acknowledged that Raven could use that very small but extremely powerful word—*No!*—was everything. It was a word that was still very much a new and precious thing in Raven's life.

"I should p-probably get back upstairs," Raven finally managed to force out. "The boys are watching television, but...well, you know, never t-turn your back and all that."

"Yeah."

Raven moved to step around, but Mark's voice stopped him as he was about to pass.

"So where should I meet you tomorrow?"

The heat from Mark's body brushed against Raven's senses. It was breathtaking and he found it hard to concentrate on what Mark had said. Instead he wanted to stand very still and soak in Mark's proximity and the spicy scent that surrounded him. It was an intense, delicious and scary reaction all at the same time.

"Raven?"

"Huh?"

"I was just wondering where I should meet you for our run tomorrow."

"Oh! Um..." Raven took a deep breath and tried to focus, but the big, earnest puppy dog eyes were doing a real number on him. "I p-promised to take Wolf to p-preschool tomorrow."

"Okay. Should I meet you here then?" Mark asked, seemingly oblivious to Raven's internal chaos.

"I...um...I usually start my r-run from outside the boys' p-preschool. Do you know where that is?"

"Yeah. I could meet you there if you like."

"Okay."

Wow! That felt good. That felt really good. Talking to Mark and trusting him with little details of his routine. Agreeing on a running date. Standing slightly too close and a little breathless. It was normal and natural and wonderful. Well, normal and wonderful in an all-tied-up-in-giddy-excited-knots kind of way as they continued to stare at each other.

Raven couldn't believe how ready to take on any challenge he felt right now.

"So, I guess I'll see you tomorrow morning," Mark finally murmured.

"Yeah. I...ah...I really n-need to get back."

"Yeah, me too."

Neither of them made a move to go anywhere, however. It was an exciting rush to think Mark was as reluctant to leave as he was.

"Night, Raven."

"Night, M-Mark."

Raven turned to head back upstairs.

"Hey, Raven."

"Yeah?"

"Thanks for letting me tag along on your run tomorrow. I'm really looking forward to it."

Raven studied Mark. Old habits of looking for teasing or sinister motivations died hard apparently. But there simply wasn't anything like that on Mark's face. There was just genuine happiness and a little vulnerability. "Yeah, m-me too."

And amazingly enough, it was true.

Chapter Eight

Mark stood beside Zak under the shade of the trees that bordered the park and took another sip of his soda. March had flown by in a rush of work, settling in a new chef—Jayden—and seizing every opportunity he could to get to know Raven. Now, the first week of April and with spring well underway, Mark found himself idle, watching the madness that was the first official 'Annual Sandpipers Restaurant Family and Friends Picnic'.

It had been a long day of games, fun and good old-fashioned craziness. And much to Mark's surprise, he had thoroughly enjoyed it. Right now, there was a heated game of croquet of all things—or something vaguely resembling it—playing out on the lush grass in front of them. A wild, disorganised and fiercely competitive affair, it had to be one of the most bizarre, madcap games of *anything* Mark had ever witnessed.

There were no rules—or at least none that he could make out—and cheating seemed to be a legitimate way of winning so long as you either didn't get caught or could argue your way out of any disputes that arose. Hoops and mallets and fist-sized coloured balls were being abused in all directions. And although he was pretty sure croquet was never intended to be a contact sport, it didn't appear to be stopping the gang from Sandpipers getting physical with one another.

So far he'd seen everything from jostling to tripping. But everyone seemed to be having a great time as the game descended further and further into chaos. It was certainly an absolute riot to watch.

Having begged out—pleading an old football injury to a chorus of light-hearted derision—Mark was able to just sit back and observe to his heart's content. He couldn't help smiling as the teams battled it out. But it was Raven he really wanted to stare at and enjoyed watching the most.

Something had happened over the last month. Something subtle but powerful in the way Raven held himself and had started to interact with the people around him—at least the people he knew. Gone was the tight nervousness and the avoidance to the point he wouldn't look anyone in the eye for more than a few seconds. Now Mark often caught Raven's dark eyes watching him, and bolder and bolder smiles every day. Hell, Raven was even relaxed enough today to laugh out loud with everybody else as Lark dashed past to 'accidentally' knock Dave's mallet just as he went to make a tricky shot.

Mark couldn't help feeling a swell of pride as he watched a grinning Raven help Wolf make his next shot around the tussle that ensued between the two. Raven was stronger and more resilient than most would give him credit for—Raven included, he suspected. He'd found his feet and an unlikely circle of friends within the odd mix that made up the Sandpipers Restaurant family.

And strangely enough, Mark understood completely. He felt as if he'd found the same thing in a lot of ways. What had started out as just another job with an admittedly good crew had gradually morphed into something more. He'd started to form a sense of connection with these people too — something he hadn't felt since Lucy and Evan had moved away nearly twelve months ago.

As for his connection to Raven, the past few weeks had been pretty incredible in that regard too. They ran most mornings together now. And man, could Raven move. Not that he minded when Raven got into the zone and started outdistancing him. The view from behind was amazing. Mark had many a night-time fantasy involving Raven and his tight, black running shorts. Although, they never stayed on for long in his dreams. Not like in reality.

He had to admit his cock was becoming more and more unruly and insistent every day. But he could hold it…quite literally as it turned out, because it was the only action he was seeing right now. And he didn't expect that to change anytime soon.

Mark quickly tried to divert his mind to other things before he ended up embarrassing himself in front of the entire restaurant staff.

He thought about the handful of formal dates they'd been on over the last few weeks. None of them had been as intense as the first — thank goodness. Mark felt like they'd finally started to relax while out together. They talked about ordinary, mundane things — what books they'd read, what movies they wanted to see, places they wanted to visit. Things he suspected most couples getting to know each other talked about —

which was good. Hopefully it would lead to more, but for right now it was…good.

Damn! Who did he think he was kidding? He wanted Raven with a passion. *Right now!* And the more he tried to deny it, the more he found himself dwelling on the need. He felt guilty because he'd promised himself they'd take things slow and he didn't want to push Raven. But he ached something fierce. He was only human, after all, and Raven was sexy as all hell.

Fortunately, his frustrated musings were cut short when Lark let out a wild, indignant cry. Apparently Brody had used Lark's distraction to set the man's croquet ball back several hoops. Lark stopped struggling with Dave and began chasing after Brody, whose escape was somewhat hampered by his amusement.

"Less laughing more running, Brody," Zak called out, clearly enjoying his lover's antics. "He's going to kick your ass if he catches it!"

Mark smiled. "I'm going to take a wild stab in the dark here and guess this whole croquet game thing was one of Lark's ideas."

"How'd you know?" Zak asked, grinning broadly as Lark finally caught Brody and tackled him to the ground to tickle him mercilessly.

"Just a hunch."

They both chuckled as Raven not so subtly used the distraction to advance Wolf and Ryan's ball several hoops—much to the boys' boisterous delight.

It was wonderful to see Raven slowly coming out of himself like this. It had been the best part of the whole afternoon actually.

Just as he thought it, Raven looked across and smiled at him—a full, uninhibited and glorious thousand-watt smile that arrowed straight to Mark's heart. And Mark fell right into it. Then Wolf and Ryan snagged Raven's arms and dragged him away, breaking the moment.

Mark didn't begrudge the boys Raven's attention for a second. In fact, he was somewhat grateful. He wasn't sure he could have withstood anymore of that look without doing something stupid...like marching right over and planting a kiss on Raven's beautiful lips. As it was, he was struggling against popping wood and probably gaping like a landed fish.

Zak cleared his throat, drawing Mark's attention away from Raven and the boys to face a very knowing grin. "So, how are things going between you and Raven?"

"Good," Mark replied, forcing a calm he didn't feel as he tried to concentrate on Zak, giving his brain a moment to clear and his cock a chance to settle down. "Yeah, slow, but...good."

"You still running in the mornings?"

There was a wicked smirk on Zak's face now. The man knew how much Mark loathed getting up early. But to be honest, he'd kind of got used to it now. He wouldn't miss the chance to be with Raven for anything. And he had to admit he felt better for the regular exercise.

"Yeah. I'm really enjoying it, actually."

"Wow! It must be love," Zak drawled—but Mark got the distinct impression Zak was scrutinising his reaction far more closely than a simple ribbing would require.

For a crazy moment, Mark felt like he was being cornered by an overprotective father and asked his intentions. He eyed Zak. Perhaps an older brother was closer to the mark, but one just as deadly earnest about looking out for Raven.

In a weird way, it was kind of nice to think Raven had people looking out for him. In another, Mark was a bit indignant that they'd think he'd ever hurt Raven. Because he had absolutely no doubt Lark and Brody had a hand in Zak's 'little talk'.

Mark squared his shoulders. "Yeah. I mean he… it's…you know…"

Zak let him flounder for a moment, before finally letting him off the hook with a nod as he looked over at his own men. "Yeah. I know."

Lark and Brody were laughing together so hard they could hardly stand up as Brody tried to wrestle the croquet mallet away from Lark. All things considered, it was probably a good move for all concerned.

Despite Brody and Lark's noisy clowning around, Mark found himself drawn to focus on Raven again.

"I just… I want to be there for him. You know?"

"Yeah. And believe me, it's a good thing too. If you didn't look after him, Brody and Lark would want me to kick your ass. And I'd hate to have to find another head-chef after we've just gotten you all broken in and everything."

Mark let out a snort, eyeing Zak's bulging biceps warily. "Thanks."

"No problem. But honestly, it probably wouldn't even be me you'd have to worry about. Lark's a vicious little bastard when he sets his mind to it. Believe me."

Mark did believe—he'd seen Lark dealing with a late delivery last week. He was certainly glad he hadn't been on the receiving end of the 'discussion', that's for sure. He might not have a mean bone in his body, but Lark didn't take any crap from anybody either.

The game gradually started to wind down. Some players finished, but most were either busy harassing their opponents or too exhausted to care. Everyone seemed happy enough to let the match dissolve down into a messy draw for second and third place, with Wolf, Ryan and Raven's team claiming an undisputed, if somewhat dubious first.

"We'll probably take off soon," Mark said, trying not to sound too nervous as he watched the boys celebrate their endgame victory on the other side of the playing field. It wasn't easy. He could feel his shoulder and neck muscles getting tighter as he thought about the rest of the afternoon. Or more precisely the potential for it to go awry.

Zak glanced over, obviously having heard the unease in Mark's voice. *Damn it!*

"We're going to take Ryan to the pier for ice cream and a walk on the beach to wind down," Mark confessed.

"First time you've all been out together, huh?" Zak asked, astute as ever.

"Yeah."

"You'll do great."

Mark took a deep breath and let it out slowly. "Hope so."

Zak snorted. "Know so. Ever since you handed your watch over before that first date and brought Raven back right when you said you would, Ryan looks at you like you can walk on water."

Mark felt his cheeks fill with heat. "He's a good kid."

"Yeah, he is. And so is his dad."

Mark merely nodded. Raven definitely was good. And good for him too, in so many ways. Mark was very aware of how much was riding on this afternoon.

* * * *

Raven felt another unexpected laugh slip out as Ryan put their team's bright blue croquet ball through the last hoop and started a zany victory dance with Wolf.

While it still startled him a little every time he heard himself make the sound, it was a pleasant surprise and slowly he was getting used to laughing. It happened a lot when he was around the boys. Their exuberance was infectious, and all the more precious because it was the first time he could remember seeing it from Ryan. But more and more often, Raven found himself relaxing enough to smile and laugh around others as well. And incredibly, no one stared at him or looked at him strangely. They only laughed with him, not at him.

A few of the other contestants—or was that combatants?—cheered Wolf and Ryan's win. There might have been one or two dubious shots and a missed hoop or two along the way, but going by the antics of some of the other teams, Raven figured it was a case of all's fair in love and croquet. And judging by the indulgent smiles and cheers as the boys celebrated their victory, everyone was pretty happy with the end result. Especially Wolf and Ryan.

Watching the two boys together, Raven realised he should never have worried about them forming an enduring friendship. They were closer than brothers these days. They'd never leave each other's side if it was left up to them. It was quite a relief to know Ryan had someone his own age he connected to so strongly. It was one less thing Raven had to worry about. He knew from personal experience loners and the socially inept were prime targets for bullies. But he couldn't imagine Wolf ever letting that happen to Ryan.

In fact, so much about their new life here in Riversands was working out perfectly, it was hard to believe at times. But he tried very hard to simply accept their change of fortunes. There were quite enough hurdles to overcome without inventing any.

Still thinking about how lucky they were, Raven's gaze strayed to where Mark stood relaxing in the shade with Zak. Nothing could have prepared him for finding someone like Mark. The temptation to fret and fuss over just how perfect Mark seemed, compared to how completely imperfect Raven felt most of the time, was strong. And once or twice in the last few weeks since he'd decided not to dwell on it, he'd still found himself wondering—questioning whether it really was too good to be true. But he always came back to the memory of their first date together, to the vulnerability and need he'd sensed in Mark. For the first time in his life he'd felt as if he wasn't the only one nervous and anxious—like the outcome of the evening actually mattered to Mark. He'd gradually started to accept that Mark really did want to be with him...maybe even needed to be with him. It was hard to explain, but something inside said *don't pull away. Don't put up barriers and keep Mark out.*

Slowly, he'd lowered his defences and it was, quite frankly...wonderful. He felt like he was waking up for the first time after being in a coma for years—a miserable limbo of silence and self-doubt. And he was determined to savour every second.

"You about ready to say g-goodbye and head out, buddy?" Raven asked Ryan when the boys finally settled down.

"Can Wolf come with us?"

Raven studied the boys' hopeful faces. It was tempting to give in to the pleading looks, but he had other plans for what remained of the day. Big plans.

"Maybe n-next time, huh? I want us to spend some time with M-Mark this afternoon. Just the three of us."

Ryan nodded, looking crestfallen.

Wolf studied Raven for a moment, then turned to Ryan and gave him a final brief hug. "See ya later."

And with that he ran off towards Brody. Ryan really looked like he wanted to follow.

"Come on. Let's go see if Mark's ready to t-take us to the beach for ice cream."

At least that seemed to perk Ryan up a little. Together they made their way towards Mark and Zak.

"Hey, guys! Good game!" Zak greeted as they stepped up. "Well done!"

Raven smiled. "It was a lot of f-fun."

"Are you and Ryan about ready to leave?" Mark asked.

Raven nodded and held out his hand to Zak. "Thank you for inviting us. It was a w-wonderful day."

Suddenly, Lark appeared at Zak's side. "You're not leaving already, are you?"

"Raven and I have plans to take young Master Ryan out for ice cream," Mark explained, ruffling the boy's hair playfully.

"We have an announcement. Do you think you guys could hang around for just a few more minutes?"

Raven glanced over at Mark, who shrugged and nodded.

"Okay."

"Hey, everyone," Lark said, raising his voice and beckoning for Brody to join them. "Zak, Brody and I have a little something we want to share!"

He waited until everyone was gathered and listening. "Okay. Well, first off we'd like to thank you all for coming. It's been a great start to a tradition we're hoping to keep going for many years to come."

"Hear! Hear!" someone called from the small crowd.

Lark chuckled. "Yes indeed! Here's to good food, good friends and good fun!"

There was a chorus of cheers and rowdy agreement that Lark let die away before continuing. "We really do appreciate everything you all do throughout the year to make Sandpipers more than just another restaurant."

"That's 'cause we're not just *another* restaurant. We're *the* restaurant, baby!" Callum—one of the barmen—shouted to a round of wolf whistles and applause from the rest of the crowd.

"Exactly!" Lark shouted to be heard over the noise, drawing everyone's attention back to him. "You guys aren't just some of the best employees around, you're friends and family." More hearty approval and clapping greeted Lark's words. After a moment he raised his hands for quiet. "So, last but certainly not least, we want to let you all know, as Sandpipers family and friends, that Brody, Zak and I are getting hitched."

Brody laughed over the mix of surprised and excited exclamations from the group. "And you were being so eloquent."

"What Lark means is we're having a commitment ceremony. To make everything official between the three of us," Zak explained, then looked down at Wolf who stood gazing up at him. "Well, four really. We're going to make our little arrangement as legal as possible, but really it's all about us celebrating being a family."

Lark frowned and affected a pout. "That's what I said."

"It's a great excuse for another party anyway," Brody said with a huge grin as Dave slapped him on the back.

"Like the three of you need one," Andy pointed out.

"True," Lark replied over the ensuing laughter.

"So, when is this party planned for anyway?" Drew, one of the waiters, asked.

"Some of you may have seen the restaurant booked for a two day function next month—" Zak began to explain, but Lark was apparently too excited to give up centre stage.

"That's our special day! We're getting caterers in. They work, we party!"

Lark's announcement was met with another chorus of approval.

Everyone seemed genuinely excited and happy for the trio. They really did resemble one big, messy extended family with the next few minutes a happy confusion of congratulations and good natured teasing.

During the mayhem, Mark slipped up to stand beside Raven.

"You ready to go?"

Raven looked over to his friends standing in the middle of the chaos. It didn't look like they'd be missed with everything else that was going on, and there was very little chance they'd get a word in edgeways anyway. Raven figured they'd said their goodbyes, at least enough not to be rude if they went ahead and left.

"Okay," Raven agreed, feeling a nervous thrill at the idea of spending the rest of the afternoon with Mark.

"Let's walk to the beach. It's not that far."

Raven nodded. "I just need to g-grab our coats from the car."

The afternoon was cooling down rapidly, and the breeze at the beach was sure to be cool. Certainly too cold for Ryan's skinny little five-year-old body to handle.

"Good idea. You go, I'll keep an eye on Ryan."

Ryan had managed to slip away to play with Wolf again. It would be easier to just nip to the car and be right back. Faster too.

"Thank you. I w-won't be a second."

Raven hesitated, then—squeezing all his courage into a sudden burst of speed—he impulsively kissed Mark on the cheek.

Mark looked completely stunned. A rush of fear and excitement poured through Raven, leaving him feeling a little lightheaded and shaky. Had he done the wrong thing? They'd never really gone in for public displays of affection before. Part of him had wondered if Mark was holding back, waiting for him to make the first move. But another more distrustful part simply held its breath, waiting to see what Mark's reaction would be.

Raven watched, slightly wide-eyed and rooted to the spot as Mark reached out to touch him.

"Take your time," Mark said, his voice low and husky as he held Raven's chin and gently brushed a thumb over his lips. "There's no rush."

Raven was pretty sure Mark wasn't referring to his trip to the car. At least not solely. "I know, I just... I don't want to d-dawdle and get left behind."

"No chance of that ever happening. You're worth waiting for."

Chapter Nine

Raven smiled as he watched Mark and Ryan — heads bent together, so serious and intent as they concentrated on the task at hand.

Once again, Mark patiently demonstrated how to kick the football he'd bought for Ryan off the little mound of sand they'd built for it. This late in the afternoon there weren't many people around so they had a nice wide expanse of pale yellow beach all to themselves. Which was probably just as well as Ryan lined up to follow Mark's instructions and ended up kicking yet another great plume of the fine grains high into the air. The ball followed a wild arc to land a few feet away.

Technically, he supposed the ball could be considered a bribe on Mark's part. But watching Ryan scramble after the small red-brown ball enthusiastically and return with a huge grin on his face to try again, Raven didn't think it really mattered. Ryan was happy. And even better than that, he seemed to be really responding to Mark's gentle guidance. It was a huge relief.

And heaven knew Raven would be no help to his son when it came to learning the fine art of football. It had never been his thing. The closest he got to appreciating it was admiring the players and the way their uniforms fit during the Super Bowl. But Mark and Ryan had really bonded over the half sized rubber 'pigskin'.

"Okay, champ. Time to wrap it up," Mark announced when Ryan reached his side. "I definitely think you deserve ice cream after all that hard work."

Ryan looked across hopefully, and Raven smiled. "I think you b-both earned your ice cream. My t-treat."

"I thought I was the one taking the two of you out today," Mark replied.

Raven shook his head. "I want to take the champ and his c-coach out to celebrate."

Mark's expression was priceless — surprise and pleasure all mixed up together, culminating in a slow blooming smile. "Okay."

Together they slogged their way back through the soft sand, heading towards the boardwalk.

"Thank you for today," Mark said as they all fell into step together side-by-side. "I've had such a great time hanging out with you guys."

"We're the ones that should be saying th-thank you. Especially after the f-football lesson, don't you think, Ryan?" Raven prompted.

"Uh-huh! Thank you!" Ryan called as he kicked the ball ahead of them, then scrambled after it when it shot off at an odd angle.

Raven smiled as they watched Ryan fumble to pick up the ball and instead accidentally end up kicking it further away—much to Ryan's delight if the laughter was anything to go by.

Pacing themselves so that Ryan could zigzag with the ball ahead of them, Raven and Mark continued on through the sand.

"You know, I don't live far from here," Mark said a few moments later with a casual air that didn't fool Raven for a second.

Not entirely clueless as to where the conversation might be heading, Raven's breath caught in his throat, but not in a completely bad way. He'd never been to Mark's apartment. And Mark had never visited the little two-bedroom place he'd rented when he and Ryan had first arrived in Riversands either. It was an odd mix of scary and exciting to think about taking this next step in the getting-to-know-you journey with Mark.

Up ahead, the ice cream vendor they'd spotted when they first arrived came into view, saving him from having to come up with a reply straightaway as Ryan ran back to them clutching his football and bouncing with excitement. It looked like Wolf was rubbing off on him, Raven noted with an amusement that helped ease his tension a little.

"Can I go and see?" Ryan asked.

Where the boy got the energy from after a full day of playing—both at the park and the beach—was anyone's guess. Raven assessed the distance between where they were and the ice cream cart. It wasn't too far for Ryan to run ahead and still be safe. And maybe it would help wear him out a bit.

"Okay. But m-mind your manners."

"I will," Ryan called back as he took off.

"Would you..." Mark started to say then hesitated, apparently hunting for the right words. "I mean, I was wondering if you and Ryan would like to come over to my place for dinner. Maybe stay for a movie?"

"Ryan's p-probably going to be pretty tired after today once he actually s-stops." Raven hedged, giving himself time to think. "He'll more than likely fall asleep in his d-dinner."

"I've got a spare room. You're welcome to stay over."

Raven blinked and stared openly across at Mark. That was a big step.

"There's twin singles in the spare room. I wasn't suggesting..." A creeping red flush coloured Mark's neck and gradually stained his cheeks. "It's just... I've got tomorrow off. I'd really like to have breakfast with the two of you. Drop Ryan off at preschool. Go for our run. Just...you know...spend the day together."

"What about c-clothes for tomorrow? I don't have anything c-clean with us."

"I've got some stuff you can borrow to sleep in and we can wash and dry what you've got on for tomorrow at my place."

Raven took in Mark's eager expression. "You've g-got an answer for everything, I see."

"Sorry." Mark looked away, the colour high in his cheeks now. "I'm pushing too hard, aren't I?"

"M-maybe." Mark's face was a picture of shame and dejection at Raven's admission. "I'm not saying I hate it exactly," he hastened to reassure, but it was clear from Mark's expression he didn't quite believe it. "It is kind of...f-flattering."

Raven could feel his own cheeks getting hot now.

Mark shrugged as if it wasn't a big deal, but Raven could see otherwise. "I just... I hate goodbyes. Always have. And...well, I'd really like you to come over and stay with me one day. I just thought..."

Fortunately, they'd reached the boardwalk and Ryan, who was pressed up against the ice cream cart, eyeing the selections—giving Raven an excuse and time to consider his reply.

It looked like the vendor was finishing up for the day, but he'd stopped packing up—albeit looking less than enthusiastic about having to hang around any longer. Raven hadn't realised how late it was getting. The last of the sun's rays were definitely disappearing fast. A shiver of unease ran up and down his spine as the man behind the cart gave them a less than friendly look. If he'd been on his own, he would have given the man a wide berth. But Ryan was busy looking at the display and Mark seemed completely oblivious to the disapproval.

"So, w-what would y-y-you like, Ryan?" Raven asked, anxiety tightening his throat.

The man rolled his eyes and heaved a sigh.

Raven cringed. This wasn't going to end well, he just knew it. And Mark stiffening beside him only confirmed his fears.

Please don't let this get ugly! Please don't let this get ugly!

"I'd like chocolate?" Ryan announced—innocent and unaware of the mounting tension around him.

"Ok-kay. M-M-Mark?"

Shit! Shit! Shit! Not fair!

His stuttering was always ten times worse when he was nervous and under pressure. And the way the guy was looking at him now definitely made him feel both—along with slightly nauseated.

"You know what? I think I have an even better idea," Mark said, eyes never once leaving the vendor's face while he said it. "Why don't we have dinner out as well. There's a place up on the pier that makes the best hotdogs in Riversands, and for dessert we can have sundaes. I think we should pull out all the stops. It's a special treat day."

With that, Mark took first Raven's hand then Ryan's and turned them away.

Behind them, Raven heard the vendor murmur the words 'fucking freaks'. Mark jerked and tensed as if ready to spin around and... Well, he wasn't sure what Mark would do, but he couldn't let it happen. He didn't want a scene, especially not in front of Ryan.

"D-d-don't," Raven managed to whisper. "P-please."

Mark glanced at him. He looked angry and Raven couldn't suppress a shiver of fear. Instantly, Mark's expression cleared and he took a deep, calming breath.

"Okay," he finally murmured. "But only 'cause you're asking me not to."

Raven considered Mark's stormy eyes, clearly seeing how much control he was exercising over himself in that moment. The situation was incredibly crappy, but watching Mark *not* do anything—and appreciating the self-restraint that took—made him feel just a tiny bit better.

"Th-th-thank you."

"Daddy?" Ryan squeaked, sounding suddenly uncertain and slightly scared as he peeked around Mark to stare up at him.

Raven hated himself, his stutter, and the asshole vendor just that little bit more for the insecurity he saw in his son's eyes in that moment.

Damn it all to hell! And the afternoon had been going so well too!

Raven opened his arms in invitation, and Ryan climbed right up into them for a hug.

"Hey! It's all fine, buddy," Mark reassured with forced cheer. "I was just remembering the promise I made. Do you remember how I promised to look after your Daddy?"

Ryan nodded as he shifted his attention to Mark — his big brown eyes studying him with all the intensity and seriousness a five year old could muster.

"Well, I think that means hotdogs and ice creams to finish off our day together. I don't think it would be looking after your dad properly if he missed out on the best hotdogs in town. What do you think?"

Ryan leant back a little to study Raven. Raven tried to give him a smile, but he wasn't sure how successful he was. Ryan nodded anyway and looked back at Mark.

"Uh-huh! I think he looks hungry."

"Yeah. Me too." Mark got them moving again towards the pier with a light touch to the small of Raven's back and a confident stride. "So, on to hotdogs and looking after your dad then."

* * * *

Mark ran his spoon through the dregs at the bottom of his caramel sundae then popped the spoon into his mouth to lick it clean. Across from him, Raven was studying the table intensely. It hadn't escaped his notice that he hadn't looked him in the eye once since they'd sat down.

Damn! He wished Raven had let him wring that stupid asshole's neck. He'd been so mad. Still was. Words just didn't do the rage justice. The guy had been a complete and utter jerk to Raven — *his* Raven — and that was just —

His Raven. Mark stopped to consider the thought that had suddenly popped into his head and settled right in like it belonged. Yes. His Raven. His to care for and protect. And much as he'd wanted to beat the guy's head in, it wasn't going to happen. Apart from anything else, the bastard wasn't worth spitting on, never mind going to jail for. And at the end of the day, his one and only concern was making sure Raven and Ryan were okay.

Which was something he hadn't been doing a very good job of, he suddenly realised.

Making sure Ryan was thoroughly preoccupied with his chocolate sundae, Mark reached across and lightly brushed Raven's fingers where they rested on the pale, speckled laminate tabletop. It was time to start looking after his man.

"I'm sorry that guy was such a —" Mark cut himself off as he looked over at Ryan, still contentedly ploughing through his ice cream. "I mean, I hate what happened back there."

Raven's face was so red, it practically glowed. "I'm s-s-sorry I m-m-messed things up."

Mark added gentle pressure to Raven's fingers where they rested under his hand. "You didn't. Don't ever think you need to apologise for stuttering. Not to me. Not to anybody."

Raven swallowed. "You're not emb-b-barrassed?"

"No." Mark shook his head firmly. "Not even slightly."

Raven still wouldn't look at him.

"I mean that, Raven."

There was a long silence. Mark could see Raven wanted to say something — he could almost see it roiling beneath the surface. He waited patiently while Raven worked through whatever it was.

"I… I'm so…" Raven looked up at him at last and Mark was shocked to see the hard, angry light in his eyes.

"Raven?" Mark said hesitantly.

But just as it looked like Raven might say something else, Ryan heaved a contented sigh and snuggled in against his father's side.

Raven looked down at the top of Ryan's head resting against his arm, his expression softening again. "You all d-done, sleepyhead?"

"Uh-huh," Ryan murmured.

Mark could see the little boy's eyelids already starting to droop. And for a moment, Mark wasn't sure if Ryan was the only one that was drifting off to sleep—Raven was so completely still, his eyes downcast so it was hard to tell if they were open or closed.

Then Raven's jaw clenched and he looked up—straight into Mark's eyes with a fierce, determined look on his face.

"Is that m-movie night and spare r-room still on offer?"

"Um…sure. I mean, of course." Mark studied Raven but he gave nothing away with his expression now. He was all closed and unwavering. The sudden change was a little unnerving. "My place is just around the corner."

Raven nodded. "Great. Are you ready to g-go?"

"Yeah, I…ah… I mean sure. Just let me take care of the bill."

Mark couldn't help wondering what was going on in Raven's head when he simply nodded once decisively and gathered Ryan up. But then again, maybe he was being paranoid. Was he really going to question Raven's decision to come over? It was the next logical step, and exactly what he wanted. He should be ecstatic right now. So why was he feeling suddenly uneasy about it all?

* * * *

Raven carefully scooped Ryan up into his arms and gently positioned him so the little boy's head was cradled securely in the crook of his neck. And the whole time he let the anger and resentment build inside. He was determined to use it this time. He wouldn't back down and cower away from what he wanted. What he needed.

He absolutely hated his stuttering. For as long as he could remember, it had fucked up his life. But Mark was right — it wasn't something he should have to apologise for or even be embarrassed about. He refused to act like his usual doormat, pathetic, scared-stiff self this time. He was sick to death of being afraid of everything and everybody. He loathed the embarrassment that came with being pitied or sneered at, or, worse still, dismissed completely. Enough was enough.

"You all right with him?" Mark asked with a frown as he joined them at the table again, eyeing Ryan draped limply over Raven's shoulder with concern.

"I'm f-fine," Raven replied shortly. "Lead the w-way."

For once in his life he was going to do and not hesitate. He was going to reach out and grab hold of what he wanted. Seize the day and all that. And he knew right down to his core what he wanted was Mark. To be with him in every sense of the word. He wanted to prove to himself — and to Mark too if he was being completely honest — that he was like everyone else. Normal. Deserving. He wasn't going to sit back and take it anymore.

Chapter Ten

Mark caught himself pacing back and forth across the length of his small, neat living room and stopped in his tracks. He closed his eyes and shook his head at himself in exasperation. At least doing so forced him to stand still. But it didn't do much to make him feel any less edgy.

After taking a deep breath, he opened his eyes again and scanned around the room—barely resisting the urge to start straightening the couch cushions like a neurotic housewife. He *really* needed to get a grip. He didn't even know what he was worried about. This was just a nice little movie night extension of their afternoon date. Raven was putting Ryan to bed in the guest room, then they'd pick something to watch. He'd put on some popcorn and grab a couple of sodas and they'd enjoy a nice, relaxing wind-down to their day together.

Companionable. Civilised. Nice.

Mark really wasn't feeling it. In fact, he was leaning more towards jumpy and maybe just a little bit raw.

Like a bad case of sunburn—all tight and hypersensitive—only on the inside, where it couldn't be relieved by things like aloe vera and plenty of water.

He wasn't sure what it was exactly, but something had changed about Raven. And it had all started somewhere between the confrontation with the asshole on the beach and finishing their dinner. The vibes Raven was giving off now were confusing...and exciting as hell at the same time. He just hoped he could keep up with whatever was going—

Sensing someone behind him, Mark spun around. Raven stood in the doorway to the living room, staring at him with an inscrutable expression on his face. It was a little disconcerting. But on the other hand...wow, Raven looked good standing there in his home, wearing the clothes Mark had loaned him.

The T-shirt and sweats Raven had borrowed were too big, but in a weird way that was kind of the appeal. Mark suddenly got a very vivid image of Raven in the kitchen tomorrow morning—swamped in the too-big-for-him shirt, his thick black hair a glorious ruffled mess and his eyes still heavy with sleep. It was completely fanciful, but he couldn't help hoping it would come to fruition. And if not tomorrow morning, then one day.

Mark realised he was staring and forced himself to concentrate on the here and now.

"I...ah... I washed your clothes. I mean they're in the washing machine. It shouldn't be too long before they're done." *Well, that was a less than scintillating start to the evening. Damn!* "So...um... Would you like a drin—"

"N-no, thank you."

Raven started walking towards him, slow and determined with an intense gleam in his eyes. It wasn't a look Mark was used to seeing from Raven.

"Oh, okay. No drink. Well…um…" The way Raven was watching him and walking towards him—almost a stalk really—made Mark oddly nervous. "Would you like to pick a movie and I'll…ah… I'll fix—"

Raven kissed him—hard, hot, possessive, and full on the lips.

As a method of cutting off his uneasy rambling, it was certainly effective. And definitely unexpected. Raven had simply stepped right up and pulled Mark in.

And oh damn!

Oh…

The man could kiss. Mark gave him that. In fact, he was sure several brain cells shorted out and died a happy death during the sensual assault. He almost lost himself completely in the dizzying sensations coursing through his body as Raven pressed up against him. Almost.

"What—?" Mark struggled to say between kisses, but was cut off when Raven sealed their lips together once more, then opened his mouth and invited Mark in with a tempting flick of his tongue.

It was too much to resist. Mark met Raven in a wild tangle of tongues and teeth and hot, wet lips. He pulled Raven in until they were fused together from neck to knees, and Mark felt his cock stir and twitch with the contact. Against his thigh, he felt Raven's cock give an answering throb of interest.

"What are you doing?" he somehow managed to ask when they eventually came up for air.

"I'm k-kissing you," Raven breathed against his lips, then dipped his head to feather more kisses along Mark's jaw.

"I know that. But—"

Another kiss stole the words right out of his mouth.

Mark couldn't hold back a moan as Raven's wicked tongue danced along his lips then plunged between them. It was dangerously easy to lose himself in the way Raven touched him—his supple runner's body leaning in close, his hot mouth open and welcoming, and his eager hands playing across overheated skin and up into Mark's hair, to weave and tug at the short strands. It was a blissful torture.

And yet somehow, in the larger of Mark's heads, there was still enough blood left to ask questions. To wonder what the hell was going on. Why was Raven suddenly acting this way? Anger? Fear? Desperation? They didn't seem like good—or smart—reasons to rush into a physical relationship. Although, Mark could certainly appreciate the desperation. But if that's all it was, then they needed to stop now.

"Raven, slow down. We don't..."

Raven tensed and pulled away—irritation clear in his expression.

"I w-want you. Don't—" Raven took a deep breath. His voice turning soft as he relaxed into Mark again—all warm, sensual and needy. "Don't make me b-beg. I w-want this. Believe me."

"I do believe you. And I'm not saying I don't want this too. But...I'm just a little worried about you."

"Don't be. Trust me. I know w-what I want."

"It's not about not trusting or believing you." Mark took a deep breath and tried to calm his raging libido enough to think straight. "It's just... I'm not sure I understand. I mean, why? Why now?"

"Because I w-want it. I want you."

Mark wasn't convinced. There was something more to all this. Something Raven wasn't telling him. "I'm just not—"

"Because I'm sick of being w-weird and s-scared and—"

"You're not weird—"

"—and alone, okay? That's what's going on. I d-don't want to be alone anymore. Mark, p-please."

Mark's heart ached—he understood not wanting to be alone. Completely.

"You're not alone. Not anymore." He cupped Raven's cheek, trying to reassure them both with the caress. "But there's no need to rush."

"I'm n-not rushing. We've been together for w-weeks. Why don't you believe me when I say I w-want this?"

"I just—"

"Please." Raven thrust up against Mark. "I w-want to feel you deep inside me, M-Mark. Take me to b-bed."

Oh man! There were so many reasons why this wasn't a good idea. Not the least of which was, he had no clue what was really going on inside Raven's head right now—why the sudden change? But at the same time he couldn't deny the need he saw in him. And he didn't want to. What if Raven shut down on him completely?

No, he didn't want to risk that. He'd just have to make sure they kept things under control. After all, it was just another, natural step along the way towards being truly intimate. Right?

Before he could over think it any more than he already had, Mark leaned in and kissed Raven, soft and slow, making the connection a languid claiming and hoping with every fibre of his being he was doing the right thing. And for a while it seemed to satisfy them. Raven melted against him as they worked together to revel in the moment. But gradually the kisses and caresses became deeper, more demanding, more voracious.

"What about Ryan?" Mark managed, panting for breath several minutes later.

"He'd sleep through a nuclear b-blast," Raven said, running his tongue along the angle of Mark's jaw and ending with a nip on his earlobe that sent shivers right down to Mark's toes.

"Raven! Oh—!"

Raven seemed to grow bolder with each passing second. Nimble fingers started working on the buttons of Mark's shirt as his earlobes were alternately nipped and laved. But it wasn't until fingers brushed across his chest and swept over his nipples that something finally flipped inside Mark's head. Raven pushed back the edges of Mark's shirt and began exploring, and it was too much.

Mark dived headlong into the moment. He swept in and claimed Raven's mouth, while at the same time setting to work tugging the borrowed soft, grey cotton T-shirt up over Raven's head. Finally, getting him bare-chested, Mark ran his hands up Raven's sides from hip to modestly defined pecs—running his thumbs over his lean torso until they brushed against Raven's pebbled nipples.

Instantly, Raven jerked and pulled away with a gasp and wide, frightened eyes. Mark backed off, wondering what the hell had happened. Then half a dozen pale circular scars scattered randomly across Raven's chest caught Mark's eye.

What the—?

"Raven?"

Before Mark could process what he was seeing, Raven stepped up and pressed his lips to Mark's once again. And it was no soft, tender caress. It was hard, demanding and hungry — a kiss designed to distract.

Mark fought against it.

He recalled from their first date Raven's vague reference to how messed up his childhood had been. He'd even come to suspect Raven might have been physically abused by his parents. But it looked like Raven had been more than hit. These looked like...cigarette burns.

"Raven, wha — ?"

"Don't."

"But —"

"No. I d-don't want... I don't want to t-talk about it. Not now." Raven stared at him, as if daring him to push it. A stubborn set to his jaw Mark had never seen before made him falter.

He wanted to know everything about Raven eventually, with no secrets left between them. But he wanted Raven to know he accepted every part of him without question or expectation as well. And he wanted to love on the man until nothing else mattered.

Reluctantly, he had to agree. This wasn't the time.

"Okay."

"Where's the bedroom?" Raven asked now that Mark had apparently proven himself smart enough to keep his mouth shut.

"Raven, are you —"

Raven gripped Mark's face with both hands and kissed him passionately, leaving him hard and breathless when he was finally allowed up for air.

"Don't m-make me ask ag-gain." Raven's eyes were dark and intense.

Mark felt a shiver run down his spine at Raven's new kick-ass attitude. If this was what the man was like in bed, he didn't think he'd ever want to leave the bedroom again. *Speaking of which...*

Mark leaned in for another kiss as he tugged Raven forward. He wasn't going to be stupid about it and deny them what they both so desperately wanted. Not now when Raven was looking at him with such raw hunger.

Entering his bedroom, Mark reached for the light switch, but Raven stopped him.

"L-leave it."

"But—"

"Please."

Raven's eyes, illuminated by the soft glow of the living room lights, were beseeching. Mark was completely lost. He did as Raven asked and stepped into the darkened room without further comment.

Raven took a moment to glance around and Mark followed his gaze, seeing the shadowy outlines of the minimalist style he preferred—pale wood nightstands, a dresser set against one wall and a simple queen-sized bed the room's only features. The plain bedspread was an inky blue-black in the low light.

"So, ah...how—?" Before Mark could get the question out, Raven tugged him further into the room, closed the door and attacked his mouth for another deep, erotic kiss.

As the kiss continued, Raven pushed the shirt from Mark's shoulders, shoving it none too gently down his arms and tossing it away as if it offended him. His hands traced random patterns across Mark's skin, exploring and dipping lower until they came to rest at the fastenings of his pants. Pausing for only a second, Raven soon set to work on the belt buckle and button.

Somehow the dark made each touch and caress more intimate—heightening each sensation until it was almost too much. Mark's cock—now aching and diamond hard—leaked copious clear beads of pre-cum as Raven finally freed it and started stroking him off with a perfect, steady rhythm.

"Raven!"

Mark knew he wouldn't last long if Raven kept touching him like that. But Raven didn't heed the desperate, warning note in Mark's voice. Instead, he made his way down Mark's body, dropping kisses and nipping gently as he went—completely lost in his ministrations. It was exquisite, but also very obvious that Raven had a final destination in mind as he lowered himself in front of Mark and worked jeans and underwear off with sharp, determined movements.

Before Mark could catch his breath, Raven swallowed his cock.

"Oh my—" Mark gasped as he worked his fingers into Raven's silky hair and tried desperately not to cum as Raven pleasured his shaft with strong suction, teasing flicks of his tongue and the deep thrust and retreat of his hot, wet mouth.

It was too much. He didn't want it to end so soon. He wanted more. Needed more from their first time.

"Raven! Raven, stop! I can't.… I—"

Raven stood in one swift, fluid move.

Now that his eyes had adjusted, Mark could see a little more. Ambient light leaking in around the shades from the street allowed for vague figures and shapes, shadows and pale outlines. It wasn't enough, but Mark would take what he could get. And right now, as he panted and tried to get himself back under some semblance of control, he was able to appreciate the planes and angles and smooth pale glow of the Raven-shaped figure in front of him. A figure that still had his pants on.

"You too," Mark murmured as he reached out and gently caressed along the line where Raven's flat stomach disappeared into his pants. "Take them off."

Mark held his breath and waited, desperately hopeful but letting Raven make the final decision to join him.

Slowly, Raven reached down and released the button, lowered the zip and eased his pants and underwear down his thighs. Mark felt a pang of regret that there wasn't enough light to see details. *One day*, he promised silently. One day he would see Raven in all his glory.

"How do you—" Mark started to whisper, but before he could finish, Raven tugged him across the room to the bed and pushed him onto the mattress, following him down as he went.

They bounced, and Mark let out a grunt as Raven landed on top of him. But it was more surprise than anything. He liked this side of Raven. He liked it a lot. Then Raven adjusted to straddle him properly and Mark forgot everything but the way Raven's groin pressed into him. The way their cocks lay together and worked over each other as Raven settled on top of him. The way Raven's hands pinned his to the bed.

Then Raven stilled above him.

"M-Mark?"

"Yeah?"

"I...ah... I—"

Mark blinked at the sudden hesitancy in Raven's voice. He tugged a hand free and carefully ran it along the side of Raven's face and up into his hair. "Are you okay?"

Raven nodded, but he still didn't move.

"We don't have to if you're not ready." The words had to claw their way out of him, but Mark meant every one. They could stop now and he would never cry foul or call Raven a cock tease.

"No! I w-want to. It's just..."

Raven's voice died away, leaving Mark to try and fill in the blanks.

Maybe...

"Have you ever been with a guy? I mean...like this?"

"Yeah, but..." He felt Raven snuggle into his palm. "N-not for a long time and...only once. It w-wasn't very..."

Mark's heart began to pound. The trust Raven was placing in him in that moment...

He gently pulled Raven in for a kiss—a hit or miss affair at best in the dark. It nevertheless seemed to cement something between them. Within seconds they were back to hot and heavy—need and lust driving them on.

"I'll make it good for you," Mark swore between urgent kisses. "I promise. I—"

Raven cut him off with another deep kiss as he laced their fingers together and began a slow grinding motion over Mark smearing pre-cum between them as soft moans filled the room.

"Mark!"

Oh yes! Mark loved the sound of his name mingling with so much desire slipping out between Raven's lips. He pulled his hand free to fumble with the top drawer of the bedside table—not wanting to break contact with Raven's mouth or disturb the delicious friction of their hard shafts rubbing together as he hunted blindly for supplies.

"Damn!"

"W-what?" Raven asked, sounding worried.

That would never do.

"It's okay. Just hold on."

Mark struggled to sit up a little without dislodging Raven. It was difficult, but worth the effort. Finally he managed to snag the lube and a condom.

"Hold out your hand." Raven hesitated for a moment, then did as he was asked and Mark coated his fingers with slick. "I want you to help me get you ready."

Raven made a soft sound—somewhere between a gasp and a moan—that sent a prickling rush of heat and need racing over Mark's skin.

Guiding him back, Mark used Raven's own finger to circle and rub lube around the small tight opening of his body. Raven arched into the touch eagerly.

"Oh! That f-feels…"

"You like it?"

Raven sat up straighter and pressed down into their fingers, unconsciously searching for more. "Y-yeah."

Mark grinned into the darkness. Raven was a delight—glorious and sensual. Who would have known? Well…he'd known Raven was more than met the eye all along, but this was an especially welcome discovery. Raven all lost in passion was sexy as hell.

Still smiling, Mark pushed gently against Raven's finger and was thrilled with the deep groan he received in reply. Once he felt the tip of Raven's finger breach the barrier, he released the pressure and let Raven feel his way forward at his own pace—stimulating and slowly opening himself.

Eventually, Raven's hips began to move, riding the sensation and his own digit.

Mark grinned into the darkness. "You like that?"

"Yeah. B-But..."

"But you want more?"

"Uh-huh."

Mark circled Raven's hole, feeling where the finger was buried into the second knuckle. Still slick with lube, he slowly added his own finger in beside Raven's.

Raven moaned and gently rolled his hips.

"Yeah?"

"Oh yeah!"

Mark let Raven get accustomed to their fingers thrusting and retreating together for a while, then added a third. At the same time he wrapped his free hand around Raven's cock and stroked the long thin shaft as he gradually stretched Raven open until his soon-to-be lover was desperate and moaning.

Pre-cum was leaking fast and free from Raven's cock down over Mark's knuckles now.

"Mmm... I love the way you respond to me."

"You d-do?"

"Yeah. All this delicious pre-cum just for me. One day I'm going to lick your cock right to orgasm. I'm going to watch you cum just from the feel of my tongue on your balls and shaft and running over your tight hole."

Raven's hips thrust forward. It was time.

Mark reached for the condom. Raven—clever man that he was—needed no guidance now. He adjusted himself and waited until Mark touched the tip of his latex-covered cock to Raven's waiting hole, then slowly lowered himself onto the thick shaft.

Mark moved to grip Raven's hips and support him, but Raven intercepted him. He interlocked their fingers and used their joined hands to brace himself as he bore down on Mark's cock. It was so hot Mark almost came right there and then. He loved this bold, assertive side of Raven in bed.

They worked together, inch by blissfully torturous inch, until Raven was fully seated on Mark's cock. As Raven stilled and breathed through the pleasure-pain, Mark thanked whatever gods looked after horny gay men for the moment to get himself under control. But it didn't last anywhere near long enough.

All too soon Raven was rolling his hips, moving tentatively up and down Mark's cock, quietly driving him insane.

"Raven!" Mark arched up into his lover's body. "Oh I need more! I need you to move, baby. I can't—"

Raven responded instantly, as if Mark's desperate plea had been the last, reassuring piece of the puzzle. He started to ride Mark in earnest. A steady, timeless rhythm that built and built as he lifted up almost to the point of losing their connection then sank back down over Mark's shaft.

Together they climbed higher and faster. Mark thrusting up, Raven pushing down. Hands locked together as they struggled to hold onto every glorious second.

Then Raven's ass clamped down around him in orgasm and it was all over.

Mark's world went momentarily white as cum exploded out of the tip of his cock and filled the condom in Raven's ass with his seed. Distantly, he heard himself cry out Raven's name.

Raven, in contrast, was completely silent as he orgasmed. The crushing grip of his hands, the tight clamping of his hole around Mark's cock and the shape of his body in shadowy relief—neck hyper-extended and head thrown back in ecstasy—followed by the warm, wet splatter of his cum across Mark's belly and chest marked Raven's passage into rapture.

Finally, Raven collapsed, gasping for breath and smearing his cum between them. Mark managed to free a hand to hold the base of the condom as he slid from Raven's body. He stripped it off and dropped it into the wastepaper basket beside the bed—not overly concerned if he missed.

Practical necessities dealt with, he draped his free arm over his lover's lower back to savour the orgasmic echoes of their first lovemaking. But Raven immediately started to squirm. He levered himself up and started searching around the bed then pulled the sheet up from the end and wrapped it around himself.

"What's wrong?" Mark asked, worried by Raven's silence and the sudden tension invading the room.

"I...ah...b-bathroom?"

"Oh! Through there." Mark pointed out the door and watched as Raven picked his way carefully across the room—wishing the whole time he'd lose the sheet. In the low light, without the sheet draped across his left shoulder and trailed down to drag across the floor, Raven's ass would have made a delectable display. "The light switch is on the left."

The toilet flushed, water ran and a few minutes later Raven was back—a wet washcloth in hand that he held out for Mark to use. Once Mark was done, he returned it to the bathroom.

When he came back this time, Raven hesitated by the bed.

"Are you okay?" A sense of dread overcame Mark as he stared up at Raven hovering above him.

"I can't stay. I have to g-go to Ryan. I don't want him getting scared waking up in a strange p-place on his own," Raven said, voice heavy with regret.

Mark nodded with relief. He was disappointed, of course, but he understood. And it was nice to think Raven might be as reluctant to leave as Mark was to let him go. It was a good sign.

He opened his arms in invitation. "Just...can I hold you for a minute before you go?"

He'd always been a cuddler if he could get away with it. Right now he had a feeling they could both use the contact.

Raven lay down on the mattress, sheet still wrapped around him like a toga, and cautiously moved into Mark's embrace. Raven's head tucked neatly under his chin, and Mark encouraged him with a gentle squeeze as he draped an arm around Raven and snuggled in.

"You cold?" Mark murmured into the top of Raven's head.

"A l-little."

Mark shifted just enough to drag the blanket up to cover them.

"Th-thank you," Raven whispered, relaxing into Mark's arms and burrowing in properly.

Mark sighed with relief and let go of the worry that had been plaguing him since the diner. It looked like everything was going to be fine after all. Better than fine, in fact. Raven was now officially his lover, and Mark couldn't have been happier with the world as he drifted off to sleep—content and finally settled with Raven held close in his arms, at least for a little while.

Chapter Eleven

It was snowing again. A soothing pattern of falling flakes outside the apartment window that slowly formed a pretty white blanket over Chicago...at least for now, before the reality of city living had a chance to taint it. Even the normally bustling street below was quiet and peaceful, most sensible folks having been driven indoors.

Raymond hated it.

Being cooped up inside always made things worse. It was harder to escape. Harder to avoid a confrontation. And any dirt on the floors would turn to messy, muddy marks with even the slightest amount of snow being trekked in.

The hairs prickled on the back of his neck. He spun around, afraid he was no longer alone, but there was no one there.

Raymond swallowed around the sudden knot of fear in his throat. So many times it had started with something as simple as dirty floors or an unexpected delay. But then there were the times when it started for no reason at all. First, there would be the yelling and the scolding. Then the random slaps and sometimes, if he wasn't paying attention, the unexpected excruciating agony of a cigarette burn. It was like living on a knife's edge – precarious, never sure when the blade was going to cut you to ribbons.

Raymond wrapped his arms around himself. Maybe today would be better. Maybe nothing would go wrong. He was so tired – worn down to a shadow. He should just try to enjoy the calm while it lasted.

Somewhere deep in the back of his mind, he knew this wasn't real. At least not present-day real. It wasn't the first time he'd found himself reliving this particular scene. But the house felt so solid and familiar it sent a shiver down his spine. White floors. Pale walls. Art he'd never understood or appreciated.

"Raymond!"

Oh shit!

"Raymond, I thought I told you to leave your boots outside?"

Oh God!

Raymond could hear the sound of boiling water in the kitchen. He struggled against the urge to cry or vomit all over the multi-coloured rug beneath his boot-clad feet. Terror squeezed him so tightly he could hardly breathe.

"Can't you do anything right? Get in here and clean this mess up!"

Raymond broke out in a cold sweat. There was still the fresh sting of a cigarette burn aching and throbbing on his chest. But when he walked into the kitchen he knew there was far worse awaiting him. He could hear the echoes of his own screams as the boiling water hit him even now. He'd walk into the kitchen. There would be angry, hateful words, slapping and then the water from the stove.

He couldn't do it. Not again.

"Raymond!"

No! He turned to run before it was too late, but he wasn't moving. His legs pumped, but he didn't move.

Oh God! *It hurt so bad. And then would come the infection when he couldn't look after the burn properly by himself. Because he sure as hell wasn't going to tell anyone about it.*

No! I can't! I can't do this! Not again!

"Raven!"

Images and memories fast getting the better of him, he felt his breath get caught up in his chest as he struggled to get air into his lungs. The sensation was quickly followed by a moment of panic. For all the world it felt like a large, clawed hand was digging into his throat and squeezing his neck. It tightened its hold every time he tried to draw oxygen into his body. He couldn't even scream now.

Squeezing. Crushing his windpipe.

He had to get out of here. He had to –

"Raven! Raven! Wake up! You're having a nightmare."

Raven fought with all his might, finally able to move.

"Raven!"

The voice wasn't right. The room wasn't cold and he couldn't hear the water boiling in the kitchen anymore. But that wasn't going to stop him getting away. He continued to struggle against whatever pinned his legs.

"Raven, you need to open your eyes. It's just a dream. Wake up."

Something touched his shoulder. He pulled away and raised his arm up over his head. Blinking rapidly, he tried to focus his bleary eyes and work out which way it was coming from this time…and he slowly started to realise he was in a bedroom, not a kitchen. It didn't make sense. It wasn't even somewhere he recognised, which was reason enough to keep his heart pounding.

Where the hell — ?

"It was just a dream, Raven. You're okay."

Raven looked over to see Mark staring at him. Not touching him anymore — thank the Lord — but close and...

Naked.

Oh!

"Hey," Mark murmured, his expression full of concern.

Raven felt the bottom drop out of his world. He'd had the dream. And a panic attack. In bed with Mark. After...

He wanted to disappear, just fade away until he didn't exist anymore. He was so thoroughly humiliated he didn't even want to keep his eyes open, but at the same time he couldn't risk closing them again.

Glancing around he suddenly realised he could see. It was morning. He'd spent the entire night in Mark's arms. He hadn't checked on Ryan. He'd had the nightmare and woken Mark up with his craziness. *Shit!* After everything he'd done. After trying so hard to get it right.

Shame, anger, bitterness and the threat of tears crashed in on him. Raven pushed and shoved frantically at the sheet he'd wrapped around himself last night, now twisted up and bunched around his legs. At least he was still covered.

"Hey, it's okay," Mark said, reaching out. Raven cringed away before Mark could touch him. "It's okay. Just take it easy."

"I n-need to go. I...n-need to ch-ch-check on Ryan."

I need to get out of here!

"Okay. But just slow down. Take a minute. You're okay."

No, he wasn't. He really wasn't. Raven scrabbled against the mattress to get away. He needed to get up and get the hell out. Now. He forced himself to concentrate on Ryan—on what he needed to do to look after his son, to get him ready for the day and off to preschool. He focused everything he had on that and nothing else.

"I n-n-need to get Ryan some breakfast. And I… I mean, is th-that ok-kay?"

"Yes, of course."

Damn! Mark sounded worried and maybe a little hurt. He didn't want that. Didn't want that at all. But…he couldn't deal with it right now.

"Th-thank you."

"You're welcome. I'll…um… I'll get it while you check on Ryan if you like. Is cereal and toast okay?"

"Yes. Th-thank you." Raven fumbled his way into a shirt, keeping busy and avoiding Mark's eyes.

He felt himself flush as he realised he'd accidentally slipped on the shirt Mark had been wearing last night. He had no idea where the one he originally borrowed was. One thing he was certain of, however, it wasn't the only reason he smelt strongly of Mark right now. His cheeks heated to scorching as he mumbled that he needed to take a shower.

"Oh! Um…yeah. Sure. You know where the bathroom is, right?" Mark faltered out as he started his own hunt in the mess of clothes on the floor. "I mean…yes, of course you do."

"Yes. Th-thank you." He felt like one of those birds dipping in and out of a glass of water—*yes, thank you, yes, thank you*—but as long as he kept saying something maybe he could fake his way through…and escape. "I'll just…um…g-g-go get Ryan up and d-dressed."

Without meeting Mark's eyes, Raven hurried from the room. All he had to do was keep moving. If he concentrated on putting one foot in front of the other and taking care of Ryan, he'd make it. He just had to.

* * * *

What a mess!

Mark wiped down the countertop in the kitchen and cleaned away the milk, butter and jam he'd used to make Ryan's breakfast on autopilot. He couldn't concentrate on anything but how totally out of control everything seemed to be right now.

And how the hell had that happened? Yesterday had been so good. And last night...well, last night had been fantastic. But this morning everything was tense and strained and back about a million miles from where they'd been twenty-four hours earlier. How had it all just fallen apart like that with one bad dream? And more importantly, how was he going to fix it?

The only one that didn't appear to be feeling it was Ryan—thank goodness. He was happily munching away on a slice of toast and washing it all down with a glass of milk like he didn't have a care in the world. Which was wonderful, of course—the last thing they needed was Ryan getting upset.

Mark finally fully appreciated just how extraordinarily adept Raven was at shielding the little boy. The cool, calm and collected performance he'd put on while getting Ryan ready was worthy of an Academy Award. But away from his son, Raven worried him. He was all twitchy and withdrawn and stretched tight.

Now that he thought about it, 'what a mess' didn't even begin to cover it, really.

Mark noticed Ryan starting in on his second slice of toast and that his milk was edging down towards half empty. "Do you need anything else to eat, buddy?"

He should have asked earlier before he finished tidying up the kitchen, but he'd been too distracted — apparently Raven wasn't the only one all wound up and agitated.

Ryan swallowed and shook his head. "No, thank you."

So polite. Raven really was doing an amazing job of bringing Ryan up. He knew first-hand it wasn't an easy thing to do. He also freely admitted he was more than half in love with both of them. Now if he could just work out how to fix it so Raven didn't bolt on him. And yes, he could see it was a distinct possibility after this morning's little wake up call.

Mark felt a painful squeeze to his heart just thinking about it. What was he going to do?

He placed a hand over the clothes he had retrieved from the dryer. Raven had forgotten to take them with him when he went for his shower — another small sign all was not right. But he needed to speak to Raven without Ryan — for a second, anyway. This might be his chance.

"I'm just going to take your dad his clothes. Will you be alright for a minute?"

"Uh huh," Ryan replied, chomping down happily on his toast again.

Picking up the bundle, Mark made his way to the bathroom. Unfortunately, he made it to the door well before any brilliant ideas of what to say occurred to him.

He hesitated. The water wasn't running anymore — hadn't been for a while — but he wasn't quite sure what to do. He didn't want to make things any worse than they already were. Still, Raven was going to need clean clothes, and currently they were on the wrong side of the door. And Mark definitely didn't want to leave things the way they were right now.

He knocked lightly on the wood panelling. "Raven?"

"Yes?" came a hesitant reply a few seconds later.

"I brought your clothes."

Another long pause. "Th-thank you."

Mark held his breath and hoped for the best. "Can I come in?"

There was a rustle of movement behind the thin bathroom door, then Raven cleared his throat. "O-okay."

Mark eased the door open, heart hammering in his throat as he spotted Raven standing in front of the sink. A towel was cinched tightly around his waist, and even with his arms wrapped defensively around himself, Raven was a glorious sight to behold. Pale, lean and completely beautiful, Mark couldn't imagine why anyone would want to hurt him.

Even as the thought occurred, something caught Mark's eye, reflected in the large bathroom mirror behind Raven. Approximately the size of a man's hand, the distinctive reddish-brown scar tissue of a burn covered Raven's left shoulder blade.

Without thinking he stepped forward. "What happened to your shoulder?"

Mark's imagination leapt to all sorts of terrible conclusions, especially given the cigarette burns he had seen on Raven's chest the night before. Then he remembered all the times Raven had grasped his hands while they made love. The sheet draped over his shoulder. The darkened room.

"You were hiding it from me," Mark realised aloud.

Raven retreated back against the sink in alarm, his hand flying up to try and cover the scar. He failed miserably, but his wide, frightened eyes certainly distracted Mark from Raven's shoulder.

He froze, but the damage was already done. *Damn it!* He hadn't meant to intimidate Raven, but it was hard not to react. When he'd seen the cigarette burns he realised Raven had been badly abused. The mere thought set a tight, angry surge of disgust racing through him. But this... If the burn on Raven's back had been inflicted intentionally as well, that was something else again. *And* it was evidence.

Mark clenched his jaw in growing rage. These people...they needed to be brought to trial. They needed to be punished. To pay for what they had done to Raven.

"Did you ever report it?" Mark asked, struggling to keep his voice even and calm.

"N-no." Raven edged away, eyes downcast and cheeks flushed bright red as he moved to press up against the nearby wall until Mark could no longer see his back in the mirror.

"It's not too late, you know. Even now you could —"

"No!" Raven paused to take a deep, shuddering breath. "I mean... I d-don't know what you're t-talking about."

"Then why are you hiding the burn on your shoulder from me right now?"

Raven went silent and still, swallowing before he continued on as if Mark hadn't said anything. "Thank you for b-bringing me my clothes."

"Raven, you —"

"No! Just…just l-leave it."

"But—"

"I said leave it!"

Shit! What was he doing? He shouldn't be badgering Raven. Apart from anything else, it wasn't helping. He hated that Raven had been hurt like this, by people that were supposed to love him. Not normally a violent man, he wanted to lash out and hit someone and make them pay. Then he wanted to wrap Raven up and make it all better.

But watching Raven—the way he seemed to shut down right before his eyes—he knew this wasn't the way. He was only making things worse. And he was desperate not to make things any worse for Raven than they already were.

"I'm sorry, Raven. I didn't mean…" Mark had no idea how to finish. He felt completely out of his depth and unprepared for anything that had happened this morning. "You didn't have to hide it from me."

"I n-need to get d-dressed."

Mark stepped back. He didn't know what else to do. He had no plan and no idea how to deal with something like this.

"I'm sorry." Mark suppressed a wince at how pathetic that sounded hanging in the still, humid air of the bathroom. "I'll just… I'll be outside with Ryan."

Raven nodded, staring down at his bare feet the whole time.

Mark turned and hurried from the room, leaving Raven to get dressed in peace. He needed to regroup and figure everything out before he screwed things up permanently.

* * * *

Ten minutes later, Mark still didn't have a clue what to do or say as they waited nervously for Ryan to finish using the bathroom. Now neatly dressed and clean, Raven completely avoided eye contact.

They couldn't leave it like this. It was torture being in the same room, having touched Raven in the most intimate of ways, and yet be so far away from him in every other respect now.

"Raven—"

"I think…" Raven paused to clear his throat. "I think I'll s-skip running this morning. I've g-got a lot to catch up on and…everything. I'm just going to d-drop Ryan off at p-p-preschool and get to w-work."

Mark swallowed around the lump of fear in his throat. "Are you looking after Wolf this afternoon?"

"N-no. Brody's home today."

His heart sank a little lower as Raven still wouldn't raise his eyes to look at him. Mark could feel him slipping further and further away with every second.

"So, when—"

But before Mark could finish his sentence, Ryan stepped out of the bathroom, drying his hands on his shirt.

"R-ready to go, buddy?" Raven asked—quick and tight, cutting Mark off.

"Uh-huh."

"Okay." Raven woodenly turned to address Mark again. "Thank you for l-letting us stay the n-night, Mark."

"Thank you," Ryan echoed politely.

"Rav—"

"We'll see you later, M-Mark. We have to get g-going or we'll be late for p-preschool."

As he watched Raven hurry Ryan out the door, Mark was sure of only two things—sex complicated everything enormously and he should never let his little head do the thinking.

Fuck! What a mess!

Chapter Twelve

Raven led the boys up the stairs to the apartment above Sandpipers Restaurant. He was more weary than the day's activities warranted, but over the past few days he'd kind of got used to that. He hadn't been sleeping well and everything was so screwed up inside him right now it was hard to force himself to eat properly. Even just going through the day-to-day motions was draining at the moment.

He tried not to think about it, but the way Mark had looked at him when he'd seen the burn haunted him. It had hurt watching his lover withdraw like that...which was stupid, because he'd wanted space at the time. He could just imagine what Mark's reaction would be if he ever knew the truth.

Reaching the front door and fumbling with the lock, Raven forced himself to concentrate on what he was supposed to be doing—looking after the boys—and pushed everything else away. He couldn't deal with any of it right now. He didn't want to.

"Okay g-guys, coats hung up, b-b-bags unpacked."

"But I'm so tired," Wolf whined, dumping his bag on the floor by the door, shoulders sagging pathetically.

"Oh what a shame!" Raven sighed theatrically. "And I was g-going to make peanut butter and j-jelly sandwiches for an adventurer's p-picnic in the living room. But if you're too t-tired..."

Magically, coats and bags were organised into the appropriate places and two little boys took off towards the bathroom to wash up.

A smile tugged at Raven's lips for the first time in days. At the same time he breathed a sigh of relief that it had been so easy as he headed towards the kitchen. They were good kids and their antics were almost enough to make him forget how awful he felt right now. He still appreciated not having to do battle with the afternoon routine, but if he just kept moving, maybe he'd make it after all.

His tentative optimism was short lived, however, as he rounded the corner into the kitchen and came face to face with Mark. A jolt of mingled shock and awareness zipped through him like an electric current, rooting him to the floor and drying the spit in his mouth right up. He couldn't look away, couldn't even seem to breathe as he was caught up in Mark's clear, blue-eyed gaze.

"Excellent," Lark said as he hopped off one of the bar stools pulled up to the counter.

Raven jumped. He hadn't realised anyone else was in the room until that moment.

"W-what's going on?" Raven managed to force out, finally tearing his eyes away from Mark.

"Intervention," Lark announced, picking up a plate of sandwiches and a pitcher of juice from the counter as he headed for the door. "You two need to go for a walk and sort out whatever's going on between you. I'm putting myself on kidlet duty for the afternoon."

Raven was completely dumbstruck as he watched Lark walk past him...and for once his inability to speak had absolutely nothing to do with his stammer.

"You two crazy kids have fun now," Lark sing-songed.

"Lark! W-wait," Raven called out, snapped back into action by the terrifying realisation he was in danger of being left alone in the same room as Mark. He wasn't ready for this. Wasn't ready at all. "You d-don't have to do that. There's n-nothing going on."

"Bullshit. You both look like crap. Go for a walk."

Lark left the room without a backwards glance.

"There's no point in arguing," Mark said from behind him. "We might as well do as we're told."

Raven swallowed as he worked through his options. There weren't many. Running had a certain simplistic appeal, but in the end, he probably wasn't going to get away with it—not if Lark and Mark were working together on this. At least if he went for a walk he'd be moving. He wouldn't have to look Mark in the eye while he...did what needed to be done. He'd been hoping to avoid it a little longer—the conversation that would drive Mark out of his life. Just the thought sent a wave of grief crashing over him, but they might as well get it over with.

Raven fought down the heavy weight of what he knew was coming and made his way down the hallway—aware with every fibre of his being of Mark's presence behind him.

As he passed by the living room, he paused in the doorway. Ryan and Wolf were already steadily working their way through their afternoon snack around the coffee table while Lark was busy pushing furniture out of the way in preparation for them to build a 'tent' with blankets and pillows.

"Hey, b-buddy," Raven called. "I've just got to g-go out for a bit. Lark's going to l-look after you, okay?"

"Can we come?"

"Not this t-time. You stay here and have fun with Wolf. I won't be l-long."

"Okay." Ryan took another bite of his sandwich then turned back to start chatting to Wolf again.

At least Ryan seemed happy enough with the arrangements. He wished he could say the same. The sharp claws of anxiety dug into his belly.

Raven turned and headed for the front door, Mark still silently shadowing him. Down the steps and across the parking lot, it wasn't until they were well away from the restaurant and a good way into their walk that Mark finally broke the silence.

"I just wanted to say I had nothing to do with this, in case you're wondering. Lark trapped me too."

Great, Mark didn't want to be here either. The knowledge didn't make Raven feel any better about the situation.

"I have to admit I didn't put up too much of a fight, though. We need to talk."

Raven sneaked a look at Mark to find him staring back — steadfast and implacable. Finally, Raven agreed with a small nod of his head. He didn't want to, but he had to concede the point. It was still a long minute before either of them were brave enough to break the silence.

"You've been avoiding me," Mark said.

"S-sorry. I've been...b-busy." Raven couldn't look at Mark as the little white lie slipped past his lips.

Mark glanced across at him, the look clearly saying he knew it was a load of rubbish. But Mark didn't call him on it. Somehow it only made Raven feel worse.

Raven lowered his head, watching his feet steadily eating up the distance along the boardwalk they'd inadvertently strayed onto — the boardwalk they'd run together so many times over the past few weeks. Raven took a deep breath. He had to end the torture — for both their sakes.

"It's n-not going to work out, M-Mark."

"That's funny, I thought things were working out just great between us the other night."

Raven felt himself flush. There was a slightly bitter edge to Mark's voice, but he guessed he had a right to it. It wasn't Mark's fault Raven was all screwed up.

Raven felt a tear well and threaten to spill over.

"Raven…" Mark said, soft and pained, the hint of an apology underlying the word as he reached out for him.

Raven jerked away. Just as unexpectedly as the tear had appeared, he was suddenly incredibly angry — mostly with himself.

"D-don't!"

"Raven, please. I —"

"You don't g-get it. We need to stop this."

"Why?"

"Because."

"That's not good enough," Mark snapped back. "You have to give me a better reason than —"

"Because you deserve b-better."

"What?" Mark's eyes went wide. "No! I don't —"

"Yes! L-look at me. L-look at what happened the other d-day. How can you w-want that?"

"Oh please!" Mark retorted, exasperation bleeding into his voice now.

"Don't!" Raven took a breath. "I'm s-serious."

"So am I."

Raven couldn't look at Mark. The fierce sincerity and determination were terrifying. Not in the least because Raven knew it couldn't last. One day soon Mark would wake up and realise he could do so much better.

"You asked me to trust you the other night," Mark continued. Raven turned away. Yes, he'd asked for trust, and look how it had turned out. "I'm asking you for the same thing. I want to be with you. You can't just tell me I deserve better and walk away because it doesn't work like that. I want *you*."

Raven paced away—a chaotic ball of agitation forming deep in his belly, blossoming outwards and threatening to consume him. "It's all j-just so…"

"So what, Raven?" Mark finally prompted.

Something snapped inside Raven. "So fucked up! I c-can't even get *this* right!"

"What? What can't you get right? Because from where I'm standing you've been doing grea—"

"I just w-wanted to be like everyone else. To be n-normal!"

"Raven, slow down. I don't—"

"This. Us. Being together. I wanted it. But…it's all messed up now. I had the stupid f-flash—" Raven took a deep breath. "The stupid dream. I wanted it so bad, but l-look what happened. And now…"

There might have been a sob choked off at the end, but Raven refused to acknowledge it. He felt like enough of a wuss right now without sobbing.

Raven turned away—he couldn't bear to see what expression might be on Mark's face.

"Raven, I don't want you to be like everyone else. I've never wanted you to be anyone but you."

"What, all fucked up?" Raven spat.

"Stop it! You're not fucked up. Just...just give yourself a break!"

Mark stepped closer and Raven braced himself. He could feel Mark's warmth radiating out towards him, but they didn't actually touch. And the really crazy thing was he couldn't decide if he was grateful or disappointed by that. The desire to be held and comforted was a dangerous siren's song doing battle with his deep need to be free and move and run if he had to.

Mark's voice was almost a plea when he continued. "You're smart and funny and kind. You work hard and you're doing an amazing job of raising a wonderful little boy. You're a good man, Raven. And I want you. Why can't you just accept that?"

Raven tried not to fall for the words or the gentle sentiment behind them. But it was hard. A big part of him wanted to lean in, to take and accept what Mark was saying. But he was afraid. How could they ever make it work? And even if they did, how could it possibly last?

"What if I'm never n-normal? W-what if it's always like this?"

"Raven, I'm not being flip, but what do you think normal is anyway? I'm a neurotic perfectionist with no life. I'm not exactly easy to live with sometimes, but...I want to be with you. And I'm hoping you'll still hang around even when I do get all obsessive-compulsive on you."

"It's n-not the same thing. What if I c-can't...you know. I mean I know we did before, but w-what if it happens again? Or if...w-what if it starts w-while we're... What if we can n-never be together like that without me f-freaking out and screwing everything up?"

"Then we stop. We wait. We try again. Or we don't do those things that make you uncomfortable. It's not going to be a deal breaker. I won't let it."

"How c-can you say that?" Raven asked in disbelief. Shocked into looking back at Mark, he was stunned by the candour he found in his lover's expression. "Y-you can't—"

"Please don't tell me what I can and can't do. I'm thirty-three years old. Nearly thirty-four. I've helped raise two kids and run kitchens that prepare hundreds of meals a day. I know my own mind." Raven had never seen Mark so fired up. Feet set firmly apart, shoulders back, eyes alive with conviction—Raven couldn't tear his gaze away. Mark was magnificent...and utterly petrifying at the same time. "If all I ever get to do is play on the beach with you and Ryan, and eat hotdogs and ice cream sundaes so we have to go run them off together the next day, then I'm fine with that." Suddenly Mark's voice softened, the tension in his body melting away. "I'll take whatever you can give me. I'll take you, just the way you are. If you'll let me."

The words washed over Raven, slipping inside like a thief and stealing his resolve to do the right thing—to let Mark go before he messed the man around anymore than he already had. Before Mark realised what a lost cause he was. Right now he couldn't stand himself as he weakened under Mark's persuasion. It would be so easy to cave right now. He wanted it. He wanted to feel Mark wrapped around him again. But could he handle it?

"I hate this. I j-just... I hate this."

"Do you hate me?"

"No!"

"Do you still want me?"

Mark sounded so stark and vulnerable in that moment Raven ached with it. He certainly couldn't lie. "Yes."

The relief and shy joy on Mark's face was breathtaking.

"I just... I c-can't...h-how will this ever w-work?"

Mark, moving slowly and carefully, took Raven's face between his hands and lowered his head in a sweet, gentle kiss that made Raven forget about everything else, even breathing.

"Remember how I said to you that there was no need to rush?" Raven found himself nodding, completely captivated by Mark's intense blue eyes. "There's no need to rush, Raven. Don't throw this away. Just give me a chance. Give us a chance. I'm not asking for it to be perfect. I just want an opportunity to try. I... I really care for you."

Raven's heart hammered in his chest. This was so hard—harder than agreeing to go out with Mark in the first place. Would it always be this difficult? Would it eventually be too much—?

Raven cut the thought off. Being defeatist was *always* a self-fulfilling prophecy. But it wasn't easy to stop worrying.

Mark studied Raven covertly as they began to walk again—it gave them both some time to process what had been said.

Raven looked terrible. He was still gorgeous, but there were dark rings under his eyes, and a troubled, tight look about him that worried Mark. He just wanted to wrap his arms around his lover and hold him close.

But he didn't. He wasn't sure Raven could handle it right now. In fact, he was pretty sure he couldn't. He had that fragile, brittle look about him.

When Lark had cornered him, giving him the third-degree and demanding to know what he'd done to Raven—Mark had been careful not to betray Raven's confidence. But apparently Lark was smart enough to read between the lines. And to set up a Raven trap.

For once Mark was obscenely grateful for the interference. He certainly hadn't been able to pin Raven down himself. He'd forgotten how good Raven was at disappearing and avoiding people. It hurt being on the receiving end of it again, but he pushed that thought away. Now was not the time.

"I won't t-talk about it," Raven whispered suddenly as they continued on their walk. "About…w-what you saw."

Mark felt the guilt hit him square in the gut. "I'm sorry, Raven. I should never have pushed you like I did. I just… I hate that you were hurt like that."

"That p-part of my life… It's over and d-done with. Dragging it b-back out only m-makes it worse."

"There are people you can talk to. People that can help—"

"No!" Raven took a deep breath. "I've t-tried. Professionals. Groups. It always m-makes it worse. N-no one…no-one g-gets what it was like."

Mark let silence exist between them for a moment, using it to gather his thoughts carefully and let Raven collect himself a little before he continued.

"You're stronger than you give yourself credit for," Mark finally said, not looking at him, using a considering voice barely audible above the noise of the ocean and the breeze. It could almost pass for thinking out loud. "You might not be outgoing or have an aggressive bone in your body, but I know how strong you are. Whatever you decide…I'll stand by you. If you'll let me."

They walked on. Miles of boardwalk seemed to pass before Raven spoke again. "Mark?"

"Yeah?"

"I'm… I'm g-going running tomorrow. Would you…" Raven paused and Mark held his breath, praying he would keep going. "Would you like to join me?"

Mark felt the tight band constricting his chest release. "Yeah. Yeah, I really would."

It was all going to work out. It just had to. He didn't want to be without Raven again. The last five days had been terrible—not being able to fix things, scared to death that Raven might never let him close again. Or that he might take off altogether.

Taking a huge risk, Mark reached out and took Raven's hand, giving it a little squeeze. Raven tensed, but he allowed the contact, and for a while they walked along hand in hand. It felt wonderful to be connected, even if only in that small way. Mark didn't want to lose that sense of connection ever again.

Chapter Thirteen

Mark finished off the last of his ice water and set the empty glass down on the bar as he glanced around Sandpipers Restaurant — all rearranged and elegantly decorated for the occasion.

Brody, Lark and Zak's commitment ceremony had been a tremendous success. Even the late afternoon rainstorm that had driven the formal proceedings indoors at the last minute hadn't dampened anyone's spirits. They had all simply relocated and continued on regardless.

Considering the unconventional nature of the relationship they were celebrating, the event had been much the same as any of the weddings and commitment ceremonies Mark had attended over the years. There had been the usual reverent joy as everyone listened to the trio share their promises with each other — Lark bubbling over with enthusiasm, Zak quiet and composed, and Brody nervously stumbling over his lines. Then a moment of tenderness as they shared a kiss, quickly followed by the chaotic excitement of congratulations. And finally it had all dissolved into the wild abandon of a party—beginning with hearty laughter as Wolf insisted on leading the family in their first dance together.

Now, several hours later, things had started to wind down. The buffet had been largely demolished, although dessert and coffee were still available for those that could actually fit them in. Groups of people relaxed and spoke quietly around the room. And on the dance floor, the songs had turned to slow and romantic numbers that encouraged holding dance partners close and swaying more than anything else. Brody and Zak were currently locked in a tender embrace as they rocked slowly together amongst the numerous couples following their lead.

It seemed there was nothing like a wedding, even one with slightly unorthodox numbers, to bring people together. An ache of longing started deep inside Mark as he gazed across to where Raven was speaking quietly with Jaime. As if conscious of being watched, Raven looked over and offered a smile that went straight to Mark's gut...and sent a curl of heat dancing a little lower down too.

Mark's heart pounded with a strange mixture of apprehension and desire. It had been several weeks now since 'the sleep-over incident' as he'd started to think of it. Slowly things were starting to get back on track between them. But while they'd settled into an easy companionship—one he certainly didn't want to mess up—he still couldn't deny he craved more right now.

He wanted so badly to ask Raven to dance—to hold him so they could move together as much more than just friends. He just didn't know if he should push that boundary. If Raven agreed to dance, it would be the first time they'd 'advertised' to the world, so to speak. Not that most people at the restaurant didn't know or guess they were together — or at least were trying to be — he supposed. Still, while not exactly shouting it from the rooftops, it would be a fairly blatant declaration.

Unable to stay away any longer, Mark crossed the space that separated him from Raven. And yet, when he got there he still hadn't quite worked out what he was going to do. Hesitating in front of Raven and Jaime for a moment, he finally cleared his throat — ready to take the plunge.

"May I have this dance?" He'd meant it to sound light-hearted, but instead it came out strained and oddly formal.

He sounded ridiculous, even to his own ears.

"Go on," Jaime said, nudging Raven with her elbow. "I'll keep an eye on the kids."

Ryan and Wolf were busy devouring their second piece of cake, both little boys starting to look decidedly sleepy.

After a small pause, awkward but tinged with a thrill of excitement, Raven nodded. Before anything could interrupt or come between them, Mark led Raven to the dance floor, took him in his arms and began a slow sway. The feeling was exquisite.

"Thank you," Mark breathed against Raven's temple, relaxing into the moment with a sigh of relief.

"You're welcome," Raven replied, barely a whisper — as if he too was afraid to break the spell.

They stayed that way — more embracing than dancing — through the entire song and on into the next. If it was a dream, Mark never wanted to wake up. It was perfect — the feeling of Raven pressed close and held securely in his arms.

"I'll need to take the boys up to get ready for bed soon," Raven murmured.

"You're staying the night?"

"Yeah. The guys have booked a room at The P-Paragon. They'll be back Monday afternoon. I said I'd look after Wolf and keep an eye on the p-place for them so they could relax." Raven blushed. "It was sort of p-part of my gift to them."

Mark soaked in Raven's spicy, warm scent. "It's nice they get to spend some time together on their own. You're a good friend."

Raven's blush darkened at the compliment, but it was accompanied by a shy smile.

"I'm going to head out soon too," Mark said a moment later, as they continued to sway to the music.

Raven nodded, but at the same time Mark felt him inch a little closer and hold just a little tighter. Damn it felt good, and made it even harder to leave.

Mark sighed in contentment and closed his eyes as they continued to move together.

"It's your fault, you know," he murmured. "If I don't get my rest, I won't stand a chance of keeping up with you on our morning run, lightning."

Raven snorted. "Yeah, because you're so old and d-decrepit. You're the one that m-makes us run on sand for resistance t-training."

Mark chuckled, enjoying the fact they could laugh about him being older where once it had worried him. It gave him hope they could work out all their issues, given time and a little trust.

"So will I see you for our regular Monday run?"

"Uh huh. I'm d-dropping the boys off at p-preschool then I'll be ready to go."

"I'll meet you at the preschool as usual then?"

"Sure," Raven replied, all husky and rough.

Mark felt his cock perk up and take interest at the sound. Fortunately, the song ended and he was able to step back. He wasn't quite ready to wade into those murky waters. Things were going well between them, but he wasn't sure Raven was ready for anything more physical. He didn't want to risk messing things up again.

Mark cleared his throat, resisting adjusting himself and giving the game away. "I better get going."

Raven looked over to where Jaime was still watching over the boys. She gave them a smile and made a little shooing motion with her hands.

"Looks like I can w-walk you out," Raven said with a smile.

"I'd like that."

But as they stepped into the foyer, Raven stopped him.

"M-Mark?"

All too eager to delay his departure, Mark turned to face Raven, only to start worrying when he saw how serious his expression was.

"What's wrong?"

Before Mark's imagination could run away on him completely, Raven reached up and pulled Mark in until their lips touched in a sweet, undemanding kiss. The sensation was still electric. Tingles erupted and coursed through his body at the feeling of Raven's mouth under his. The light pressure that Raven used to keep their lips joined was a heady rush…almost as overwhelming as the endless moments of the kiss itself.

More than anything he wanted to deepen the kiss. He wanted to crush Raven against him and ravage his mouth and then trail his lips lower. He wanted to mark Raven's neck and feel the sweet curve of his ass in his hands. But he couldn't. Too much too soon and he was sure it would all come to a crashing end. And Mark didn't want that—couldn't even stand the idea in his head for more than a second.

When the kiss came to an end, Mark pulled away just enough to see Raven's eyes closed, his lips parted as if begging for more. He lowered his forehead to Raven's as his eyes opened—a stunned look of wonder clearly showing in their depths—resisting the temptation to take more. It was good. For now it was enough.

"I want to t-try again," Raven breathed across his lips. "Being together. As l-lovers I mean."

Mark couldn't have been more surprised if Raven had clubbed him. Or more aroused. "Raven—"

"Not now, but…maybe sometime s-soon. I'm not rushing. I'm not m-messed up this time. Well, no more than usual."

"I—"

"When it feels right," Raven explained quickly. Then his expression faltered, his dark brown eyes clouding with worry. "That is…if you… I m-mean if you w-want to."

Mark groaned and closed his eyes. "Oh man! You're killing me here. Of course I want to."

To prove it he pulled Raven in closer and let him feel the hard ridge of his erection pressed up between them.

Raven gasped before a tentative, wicked grin came out to play and he leaned into Mark, subtly rubbing himself against the length of his full cock. "Ah! But what dreams may c-come."

Mark moaned and pressed back into Raven. Even he knew enough to recognise it as a quote from Shakespeare—some reference to death or something.

But the 'little death' was about the only thing on his mind right now.

"Wet dreams," Mark mumbled.

Raven laughed. And it was glorious to hear.

Laughter bubbled up out of Raven's throat. It was amazing how easy the sound came now. Then again, he wasn't sure why he was surprised—Mark always made him feel good.

How had he ever got so lucky?

The last few weeks of Mark's patience and persistence had worn him down...and then built him right back up again. He still worried. He'd probably never stop completely. He still had moments of insecurity and doubt, but he was slowly feeling strong enough to try—brave enough to see what happened. He tried not to question why Mark wanted to be with him or wonder if it would last. That was a steep and slippery slope to disaster.

Most importantly of all, at least as far as Raven was concerned, Mark had kept his promise and never asked or spoken of the scars. And that was the final key. If he didn't have to reveal his shame, if he could just forget about it and move forward, it would work. Really it would.

"I better go," Mark said, still with his forehead pressed against Raven's.

"Yeah."

Stepping back with obvious reluctance, Mark pushed through the door and stepped out onto the footpath. The earlier storm had left behind that new, fresh washed dirt smell that always thrilled Raven for some reason. It was just so potent and invigorating. He'd never particularly liked rain, but coming outside afterwards was like waking up to a whole new world of possibilities.

The row of streetlamps that lit the way to the parking lot reflected off the puddles and raindrops that had been left behind. And in the lee of the door, they were cosseted and secluded.

"Don't come out," Mark said.

Raven frowned. He wanted to make sure Mark made it safely to his car. It was a crazy, protective instinct that just appeared from nowhere, but he wouldn't be able to rest if he didn't know Mark was safe.

"Where are you parked?"

"Just over there."

Sure enough, he could see Mark's dark blue SUV parked close, directly under one of the nearby lights. Raven liked that. Mark was careful and conscientious. It was…reassuring.

"I'll see you tomorrow," Mark said, breaking into his thoughts.

"Yeah."

Mark leaned in and dropped another sweet kiss on Raven's mouth.

"Night."

Then Mark was gone with a smile full of promise. It left Raven hard. A promising sign, even if it was uncomfortable.

Chapter Fourteen

As the gate to Riversands Preschool clanged shut behind him, Raven scanned the area, searching for Mark. Feet crunching across the gravel of the parking lot, his gut tightened when he didn't spot anyone but the usual harried mothers with toddlers in tow and a father whose business suit seemed to have had an altercation with a cereal bowl recently. Normally, Mark was right there waiting for him, but today he was nowhere to be seen.

Raven's mind launched into overdrive, bombarding him with possibilities. Had something happened? Maybe Mark had simply changed his mind about running today. But did it have anything to do with their conversation the other night at Sandpipers? Had Mark—?

Fortunately, before he managed to get too worked up, Raven spotted Mark—crouched down retying his shoelaces beneath the 'Welcome to Riversands Preschool' sign at the entrance. Raven's heart rate instantly picked up as their eyes met—and he hadn't even started his warm-up routine. The genuinely happy smile that lit Mark's face, the tight, corded lines of his body—it was a breathtaking combination.

"Hey! You all ready?" Mark called as Raven approached.

"Yes."

Yes, he was ready—ready to try again with Mark in every sense. The look in Mark's eyes suggested he hadn't missed the emphasis Raven put into his answer.

Mark cleared his throat, colour rising in his cheeks. "You…ah…you feel like taking it across the sand today?"

Raven nodded. He wasn't sure he could get his voice to work again, and the heated look in Mark's eye certainly didn't help in that regard. He couldn't deny it went a long way to making him feel better, however. And it sure did stroke his ego and calm a few of the nervous butterflies that had started swarming en masse in his belly.

They quickly worked their way through their warm up routine—the whole time eyeing one another with increasingly heated stares—then, sharing one last intense glance, they started their run. Normally, Raven was completely focused on the job at hand, but today he just couldn't concentrate. He was all about the man running at his side. The quick in and out of Mark's breath as they built up speed. The flashes of tanned skin he caught out of the corner of his eye as arms and legs pumped. The sharp, musky scent he'd come to crave as the exertion heated Mark's skin. It was utterly distracting.

In no time at all, they'd made it to the boardwalk and after a few hundred yards, Mark led them onto the sand where they used the softer surface to really build up a sweat. It was hard going, and Raven finally found himself settling into the rhythm—effort succeeding where willpower had failed.

Then Mark reached across and snagged his wrist. With a gentle but determined grip, Mark steered them under the boardwalk.

The shade was a welcome respite from the sun. It was cool, quiet and secluded. But Raven wasn't really aware of any of it as they stood staring at each other, panting for breath. Instead, all his attention was on the heat and need he saw in Mark's eyes—a desire that mirrored his own.

Finally—perhaps as worried as Raven that words would simply get in the way—Mark stepped in and closed the distance between them with a kiss. Without a second's hesitation, Raven kissed him right back. He thrilled to the freedom he found in giving every bit as good as he got, losing himself in the sensation of Mark's lips against his own. The hot wet sweep of their tongues as they set to tasting and exploring each other was exquisite. A curious mix of exhilaration and relief rushed over Raven's skin in waves of sensation that blocked out everything but Mark.

With a gasp, Raven felt the press of Mark's cock against his belly. Caught up in the moment and feeling inexplicably bold, he ground his own stiffening shaft back against Mark.

"Raven," Mark groaned as he pulled away—eyes closed, head thrown back in what could only be described as excruciating bliss.

Suddenly, Mark was kissing him again—harder and more demanding this time. It did nothing but inflame Raven's own runaway desire.

"There's no way I'm going to be able to run any farther," Mark murmured between kisses. "Not like this."

Raven moaned into Mark's mouth as he sealed their lips together again. He felt his cock throb in his running shorts, now full and aching. He didn't want to run either. Didn't even want to think about it. All he wanted was the hot, hard man in front of him and a horizontal surface. Now!

"Mmm...you smell so good," Mark mumbled as he trailed kisses up the angle of Raven's jaw while they caught their breath.

"Sweaty," Raven panted back.

"Yeah."

Mark ground their cocks together again and Raven couldn't take it anymore.

"M-Mark! I need... I n-need..."

"Yeah, me too."

"Not here. We n-need to take this...somewhere...somewhere n-now!" Raven couldn't have kept the desperate edge out of his voice if he'd tried.

"Raven, are you..." Mark groaned, but all the while he rained kisses down on Raven's lips and jaw, working their cocks together. "Are you sure? Really sure?"

"Yeah! Yeah, d-definitely." Raven gasped as Mark kissed the sensitive spot below his earlobe. "Oh! D-Definitely sure. M-Mark!"

"You taste so good."

"Mark! P-Please!"

He couldn't believe how much he wanted this. With a lightning like flash of realisation, he finally accepted he could trust Mark. It was more than just words and hoping for the best. He really did believe it. He knew, even if something happened and he did freak out, Mark would be okay with it. They would deal with it…together.

It was an amazing feeling—one that went straight to Raven's already demanding cock. The ache was almost unbearable now.

Mark kissed him again. "Your place is too far. We'll never make it." Mark continued to kiss him between the words, making it hard to think, never mind reply. "Come back to mine. It's closer."

"Closer is g-good," Raven managed breathlessly.

"Yeah."

"Now. Need… Oh! Need to g-go."

But it was another long, hot kiss later before they could actually force themselves to leave.

* * * *

Mark was almost frantic with need by the time they reached his front door. Every second felt like a lifetime. Raven's shy advance and subsequent heated responses had opened a floodgate on the desire that had been steadily building inside him for the gorgeous man currently crowding and rubbing against his side so wantonly. And yet, at the same time, somewhere in the back of his lust-clouded mind, he was very conscious of the need to calm down. To handle with care.

But even as he told himself to go slow, the keys jingled in his hand and he fumbled desperately with the lock. He just couldn't help it. He was wound so tight something had to give.

Fortunately it was the door. He quickly stumbled inside, Raven hot on his heels, and slammed it shut behind them. Mark turned to take Raven into his arms, but instead found himself pushed back against the wall.

"Need you," Raven managed between urgent kisses.

Mark had to admit he was a little surprised by Raven's sudden, passionate onslaught but at the same time he was incredibly grateful for it. It was a relief to know Raven was every bit as eager and keyed-up as he right now.

A burning need sizzled and sang inside Mark as he returned Raven's kisses, urging him on and demanding more. With desperate, jerky movements they pulled at each other's clothes, exploring under soft cotton to fondle and tweak peaked nibbles, tugging up shirts to find hard, masculine planes and stroking over the hot, naked flesh.

"Oh, Raven! So good."

Not wanting to lose contact for even a second, Mark continued to tangle his tongue with Raven's as he backed his way down the hallway towards the bedroom, dragging his deliciously excited lover with him as he went.

Struggling to toe off their shoes along the way, they staggered like drunks on New Year's Eve—lust being the ultimate intoxicant. Finally, after bouncing off walls and a near miss with the hall table, Mark threw open the door and drew Raven into his bedroom, kissing him all the way.

Calm and control were long gone now. In a flash, Mark whipped his shirt up over his head, pushed his running shorts from his hips and reached for Raven. But the sudden stiffening of his lover's body halted him in his tracks.

"Raven?"

Raven stared back at Mark—eyes wide, breath ragged and his fingers white-knuckle tight around the hem of his T-shirt. It took a moment for coherent thoughts to filter back into Mark's lust-fogged brain, but finally he realised—or at least suspected—what might be wrong. The room wasn't dark the way it had been the last time they found themselves here. Late morning sunlight poured in around the edges of the shades, illuminating everything in a clean, mellow glow.

As Raven's gaze strayed around the room—as if seeing it for the first time and conveniently avoiding Mark's eyes—Mark felt his suspicions were well founded.

"Don't hide from me," Mark said, stark and simple, praying he was reading the situation right.

For several long seconds he held his breath and waited, worried he might have made the wrong call and uncertain what would happen next.

Raven swallowed, then slowly lifted the hem of his T-shirt up over his head and let it fall to the floor, followed quickly by his shorts. His hands dropped to his sides and he stood silent and still in front of Mark, completely naked with a hesitant expression on his face as if waiting for judgement.

Slim and pale, Raven nevertheless looked absolutely magnificent to Mark in that moment of austere courage. Careful not to move too quickly, he leant forward and kissed one of the small circular scars on Raven's chest. Raven tensed, and for a second he thought he'd gone too far. When Raven didn't push him away or move to cover himself, Mark cautiously placed another kiss beside the first.

Scared he would be stopped at any second, Mark continued kissing his way over Raven's chest. Moving steadily higher, he pressed his mouth to the column of

Raven's neck, then along his jaw and finally let their lips meet in a languid caress.

Gradually Raven relaxed against him. Mark wanted to crow in triumph. Instead, he concentrated on making the kiss all it could be. Slow and tender, building to deep and thorough and finally moving to a heated claiming filled with all the longing and ill-suppressed passion Mark felt growing inside him. It was only then that Mark realised he might have a problem or two of his own to deal with.

Somewhere along the line, as they'd moved from intense and furious to gentler, more cautious lovemaking, his erection had faded. Mark tried not to panic. He didn't regret having slowed things down when Raven had hesitated. He'd thoroughly enjoyed the soft kisses he scattered across Raven's chest, neck and jaw. And continuing to kiss him now was wonderful. Unfortunately, no matter how much he wanted Raven, how desperate he was to connect physically with his lover, or how sexy Raven looked—his lips all swollen from kissing, his eyes clouding with renewed desire—he couldn't seem to get his cock to rise to the occasion...so to speak.

After coming so close to losing Raven the last time they'd made love, he'd been desperate to make everything perfect. He'd tidied and cleaned to within an inch of his life this morning, just in case. Fresh sheets. Clean towels. Furniture polish. The works. All the while telling himself not to let anything screw it all up again. If he got this right, things would all start to fall into place for them, he just knew it. Unfortunately, at the moment his cock just wasn't playing the game. Right now—only half hard and growing limper by the second—it wasn't likely to be pleasing anyone. And with his brain kicked into high gear, working furiously to try and overcome the problem, it seemed determined to stay that way.

Mark surreptitiously reached down and stroked along his semi-erect shaft. Fear crept in around the edges of excitement as the extra stimulation didn't seem to change anything. If he didn't get it together soon, he'd ruin everything.

Then he spotted it, the lube sitting out on the bedside table where he'd carefully placed it this morning—just in case—and inspiration struck. He reached out and snatched it up like a lifeline and pasted what he hoped was a seductive smile on his face.

"I think it's my turn this time."

"W-what?" Raven stammered, looking momentarily stunned by the suggestion.

Mark forged ahead. He crawled across the bed on his hands and knees to the middle of the mattress and lowered himself to his elbows. Lube still in hand, he took a deep, steadying breath. He felt incredibly exposed and vulnerable in that moment. The cool air caressed his perineum, making him hyperaware of his position—head down, ass up, his cock and balls hanging between his legs.

Determined to follow through with his plan now he'd started, Mark flipped open the cap of the lube and took a generous amount of the slippery gel onto his fingers. Adjusting his stance, he glanced over his shoulder as he reached back...and found Raven staring at his ass.

Heat filled his face, but at the same time he couldn't deny Raven's unwavering focus was completely hot. Suddenly, what had started out as a spontaneous ploy to cover his embarrassing performance anxiety was morphing into something very different. It had been quite a while since he'd been in this position, but seeing the look on Raven's face, the idea of taking Raven inside him sent a thrill of excitement dancing along his nerve endings.

Mark shivered and closed his eyes as he ran a finger around his hole. He pushed in and exhaled on a low moan.

"M-Mark?"

Mark's eyes snapped open. Even lost in the pleasure of fingering himself, he could hear the uncertainty in Raven's voice. And concern had definitely edged its way into his lover's expression, which was the very last thing Mark wanted.

He twisted around and settled his ass on the mattress to face Raven.

"What's wrong?"

"I've n-never…that is…I've n-never done this before."

"You've never topped?"

Raven shook his head.

Shit! Apparently the ploy had been met by another unexpected hitch. Ironically enough, his cock had hardened up nicely as he'd relaxed and prepared himself for Raven. There was a distinct sense of disappointment knowing he might not get to take Raven's cock in his ass after all.

"You don't have to if you don't want to," Mark said, carefully watching Raven's reactions.

Raven was looking at his feet now — not meeting Mark's eyes and giving nothing away in his expression.

"Do you want to?" Mark asked, keeping his voice carefully neutral.

"I'm n-not sure."

Raven's cock was still hard. Clear beads of pre-cum glistened at the head of his shaft. Acting on instinct, Mark leant back on his elbows and bent his knees up to expose his hole once again. He was rewarded with an intense, heated gaze from Raven. Pre-cum slowly trickled from the slit of Raven's cock down the length of his shaft.

Mark decided to go with a simple truth. "I want you to fuck me, Raven."

"Really?"

"Yeah." Mark groaned and arched his neck as he pushed two fingers into his ass to the second knuckle. Yes, he was laying it on a little thick, but it wasn't a lie—he ached to feel Raven moving inside him. "Please."

"But...what if I h-hurt you?"

Mark glanced up at Raven and fell a little more deeply under the man's spell as he suddenly realised what this was all about.

"You won't. At least not in a bad way." Raven still didn't look convinced. Mark let his expression soften as he halted his preparations. "Trust me to tell you if you do, Raven. I want this. I really do."

"Okay," Raven finally whispered.

Mark held out his hand to Raven. "Come here."

As Raven hesitantly crawled over him, Mark lay back, encouraging Raven closer. Slowly, Raven lowered himself so their bodies met chest to chest, groin to groin. With Raven cradled between his legs, Mark let out a soft moan of pleasure and pulled Raven in for a thorough kiss.

It was amazing and yet nowhere near enough all at the same time. He wanted more. His cock and balls ached for release. His hole—sensitised and stretched by his fingers—felt empty.

Pushing up against Raven's body, Mark rubbed their cocks together, working them over each other until their pre-cum mixed and created a slick wetness between their bodies. But it wasn't enough.

Between passionate kisses, the slide of heated flesh and questing hands, Mark murmured the word 'condom' as he groped for the packet he'd left out on the bedside table earlier. He wasn't above begging at this point. Fortunately, Raven seemed just as eager and sat up to receive the little square packet Mark handed him.

Between the two of them they covered Raven's long, slim cock with the thin layer of latex and smeared more lube up and down the straining length of his erection. Then everything stopped.

There was a suspended moment when they simply stared at one another, letting the realisation of what they were about to do sink in. No words were spoken or needed — the look they shared said everything.

Then Raven adjusted his position, his hand steadying his cock as he carefully manoeuvred between Mark's legs.

"Ready?" Raven whispered.

Mark nodded. "Yeah."

Seconds later, Raven's cock nudged at Mark's hole, slipping over and around its goal before finally pushing the very tip inside. With infinite care, Raven gradually filled him up using little thrusts and tiny forward movements until they were finally joined.

"You okay?" Raven panted.

"Yeah. Just…give me a moment." More than allowing his body the chance to get used to the stretch and burn of having Raven's cock buried in his ass, Mark wanted a chance to savour the sensation of being so perfectly filled.

But all too soon he needed more.

Mark rocked his hips, encouraging Raven to move inside him. "Okay."

Together they built the speed and intensity of the thrusts and retreats until Raven was rolling his hips, rhythmically pounding into Mark's ass and rubbing over the hard swell of Mark's prostate.

Mark arched and gasped as pleasure shot through him.

"Raven! Oh...more..."

As if catalysed by the words, Raven lunged into Mark, nailing his prostate again and again, and Mark came—long jets of cum bursting out of his cock and splashing up between them.

For the first time in his adult life—hell, since he was sixteen and his family had come crashing down in a twisted mess of metal and sirens—Mark let go. He let Raven take over and do whatever he wanted. He trusted Raven. More than that, he needed Raven. He needed this. Everything just uncoiled itself inside him and he relaxed completely—lost in the moment of euphoria.

Finally, with one last thrust and a grunt of pleasure, Raven joined him in orgasm, and it was the most amazing moment Mark could ever remember. Head thrown back, eyes closed, neck muscles corded and chest heaving with effort, Raven was the very picture of bliss.

Slowly, Raven collapsed on top of him, still panting for breath. Eventually, after several minutes, Raven lifted his head and planted a soft kiss against Mark's lips.

Mark's eyes stung suspiciously and he was pretty sure, judging by the expression on Raven's face, there were tears in them. Before Raven could panic, Mark reached up and stroked the rounded swell of Raven's shoulder, carrying the caress further up his neck and ending by cupping Raven's cheek.

"Thank you." Mark felt raw and laid bare as he said it, but it was worth it for the look that appeared on Raven's face.

"So beautiful," Raven breathed.

As Mark gazed up at Raven—all glorious, flushed and mussed from their lovemaking—he knew. "You're the beautiful one."

Raven looked away. "As l-long as I keep my m-mouth shut."

Mark blinked.

What the hell?

"Who told you that?"

"Doesn't matter," Raven murmured.

Mark took a moment to study his lover, a barrage of thoughts and emotions jostling for space inside his head, ranging from confusion to anger that someone would ever say something so hurtful to the sweet man above him. But the flush of embarrassment and tight way Raven held himself, possibly regretting his impulsive words, overrode all of it. Raven didn't need him to overreact or probe for explanations right now.

"You're right." Mark reached up to gently push back the hair that had fallen into his lover's downturned eyes. "An idiot like that doesn't matter."

Raven seemed lost for words. Instead, after a moment, he bent forward and took Mark's mouth in a kiss. And Mark opened for him immediately, welcoming Raven's tongue inside even as the cock in his ass softened and slipped away, leaving a sense of loss in its wake.

"I want to do that again," Mark said when Raven finally let him up for air.

Raven's smile was glorious.

"Yeah, me t-too," he whispered, moving in for another quick kiss.

"What did you have planned for the rest of the day?"

"Nothing I c-can't put off. I have to p-pick the boys up at three and wait for the g-guys to get home. But until then…"

"Mmm…until then you're mine."

"I like the s-sound of that."

"Yeah." Mark did too.

Chapter Fifteen

Mark parked his SUV in front of Raven's apartment building and glanced up into the rear view mirror. In the dim pools of light and shadow created by the streetlights he could see Ryan still sound asleep in the back seat—head resting heavily against the side of his booster, face angelic and relaxed. He hadn't even stirred as they'd pulled up.

Mark smiled across at Raven. "Looks like we wore the little guy out."

Raven rotated in his seat, his face softening as he took in the sight of his sleeping son. "Yeah."

"It was nice of the guys to invite us to dinner," Mark said, hoping to prolong their goodnights.

Raven turned back to face the front, eyes downcast as he fussed with straightening his jacket. "I'm g-glad they enjoyed their t-time away."

"Uh huh."

Mark ran his thumb over the steering wheel. Zak, Lark and Brody had invited them to stay for dinner as a thank you to Raven for taking care of Wolf over the weekend. And it had turned out to be a wonderful evening with their three, still starry-eyed and slightly debauched-looking friends. But now it was time to say goodnight to Raven. And damn it was hard. Mark really didn't want to let him go.

"Thank you," Raven suddenly whispered.

"What for?" Mark asked, surprised by the depth of feeling in Raven's voice.

Raven looked down at his lap, rubbing at a non-existent mark on his pants. "For bringing us h-home. And for everything. I m-mean...today."

Mark grinned, remembering the morning that had stretched out into early afternoon, making love to Raven. "Oh, you're very welcome. Believe me."

Even in the low light, Mark could see Raven's blush. But at the same time Raven smiled, and it was the most tempting, wonderful thing Mark had ever seen. He couldn't have helped himself if he'd tried — he cupped the back of Raven's head, drawing him in for a long, slow kiss.

"Will you stay?" Raven murmured when they finally pulled away from each other.

Mark was a little shocked. He hadn't expected Raven to offer something like that.

His brain wasn't really in gear when he asked, "Are you sure?"

"Yeah."

He wanted to whoop out a cheer but wasn't sure how Raven would take such a display. And he certainly didn't want to risk waking Ryan. He had plans for the rest of the evening now and not much patience with any delay in executing them.

"Do you think we can get Ryan inside without waking him up?" he asked instead.

"Yeah. He's a p-pretty heavy sleeper once he's out."

"Mmm...you wouldn't believe how glad I am to hear that right now."

Raven smiled, shy and wicked all at the same time. "Oh, I think I w-would."

If Mark's cock hadn't already been hard enough to drive nails, he would have stiffened right up at the look on Raven's face in that moment—a look that said all sorts of things to the primal instinct to claim his lover over and over again.

Then Raven kissed him, and Mark couldn't help the little moan of appreciation that slipped past his lips.

"Let's get him upstairs. Then we can get into something a little more c-comfortable," Raven said, still grinning.

"Mmm...did I mention how comfortable you're looking tonight?"

Raven laughed. "Oh that was t-terrible. I was thinking about b-bed."

Mark stole another kiss. "I like the way you think."

It was difficult, but after one last lingering taste Mark forced himself to stop kissing Raven and get out of the car. Eager to get in and settled, he hurried around to help get Ryan and his gear out. It astonished him how much stuff one little person needed for six hours of preschool. He couldn't remember Lucy and Evan needing as much at the same age. But then again, it was a while ago now and had sort of passed in a blur even at the time. Mark was determined to pay more attention this time.

Distracted by his thoughts and watching Raven as he hopped out and moved to open Ryan's door, Mark was startled when a woman stepped out of the shadows. It was rather late for her to be wandering around on her own, even in this relatively quiet neighbourhood. He was just about to ask if he could help — thinking she might be lost or in some sort of trouble — when Raven let out a startled gasp.

"M-M-Maria."

"Hello, Raymond," the woman drawled as she sashayed towards them.

The sound sent a shiver down Mark's spine. What the hell?

"W-w-what are you d-doing here?" Raven stammered as he took a step back.

"Looking for you, of course." The smile she gave Raven in that moment could only be described as predatory.

Who was this woman? And why was she looking at Raven as if she was a very large cat that had just worked out how to get into the canary's cage? Without thinking, Mark moved to stand beside Raven.

"H-how did you find m-me?" Raven asked, looking decidedly pale and a far cry from the laughing, carefree man of a few minutes earlier.

"Your brother helped me. If he hadn't told me about your little writing sideline I might never have found you. He wasn't very happy that you up and left town like that, by the way."

Raven definitely looked shaken now.

What the hell was going on?

Mark studied the woman as she stood in front of them. Short and rather petite, she looked to be in her early thirties, certainly not any older than thirty-five. With long curly dark brown hair and a lovely smooth caffé latte complexion, she was quite pretty, really. But there was something hard and bitter about her eyes — like unsweetened dark chocolate.

Maria returned his scrutiny before stepping forward and extending her hand in greeting. "Hello there. You'll need to forgive Raymond. He has trouble with the little social niceties sometimes, so I'll introduce myself. I'm Maria. Raymond's wife."

Mark felt like he'd been kicked in the balls—that same gut-churning agony hit him hard as the words landed between them. "Wife?"

"No! M-Mark, it's n-n-not like—"

"He didn't tell you about me, I take it?" Maria looked down her nose at Raven—an impressive feat considering she was a good half a head shorter. "I can't say I'm entirely surprised."

"You said your wife was dead," Mark managed to squeeze out past the lump in his throat and the fog of betrayal clouding his mind. No wonder Raven had looked so pale and distressed when he'd seen her.

"I n-never said she was d-dead. I said she was g-gone," Raven managed as he looked back and forth between Mark and Maria. "And she's my *ex*-w-wife!"

Maria's eyes narrowed. "Don't lie to the man any more than you already have, Raymond. The game is well and truly up."

"N-no! I d-divorced you."

"Since when?"

"When you t-took off with your art d-dealer, chasing fortune and f-fame."

"You're lying."

"N-No! I'm n-not!"

"Raymond! Stop this. You're only mak—"

"D-don't call me that! It's R-Raven!"

"Raymond, please. You're acting like a child! You've been caught and—"

"You r-rode out of town and n-never looked back, leaving m-me trying to scrape together enough m-money for food and r-rent, and *I'm* the ch-child?"

Mark was confused and hurt as he listened to the two of them argue back and forth—not knowing which way to turn or what was coming next. He was finding it hard to concentrate past the pain of deceit that battered at him. How could he not know any of this about Raven?

Suddenly, Maria let out an exasperated sigh.

"Raymond, please," she said, a soft, pleading note in her voice now. "It was a mistake. I know that now. I—"

"N-no!" Raven shook his head vigorously. "It was the b-best damn thing that ever h-happened to me! Or R-Ryan!"

Maria's eyes flashed with fury. "Raymond—"

"Daddy?"

Mark spun around to see Ryan slide out of the car and come to stand beside them.

"Hey, sweetie," Maria cooed.

Ryan drew back, cowering behind Mark's leg as Raven stepped in to block Maria's approach.

Her eyes darkened with anger as she fixed on Raven again. "Have you been poisoning him against me?"

"He d-doesn't know you," Raven snapped. "You l-left when he was three."

Maria glanced between Mark and Raven, then all the tension in her body and fire in her eyes slowly bled away until she looked small and sad. "I'm sorry, Raymond. I never meant to hurt you. I just… Everything was so messed up. Suddenly there was Ryan and my artwork wasn't selling so well, and… I just couldn't cope. But I never meant to hurt you. You know that, right? I just…" Maria looked down to where Ryan still hid behind Mark's leg. "I just want a chance to get to know Ryan. And maybe…maybe we could try to be a family again."

Mark's heart felt like an arctic blast had rolled through it, as Maria's words fell between them.

"I'm sorry," she continued. "I know I messed up. I just want a chance to make things right."

"You l-left us."

"I know, baby. But—"

Raven's hands clenched at his sides. "No!"

"Raymond—"

"It's R-Raven!"

"Can't we talk about this?" Maria's eyes darted to Mark. "Privately."

"He th-threw you out, didn't he?" Raven said, straightening to stand a little taller. "Your fancy art d-dealer got sick of you."

Maria's eyes narrowed, the angry spark returning in an instant. "That's enough—"

"No!" Raven repeated.

"He's my son too, you know. I never agreed to any divorce and I certainly didn't agree to you taking him thousands of miles away. I have rights—"

"You g-gave them up the day you w-walked away."

Mark wanted to scream at them both to just stop. The barrage of noise and confusing emotions was too much. But he couldn't seem to make his mouth move. Finally, he looked down at Ryan—all wide-eyed and terrified as his parents fought. It unlocked Mark's vocal cords like nothing else could.

"Guys, you're scaring Ryan. You need to stop."

Mark wasn't surprised when Raven immediately clamped his mouth shut—he was only glad Maria decided to do the same.

"You need to sort this out between you," Mark said with a calmness he didn't feel as he glanced back down at Ryan pointedly. "But this isn't the time or the place."

The look on Raven's face was like a knife to Mark's heart—a strange mixture of hurt and betrayal. He steeled himself against it. This was bigger than the two of them. Like it or not, Raven and Maria were connected through Ryan. Raven and his wife—*ex*-wife…whatever—needed to work things out between them or it was Ryan who would suffer. Mark couldn't think about anything beyond that right now.

"Yes," Maria said, taking Raven's arm as he stood staring at Mark. "Your friend's right. We should figure out a better time and place."

Mark ignored the triumphant look on Maria's face as she led Raven a little way off. As long as they sorted out a time and place that didn't have Ryan anywhere near the firing line, that was the only thing that mattered right now.

"You promised you'd take care of my daddy." Ryan suddenly said, his voice full of accusation as he looked up at Mark.

His heart ached. Ryan looked so scared right now.

"Ryan, I—"

"You promised!"

"Your mom and dad need to talk and sort things out, buddy."

"You promised," Ryan whispered again, tears welling in his eyes.

Something in the way Ryan looked up at him, in the trembling note of fear he heard in the little boy's voice, started to worm its way into Mark's brain. Glancing over at Raven, he suddenly noticed his lover looked almost as pale and frightened as Ryan.

Echoes of the words Ryan had spoken at Wolf's birthday party so many months ago began to replay in Mark's mind. *'You're not allowed to hurt him. Friends don't hurt each other'.*

Oh my — !

It was like a blindfold had suddenly been ripped away.

Mark rushed forward, but it was already too late.

"You lying bastard!" Maria snarled.

As if in slow motion, Mark watched Maria lash out. The smack of her hand to Raven's cheek was loud and shocking. But it wasn't alone. Without pause, Maria slapped Raven again.

"You were holding out on me the whole time, weren't you? You son of a—"

Before she could land another blow, Mark wrapped his hand around her wrist, locking it in place. Maria looked stunned. He had to assume no one had ever tried to stop her before.

Glancing over to Raven, Mark was shocked to see a smear of blood at the corner of his mouth.

There were so many things Mark wanted to say in that moment, but he settled for just one as he swung his gaze back to Maria.

"You need to leave."

"You can't tell me—"

"Leave or I'll call the police." Mark kept his voice completely even and calm.

Out of the corner of his eye, he noticed Ryan creep up to wrap his arms around his father's waist and bury his head against Raven's side. Maria yanked her arm out of Mark's grasp and he released her readily, but refused to take his eyes off her for a second.

"You'll regret this," Maria said as she straightened her jacket and stepped back. "We'll see what a judge has to say. Especially when I tell them about the two of you. Don't think I don't know what's been going on here."

Mark thought he saw Raven pull Ryan a little closer, but he couldn't look away to check on them properly as he focused all his attention on making sure Maria truly left.

He couldn't believe he'd almost made the biggest mistake of his life. He'd been so close to letting her sink her claws into Raven. If what he was beginning to suspect was true —

"I th-think you should g-go."

Mark jerked in surprise and turned his head to see Raven looking at him — the blood cleaned away from the corner of his mouth, his expression withdrawn and shuttered against him.

"Raven, please. I'm sorry. I thought —"

"I know w-what you thought."

There wasn't a trace of emotion in Raven's voice, and it chilled Mark to the bone.

"Raven, I'm sorry." Mark looked down at where Ryan still clung to Raven, remembering the promise he'd made and broken. "I made a mistake, okay? I'm sorry."

"It's n-not about that," Raven said as he began guiding Ryan away. Mark noticed his hands were beginning to shake a little. "I just... I n-need to get out of h-here. I h-have to... I h-have to w-work out w-what to do."

Mark was terrified when, instead of heading towards the apartment building, Raven walked towards the parking lot, fishing his keys out of his pocket as he went. Mark had the sinking feeling working-out-what-to-do meant running away to Raven.

"Don't. Don't take off. Stay here and fight. Let me help you."

"Please, I j-just... I n-need to g-go."

Raven had reached his car as he spoke. He unlocked the back and lifted Ryan into his booster seat. Ryan, looking lost and frightened, stared at Mark as Raven silently worked to strap him in.

"You have friends and people who will help you here, Raven. Let them. Please don't go."

Raven shut Ryan's door and headed around to the driver's side without a word.

"Raven—"

"I... I n-need to go, Mark."

"Please, don't do this. Don't shut me out. I'm sorry. I didn't understand—"

"M-Mark, d-don't..." Raven closed his eyes and took a deep breath. "Don't m-make this any harder than it has to b-be."

"It doesn't have to be hard. Why does it have to be hard?"

Mark could hear the edge of panic in his voice, but he couldn't help it. It didn't help that his question was met by silence as Raven eased himself into the driver's seat. He was going to run. Mark just knew it.

"Where will you go?"

"I d-don't... I just... I don't know," Raven said as he turned the key in the ignition.

"Don't run. Please, don't—"

"Mark, just...just g-give me some room to b-breathe."

With that, Raven pulled his door closed and backed out of the parking space. Watching Raven pull away without looking at him while Ryan's pale face tracked him with sad intensity, Mark felt as though a cold, hard rock had replaced his heart. He put his hands on his hips and took several deep breaths, bowing his head as he struggled to keep it together.

As he glanced down, he saw the crushed remains of several cigarette butts littering the ground. He realised he was standing in the exact same spot where Maria had been waiting for them and he felt physically ill.

Chapter Sixteen

Mark slammed his fist down against the steering wheel in frustration as he stared at Raven's assigned parking space in front of the Oceanview Apartments building — the one that should have contained Raven's car at this time of the morning...but didn't.

Damn it all to hell! Raven hadn't come home. Or maybe he had, but he certainly wasn't there now. And who knew if he'd ever be back.

Mark's stomach rolled just thinking about never seeing Raven and Ryan again. In the last few months they'd come to mean everything to him. Where were they? Had Raven run? Had something happened to them? Raven's car was pretty old. Maybe it had broken down somewhere. Or they'd been in an accident.

Heart slamming against his sternum, Mark pushed the last thought firmly from his mind. There weren't going to be any more car accidents. He just needed to find them, wrap them up in his arms and take things back to the way they'd been before he'd dropped

Raven and Ryan home last night. Back to when everything had been right with the world.

Okay, that was not even vaguely realistic, but realistic wasn't going to keep his heart from pounding into cardiac arrest or prevent his imminent breakdown.

Screw realistic.

A horn blared, startling Mark out of his little internal tirade. Looking up into the rear view mirror he spotted the scowling face of the guy in the car behind wanting to get on with his day. It was supremely irritating when his life had gone to hell and didn't look like it was getting better anytime soon. It drove one thing home loud and clear, though. He needed to do something. He couldn't just sit here hitting inanimate objects.

Mark took a moment to consider his options, earning him another blast from the guy behind him, which he ignored. There really was only two he could come up with—drive around in circles looking for Raven by himself, or get help. Peeling out of the parking lot with a squeal of tires, Mark made for the one place he could think he might get the latter.

After ten minutes of minor traffic infringements and several more horn blasts, he pressed the buzzer to Zak, Lark and Brody's apartment. He hadn't known where else to go. Maybe they'd have an idea where to start. Or perhaps they'd heard from Raven. At the very least they'd be arms and legs to help in the search and freak out.

Long seconds passed as he waited impatiently. Where the hell were they?

Just as he reached out to press the buzzer again, Zak opened the door—a scowl marring his usually calm features. Mark didn't have the resources to spare the expression much thought right now.

"I can't find Raven! I've looked—"

"He's here," Zak replied, cool and stern.

The relief that hit Mark as those two little words registered was a powerful thing. It almost bent him double as all the air rushed from his lungs.

"Oh thank God! Is he—"

"He's fine."

Zak was still scowling and Mark's heart leapt up into his throat.

"What's wrong? What's happened?"

"I was just about to ask you the same thing."

"What the hell are you talking about? Where's Raven?" Mark moved to push past, but Zak blocked his way.

Mark fought hard against the growl that threatened to rumble up from deep inside him.

"May I come in?" he forced out instead from between clenched teeth.

"I don't know. You tell me."

"What's that supposed to mean?"

"It means that Raven got here ten minutes ago so messed up he could hardly breathe, never mind talk. I want to know why before I decide whether or not to let you in."

"You think I hurt him?" Irrational anger, the likes of which he had never experienced before, bubbled up inside Mark, threatening to explode right out of him and all over his friend…and boss.

"Honestly, I don't know what to think," Zak replied with infuriating calm.

Just as suddenly as the rage had hit, Mark felt all the blood rush from his head and make a beeline for his feet. "Oh God! Where's Ryan? Is he alright?"

Zak's eyes narrowed. "I saw Ryan at preschool this morning when I dropped Wolf off. He looked fine."

A heartfelt sigh of relief escaped Mark. For a moment he thought Maria might have got to them and...well, he wasn't sure what she was capable of. But he was damn sure it wouldn't be good.

"What the hell is going on, Mark?" Zak demanded, frown firmly in place now.

Mark tensed. Suddenly put on the spot, he wasn't sure what to say. "How much has Raven told you?"

"Nothing. Like I said, when he got here he couldn't string more than three words together. He was shaking so bad I thought the poor guy was going to pass out."

Mark ran his hands through his hair. Truth be told, he wasn't feeling too good himself. He wasn't sure what to tell Zak. He only knew he refused to add betraying Raven's confidence to his list of sins. There was no way Raven would want anyone to know everything. Hell, Mark didn't know everything. All he knew was he desperately needed to see his lover. Even if he couldn't touch him or hold him or make everything better, he needed to make sure Raven was okay. Or as okay as he could be right now.

"Please, just let me come in. I need to see him." Mark looked up at Zak, not too proud to beg if it got him in the door. "I'd never hurt him. You know that."

After several tense seconds of scrutiny, Zak grumbled something about not knowing jack shit right now then stepped back to let Mark in. Trying not to think about the very real possibility that Raven might not actually want to see him, Mark followed Zak down the hall.

It wasn't a long walk. Before Mark was entirely prepared, he was in the living room. And there he was. *Raven.* Sitting on the couch with Lark pressed up close on one side and Brody handing him a steaming cup of coffee on the other.

Suddenly Mark couldn't move. Raven looked wonderful, simply because he was here and not halfway across the country, but at the same time he seemed so damn scared it was hard for Mark to breathe as he stared at his lover. He certainly didn't have a clue what to say. He wanted to hug him and scold him and shake some sense into him all at the same time. Instead, he just stood in the doorway, drinking his lover in.

Raven had glanced up as they entered the room and stared back, apparently just as lost for words. Lark, on the other hand, appeared to be working his way up to pissed as he glared at Mark, while Brody looked both confused and concerned as he glanced between them.

"I think I n-need a lawyer," Raven finally whispered.

Brody's expression of concern intensified. "Raven, what's going on? You're scaring me here."

"She's g-going to try and t-take Ryan away from me. I n-need a lawyer. Someone that d-doesn't lose. I c-can't lose him to her."

The urge to wrap Raven up in his arms, beg forgiveness and go forth to slay the dragon was so strong, Mark actually found himself taking a step forward. But there was no room to manoeuvre between Lark and Brody. And he wasn't exactly sure how to word an apology for his assumptions, especially in front of their friends. Finally, but crucially, he had absolutely no idea how to make things better.

"Who's trying to take Ryan away?" Brody asked, his voice rising in fear.

"My ex-w-wife. She c-caught up with me last n-night and—" Raven took a deep, shuddering breath. "Ryan is m-mine. I won c-custody and I c-can't let her take him."

Zak—ever the practical member of the family—settled on the edge of the adjacent couch. "So you've got sole legal custody of Ryan? Is that right?" Raven nodded. "Am I right in thinking that happened for a good reason?"

Again Raven nodded. "N-no one could f-find her. She r-ran out on us."

Mark had to wonder if that was the only reason the courts had awarded Raven sole custody, but he kept his mouth firmly shut.

Zak ran his hand over his close-cropped hair as he looked around the group. "I don't know for sure, but I don't think there's much she can do to take Ryan away from you if it's a court order that you have custody."

"I'm still w-worried."

"Of course you are," Lark said, wrapping an arm around Raven's shoulder. A confusing mix of gratitude and jealousy lanced through Mark. He wanted to be the one wrapping Raven up in his arms right now. But he wasn't sure the gesture would be welcome. The words 'give me some room' still echoed loud and clear to Mark as Raven refused to meet his eyes.

"I'm sorry to d-do this to you g-guys when you're supposed to be enjoying your h-honeymoon." Raven looked down, pale cheeks turning red.

"Nonsense," Lark said. "I'd be pissed right off if you hadn't come. We look after our own, right guys?"

Brody and Zak nodded their agreement.

"I just... I know you guys had that p-problem a while b-back and needed a lawyer. I thought... I thought you m-might be able to recommend someone."

"We'll get onto Mac straight away. He's a kick-ass lawyer," Lark said, looking to Zak.

"Yeah, he's really good. He's helped us for years." Zak and Lark shared a look Mark couldn't quite read. But at the moment it was the least of his concerns. "I'll go call him now."

As Zak left, the tension in the room ratcheted up several thousand notches. The silence settled loud and heavy over them all. Lark still eyed Mark. The fierce protectiveness coming from the normally easy-going twink making Mark even more edgy. Brody, on the other hand, appeared uncertain as he continued to look between them.

Finally, Mark couldn't stand it anymore. He opened his mouth to ask for some time alone with Raven, but Brody beat him to it.

"Lark, maybe we should take a look at that fresh herb order. Didn't you say you wanted to get it in to the supplier this morning?"

"It can wa—"

"I think we should do it now, Lark."

For a moment, Mark didn't think Lark was going to budge. His eyes, normally bright with mischief, were hard and unyielding as he looked first at Mark, then at Brody and finally at Raven. "Will you be okay?"

Raven swallowed before giving a single nod.

"All right then. We'll be in the study if you need us," he added, speaking directly to Raven.

Mark resisted the urge to shake his head. Not subtle, but at least they were leaving. He really needed to sort things out with Raven.

Alone.

Raven lifted the mug of coffee he suddenly discovered in his hand to his lips and took a tentative sip of the sweet, strong brew. It was a welcome distraction from having to meet Mark's eyes.

"I thought you'd run."

Raven swallowed, giving himself time to think through his reply. There didn't seem to be any point in sugar-coating it.

"I th-thought about it," he admitted, still not ready to look at Mark. "I was d-driving around most of the night thinking about it. I was too scared to go home. And... I d-did think about just t-taking off."

"Why didn't you?" Mark asked, and there was a terrible note of fear and hope all mixed up together in his voice.

The answer required a deep breath before Raven could reply. "I decided you were right. I n-need to stay and fight. And I was all worked up and r-ready to. Right up until I dropped Ryan off at p-preschool this morning. Then I just... I d-don't know. I guess I kind of lost it for a b-bit. I don't remember getting h-here."

"Zak said you were pretty shaky."

"Yeah."

The silence battered against Raven—a nervous, oppressive kind of silence that tightened muscles and made him excruciatingly aware of every ashamed inch of himself.

"It was her, wasn't it? Maria was the one that hurt you."

And there it was. Raven's worst nightmare finally landing between them. As physically painful and traumatic as the years of abuse had been, the shame and humiliation of having someone know — of having

Mark know—and lay it out bare for the world to see was almost too much to live with. It was like every cut, burn, punch, slap and scream was inflicted all over again and all at once.

"Did she ever hurt Ry—"

"No!" *Damn it!* The hits just kept on coming. He would never have let that happen. How could Mark even ask? "Never. She n-never hurt Ryan. It was always just...just m-m-me."

"I didn't mean it like that," Mark rushed to explain. "I know you'd never let her hurt Ryan, but... I don't know..."

Raven nodded, his shoulders slumping. He didn't know either. He'd always told himself he'd have been able to stop Maria before she hurt Ryan. That he would have got them out so fast if she'd ever even looked at Ryan the wrong way. But now, looking back, he just didn't know. It made him want to heave up the half dozen mouthfuls of coffee he'd managed all over the carpet. The only thing that consoled him was the fact she never had.

At first he'd stayed, thinking he was doing the right thing. Babies needed their moms—God knew he wished he'd had a real one in his life. And afterwards, when the screaming and pain had died down, it was like the pressure had been released and things would be okay for a while. But gradually the okay times had got shorter and shorter, and he'd stayed because he was too scared to do anything else. He was terrified she'd get Ryan if they ever split up. Then, when it had got so bad he knew he had to do something—when he was frightened even to fall asleep at night—he'd stayed because he knew that when he did run, he needed to run so far and so perfectly she'd never find him.

When she'd taken off he couldn't believe his luck. He'd thought things were finally turning around, going his way. He should have known it was too good to last.

Raven took several deep breaths as he remembered Maria's latest attack. The venom that had spewed from her mouth last night sent a fresh shiver of dread down his spine.

"You're such an idiot. You really think you'll keep custody of Ryan? A few discreet phone calls... a tip-off or two about a child in danger from his perverted dad and sicko boyfriend... How hard do you think it'll be? I know where you live. I know where you work and who your friends are. I know where he goes to preschool..."

Oh God! He really was going to be sick.

"I thought it was your folks," Mark said, drawing Raven back from the edge of panic.

Raven concentrated on letting the words fill his head, driving out Maria's whispered threats and vile taunts. He breathed in through his nose and out through his mouth a few times before he let himself answer.

"They weren't violent. My parents. They just... They d-didn't care. Maria..." Raven closed his eyes. Even saying her name required another set of deep breaths before he could continue. "She was the first p-person that ever showed any interest in me. And I...f-fell for it."

"Where did you meet her?"

"C-college. She was p-part of the arts dep-partment.

"One of your teachers?"

Mark sounded shocked. Raven didn't see why that little titbit should be so shocking—not considering everything else Mark knew, or at least suspected, about his relationship with Maria. It wasn't like he'd been under-age or anything.

"It w-wasn't like that."

Mark just looked at him, and Raven had to duck his head in shame. Yeah, he'd been an idiot.

"She knew you were vulnerable."

Raven shrugged. Why did vulnerable and eunuch sound like synonyms to him right now?

"I guess."

"I'm sorry, Raven," Mark said. "I just... I never thought—"

"No one ever d-does. No one understands how it's p-possible. They look at her and how small she is and p-pretty and... She's not, you know. When she d-drinks and...she's not p-pretty."

He sensed more than saw Mark start to move towards him, but right now having anyone touch him was the last thing he could handle. Without thinking he shot up off the couch and hurried around it. Mark didn't comment or follow, thankfully. Raven craved space and room to move and run if he had to. It was illogical and as real as the soft leather he crushed beneath his fingers as he clung to the back of the couch.

Mark cleared his throat. "How... I mean..."

Raven wasn't sure Mark really wanted to know. Or even knew what he was asking. To be honest, he sounded just as confused and messed up as Raven felt right now.

Without meaning to, the words started tumbling out of his mouth—a torrent he'd kept dammed up inside for so long it was impossible to stop once he started to release it. "You know the...the b-burn on my back. You know how I got that? Because I was slow. I d-didn't run every day back then like I do now. I... I d-didn't get out of the way f-fast enough. She threw a p-pot of boiling water at me and... I tried to get out of the way, but...it c-clipped me on the way through. I left my b-boots on when I came inside...I t-tracked in a mess. I remember...she was screaming, 'It's not c-clean if you don't use hot w-water.' It was b-boiling on the stove and she th-threw it at me. It was an—"

Raven cut himself off. He'd almost said it was an accident. When was he ever going to stop that? It hadn't been an accident. It was never an accident, but he'd explained so many things away as clumsiness or mistakes or a minor mishap that it was almost as if it had soaked into his pores and become the truth.

"You should have told me," Mark whispered, breaking Raven's wildly ricocheting thoughts as they bounced around in his head. "You should have said...something."

Raven laughed—a harsh, brittle burst of sound that scraped against the senses like nails on a chalk board. There was an odd sense of satisfaction when Mark flinched. "Yeah. That would have gone over real w-well. Oh and hey, just so you know, my ex-w-wife regularly b-beat the crap out of m-me. Yeah, real believable and all m-manly too! Great!"

"Raven—"

Shit! He hadn't meant to be so caustic. He was just so...so...

"Just...I n-need..."

Oh God, he needed to run. He couldn't be around Mark right now. Something dark and angry was trying to punch its way out of him. He needed to run it off. Then he needed to prove to himself and everyone else he could handle things—that he wasn't the same doormat he'd been for so many years.

"Let me help you."

"No. I c-can do this."

"But I can—"

"No! I n-need to be in control of this. Not y-you. I wanted to run and I almost did, but...but then I r-realised I need to stop. I need to stand up for myself. And...I n-need to do this on my own."

"No you don't." Mark took a step towards the couch and Raven tensed. Mark must have noticed because he stopped. "Let me help you."

Raven's skin felt tight and irritating as he struggled to get Mark to understand. It wasn't easy when he was still working through it all in his own head. "You c-can't fix this."

"Don't push me away."

"Don't make me!"

Mark looked shocked, and Raven had to admit he was a little stunned by the loud outburst himself. But he refused to back down. He was serious and Mark needed to back the hell off.

"I only want to help," Mark said in the quiet, calm voice one might use to placate a madman.

"Then wait for m-me to ask."

"Stop being so stubborn. You'll end up getting hurt again."

Raven felt like Mark had slapped him in the face. The same stinging shock and burning pain rushed over him and ignited the anger he'd tried so hard to hold back.

"Screw you!" Raven spat, a fire bursting to life deep inside him.

"Raven! I didn't—"

Raven held up a hand and spun away. He paced to the window and back again. Fortunately, Mark finally had the good sense to shut the hell up.

It took a few seconds before Raven felt calm enough to speak, but when he did he made sure to look Mark right in the eye. "Don't m-make me the victim to your h-hero."

"What?"

It was Mark's turn to look like he'd been bitch-slapped. Raven couldn't find a whole lot of remorse in that moment.

"That's not what… I mean, I'm not."

"Aren't you?"

"No! I just want to help."

"No, you w-want to play hero." Mark was shaking his head and opened his mouth to say something, but Raven cut him off. "Stop trying to control this. You c-can't just fix it. It's not yours to f-fix!"

"I'm not tr—"

"Yes. You are. You said it yourself. You don't w-want me to be like everyone else. You w-want me like this." Raven gestured to himself with a derisive flick of his hand. It was all so clear suddenly—almost as clear as the incandescent rage burning him right up.

"That's not what…I meant—" Mark stammered.

"You w-want me to be the w-walking w-wounded because then you get to be the big m-man and rush to the r-rescue!" Rage overshadowed reason and threatened to swallow him whole. He needed to get the hell out.

"Raven!"

"Just leave me alone!"

Chapter Seventeen

Mark lifted out a bottle of water from the bar fridge and took a long pull of the ice cold liquid. The restaurant was finally closed for the night. The last customers had left maybe thirty-five minutes ago and there was just the low, restful hum of clean-up filling the room. But even that was coming to an end as everyone finished their preparations for the next day and started to drift away.

As a pair of waitresses — Rachel and Tina — passed by the bar arm-in-arm heading for the door and home, he waved and took another mouthful of water. It soothed his raw, parched throat. Kitchens were hot work and he felt like he'd lost a gallon of sweat. But tonight he'd welcomed the gruelling physical punishment. It was a pleasant diversion from worrying about Raven.

He closed his eyes as he rolled the chilled bottle across his forehead. *Raven*. He hadn't seen his lover since yesterday's disastrous conversation, the one that had ended with Zak not so subtly suggesting he leave while Raven talked with the lawyer—Mac someone-or-other.

With another deep gulp of water, Mark pushed down the lump in his throat that had nothing to do with dehydration. He'd never appreciated how attached he was to the little, inconsequential things he shared with Raven every day until they'd been ripped away. Seeing Raven walking towards him in the morning for their regular running date. Catching a quick glimpse of him when Raven brought the boys home from preschool. The unexpected smiles he caught every now and then that meant so much. Their late night chats over the phone about everything and nothing.

Twenty-four hours and he missed Raven terribly. He'd be worried about how pathetic that made him if he had the energy to spare. As it was, all his attention was focused on the fact he might be locked out of Raven's life forever. After the complete balls-up he'd made of the previous day, he wouldn't be surprised.

He'd worked and worried over the possibility all day. And in the end, he'd been forced to acknowledge that, yes, somewhere deep inside he'd been scared Raven would outgrow him. Every day Raven seemed to become more confident and outgoing. But he'd been thrilled to see it...mostly. It was just one tiny, dark corner of his ego that liked the idea that Raven might need him and worried that if there ever came a day when he didn't, he'd move on. And true to form, Raven had seen right to it.

Mark swallowed another mouthful of water. Something in his makeup always made him feel like he needed to be doing things for other people, especially the people he loved. If he didn't then...well, he wasn't sure what would happen, but being needed felt good. And right. And safe.

Oh God! Maybe Raven was right. Maybe he was trying to make himself 'the hero' in Raven's life in a bid to be indispensable. Mark's gut tightened and a sharp pain started up in his temples. The familiar ache of tense shoulder and neck muscles flared to life. Who could blame Raven for never talking to him again? And he didn't expect a second chance. But if he ever got one, he'd do whatever it took to make it up to Raven. He'd change. He'd—

"You nearly ready to go?"

Startled out of his painful thoughts and self-flagellation, Mark looked across the bar to see Jaime staring back at him expectantly. It took a moment before he remembered he'd promised to give her a lift home earlier in the week while her car went into the shop…again. He'd been so distracted he'd completely forgotten.

Feeling the chagrin creeping up his neck to heat his face, Mark looked away, busying himself with screwing the cap back on his water. "Yeah. Sure. Just give me a minute to get my stuff."

Out of the corner of his eye, he saw Jaime cock her head to the side as she studied him.

"You okay, Mark?"

Mark swallowed the truth like the bitter pill it was. "Uh huh."

Fortunately, just as Jaime opened her mouth to say something more, a taxi pulled up out in front—distracting them both from a potentially awkward question and answer session. Mark looked around, wondering who had called a cab. If he'd known someone else needed a lift he would have tried to organise one. Even if he hadn't been able to help himself, surely someone could have lent a hand. Taxis were too expensive at this time of night.

"Is that Raven?" Jaime suddenly asked beside him.

Mark jolted in surprise. *No. It couldn't be…*

But as he looked back out through the tall glass panels to the taxi, sure enough, Raven emerged from the back of the cab. And his stiff, hesitant movements screamed pain.

In an instant, Mark threw off the shock of Raven's unexpected arrival and rushed for the door, barely making it ahead of Jaime. Somewhere behind him, he heard Zak and Lark's voices following them out. But his entire focus was on getting to his lover.

Mark saw Raven straighten up, wince and cradle his left arm then turn to stare down at the back seat of the cab, looking lost and uncertain.

"Raven!" Mark called as he raced forward.

Raven shied away, ostensibly to protect his arm, but Mark felt the rebuff as Raven refused to look at him. He found himself slowing to a stop still several feet away.

"I'm ok-kay."

"What the hell happened?" Zak asked as the others all hurried to Raven's side.

"I f-fell down the stairs. At the apartment."

Mark's muscles locked tight. "Was Maria there?"

"Yeah."

Raven sounded hollow and empty, like he wasn't really there—this was just a recorded message and you could leave your name and number after the beep but there was no guarantee anyone would get back to you. It was a truly terrible sound that was almost immediately swallowed up by the cacophony of questions from the small crowd of wait- and kitchen-staff that had followed them out.

Not knowing what else to do as Raven continued to avoid looking at him and as their well-meaning friends created a chaos of noise, Mark peeked into the dark cabin of the taxi. He spotted Ryan stretched out across the back seat, fast asleep. Without thinking, he bent down and scooped the little boy up into his arms. Something tight and anxious loosened in him as Ryan squirmed and snuggled into his arms with a contented sigh. Then he looked to Raven and the tension was back in a flash.

Raven was so still, as if he didn't know quite what to do or which way to turn while he stared at Mark with slightly dazed eyes.

"Okay guys, come on. Let's just give Raven a second here," Zak said over the top of everyone.

As the confusion died down, Mark absently heard Brody paying the driver. He took the time to cast his eye over Ryan properly. The little boy seemed okay, breathing slow and even. No obvious signs of pain or injury. Of course, Raven was a different story entirely.

Beside him, he saw Jaime wrap her arm around Raven. "Come on, honey. Let's get you both inside."

Raven gasped.

"Your arm?" Jaime asked, her voice soft and sympathetic.

Raven nodded.

"Take them straight up to the apartment," Lark suggested from somewhere off to the right. "We'll tuck Ryan into the spare bed in Wolf's room and take a look at it."

"It's fine," Raven mumbled, sounding flat and distant.

"We'll see," Zak said, shepherding them towards the restaurant.

* * * *

Mark would never cease to be amazed by how soundly kids could sleep. Not all, granted. Lucy had been an incredibly light sleeper as a child, to the point she didn't like sleeping anywhere but her own bed. His little brother Evan, on the other hand, had been a classic example of the heavy sleeper variety—once asleep, he was out for the count until morning. By some blessing, Ryan was apparently the same. He'd barely stirred as Mark carried him upstairs and, with Brody's help, tucked him into the spare bed in Wolf's room, safe and sound and blissfully unaware.

Taking one last look at the sweet little face all relaxed and peaceful, Mark crept out, closed the door quietly behind him and took a deep breath. He could already hear the sound of frustrated voices coming from the kitchen.

"Sounds like Raven doesn't want to go to the hospital," Brody said as they moved down the hall together.

Judging by the arguing and grumbling, it was very obvious Raven didn't like the idea at all. It was possible, given his past, he'd had some bad experiences with hospitals. But like so many things he was coming to appreciate about Raven's life, Mark just didn't know for sure.

"He still needs to go."

Brody nodded. "Yeah. But it was hard enough getting him to sit down while we tucked the little guy into bed." That was an understatement. Only Lark's no-nonsense, do-as-you're-told-or-else voice and Jaime's gentle insistence had finally won the day. "I don't know how we're going to get him to actually leave and go to hospital."

With everything that was happening, it was understandable that Raven would become even more protective and paranoid over Ryan, but—

"He needs to look after himself too."

Brody merely nodded his agreement, perhaps understanding better than most what Raven was going through. He'd been the sole caregiver for his little brother for years, and by all accounts it had been far from smooth sailing up until recently.

As they approached the kitchen, they heard Zak's deep baritone.

"You need to go get checked out."

"I'm f-fine."

"No. You're not," Lark said, a snap to his voice that suggested they'd been trying to convince Raven for a while now. "I'm guessing you've broken your arm. And that lump on your head is the size of a goose egg."

"Did you lose consciousness?" Jaime asked, a soft, reasonable voice in a sea of fear-induced irritation.

"I... N-no, I was awake the whole time."

"You should still get it checked out. I think you've done something to your ribs too. You could have internal bleeding or anything," Jaime said, sounding genuinely worried.

"Really. I'm f-fine."

"Don't make me drag you down there," Lark growled, but under the exasperation it was easy to hear how upset he was.

Mark rounded the corner into the kitchen and came to a sudden halt in the doorway. The room was full of people—Zak, Lark, Jaime, Andy, Dave. Raven was only just visible as the centre of attention perched on one of the bar stools with a cold pack wrapped around his wrist and Jaime holding another to the back of his head.

As determined as he'd been less than an hour ago to try and mend his ways and not jump in unless Raven asked for his help, Mark found he couldn't just sit back and let this go on. "You need to at least go in and get the evidence recorded or..."

"Or no one will ever believe me," Raven finished, a bitter edge to his words. Mark didn't begrudge him even while he had to fight the urge to flinch. "Yeah, b-been there. D-done that."

No one said anything. They all just looked between each other in a mixture of confusion and concern, depending on how much they knew or suspected, Mark guessed.

He swallowed, afraid of what he had to say next, unsure how Raven would react to his interference. "You said it was time to stop running."

Raven was silent and still for so long, Mark was beginning to think he was going to be ignored completely. Then Raven edged his way off the stool with a slight grimace of pain. "I just... I n-need to check in on Ryan. Then...can you guys l-look after him while I g-go get this looked at?"

"Of course. You know you don't even have to ask," Brody said, still looking worried.

"Thank you."

Raven slowly shuffled past, cradling his arm in a makeshift sling someone had rigged up for him.

As Raven disappeared down the hallway, Mark reached into his pocket for his keys. There was no way Raven was going to the hospital without him.

"I'll bring my car around to the back dock."

Jaime got to her feet. "I'll come with you to the hospital."

Mark felt a flush of embarrassment. He'd forgotten all about giving her a lift home. "Damn! I'm sorry, Jaime. I forgot. Maybe someone—"

"It's fine. I want to come too. I've got friends that work the emergency department at St Andrew's." Jaime winked at him, but her smile didn't quite meet her eyes. "Trust me, it's not what you know…it's definitely who."

Mark studied her for a moment but couldn't work out any deeper meaning right now. He didn't have it in him. All he could think about was Raven in pain and possibly more injured than they realised. "Okay. I'll meet you out back."

"We'll be right down."

As he headed for the door, he heard Dave and Andy start to argue with Jaime. Apparently they wanted to see she got home safely. Mark ignored them. No one was arguing with him and he needed to get Raven to the hospital. That's all that mattered to him right now.

* * * *

Raven lay back on the thin, uncomfortable emergency room gurney and tried not to think. *Just for a few seconds,* he promised himself. Then he'd get it together again.

For the first time in several long hours, he had a moment of quiet to himself. Someone had called in Nick MacKinray, the lawyer he'd met with yesterday—his lawyer now—and from there the procession of doctors, police officers, nurses, medical technicians and goodness knew who else had just kept coming. Now he was waiting for them to find him a bed somewhere so they could observe him going slowly out of his mind with worry. All he wanted to do was get back to Ryan. But someone in a white coat had insisted he needed to stay, and Nick had convinced him it was a good idea, strategically speaking. Just in case.

Raven found himself exhausted, both mentally and physically. He absently ran a finger over the plaster covering his left arm from knuckles to elbow. It probably wouldn't have been so bad if he wasn't left-handed. Looking after Ryan like this was going to be difficult. The stab of pain as several cracked ribs reminded him sharply that his wrist wasn't the only casualty of the day underlined the conclusion. Still, as one of the white coats had pointed out, he'd been lucky. Plenty of people broke their necks falling down stairs.

He shivered just thinking about it. Ryan would have been left all alone. He really needed to think about how he was going to deal with that possibility.

At the end of the day, Ryan was the one and only reason he had agreed to talk to the police. In the past, more than one police officer had been the enemy. No one ever believed the man was the victim. Maria would only have to turn sad brown eyes on most of them and instantly they'd be looking at him like he was the scum of the earth. It wasn't fair, but then few things were. But he was so scared—not for himself, but for his little boy—that he really hadn't been given a choice. It seemed to be his best and only chance to record why she should never be given custody of Ryan, no matter what happened to him.

And in a way, he was glad Maria had finally been backed into a corner. Not glad she'd pushed him down the stairs, obviously. But in the ranting and raving she'd done, he'd realised one thing. She'd discovered she didn't have any legal recourse just like

Nick had said she wouldn't. That's why she'd come to the apartment. To bully him. If it had only been him, maybe it would have worked. But with Ryan to protect—not happening. And she'd been mad enough to spit fire...or push someone down the stairs, as it turned out.

"Knock, knock." Jaime poked her head around the edge of the curtain. "Hey, little brother, how you doing?"

"Okay."

"Can I come in?" Raven nodded, but his confusion at her greeting must have shown, because as Jaime leaned in to kiss his cheek, she whispered, "I told them I was your sister. Just in case anyone wanted to stop me coming in to see you."

"Where's M-Mark?"

"Here."

Raven focused in on Mark as he slid into the cubicle beside Jaime.

"My husband," Jaime said with a smile as she looped her arm through Mark's. "Aren't I a lucky girl?"

The grin slowly faded as she looked between Raven and Mark.

He had no idea what to say to Mark. So many things were going on right now, he wasn't sure he had anything left to deal with the mess they were in. It was a painful ache competing with a whole host of hurts.

"What are you g-guys still doing here?" Raven finally managed.

"We hung around to give you a ride back to Sandpipers," Jaime said, sounding a little nervous—as if she'd sensed the elephant in the room with them but couldn't see it. "But it sounds like they want to keep you in for observation."

Raven nodded again. "Thank you, though. I mean…I'm sorry you hung around for n-nothing."

"Not nothing, honey. We were worried about you." Jaime took his uninjured hand and gave it a gentle squeeze. "I'm glad you're okay."

"Me too," Mark added in a low rumble.

Raven couldn't look at them anymore. The sympathy and sincerity was too much when he was feeling so worn down and tired. It threatened the thin veneer of his composure. "Thank you."

Jaime squeezed his hand again. "Do you need anything?"

Raven shook his head, then wished he hadn't. The bump on the back reminded him it was there with a sharp stab of pain.

But at least it brought him back to focus. "Wait. Can you c-call the guys and let them know I have to stay in?"

"Already done," Jaime said. "We called them before we came in here. I said I'd give them an update after we spoke to you."

"Thanks. Can you… I d-don't want Ryan to w-worry."

"They'll look after him."

"I know. I just…" His thoughts trailed off. He wasn't sure what he wanted or expected them to do so Ryan wouldn't worry.

"Do you know how long they're keeping you in?" Mark asked—too quietly—then cleared his throat. "Ryan will probably want to know."

Mark was right. It was exactly the sort of thing Ryan would need. With his thing for time, he'd probably want to know right down to the number of minutes. But Raven wasn't sure himself. So many people had said so many things and asked so many questions over the last couple of hours, he didn't remember anything.

Raven shook his head. "I'm n-not sure."

"It's okay. I'll just go and see if I can find someone to tell us how long you're likely to be in," Jaime said. "We can organise to come and pick you up when you're ready to get out that way too."

"Does it count if I'm r-ready now?"

Jaime chuckled and patted his leg through the blankets. "Afraid not, honey. I'll be right back."

Raven swallowed and picked absently at a loose thread on the sheet under his right hand. His left still throbbed too much to move his fingers. The tension mounted in the little curtained room with each passing second. Finally, he couldn't take it anymore. He had to say something.

"Are you here to say I t-told you so?"

"No! Of course not."

"I wouldn't b-blame you if you did."

"Raven, I never—"

"Nick says this will help r-rush the interim p-protection orders through for us at least."

Mark hesitated, as if wanting to go back to what he'd been about to say. But finally he settled on, "That's good."

Raven was obscenely grateful. He didn't want to go back to the conversation they'd had the day before. Or was it the day before that now? It was hard to tell in the brightly lit emergency room, disconnected from time and reality. Either way, he had no idea what had prompted him to bring that particular tête-á-tête up. Masochism perhaps.

"It's just a p-piece of p-paper. But…at least I'll have something."

"You never had one before?"

Raven bristled. "You have no idea what it was like." Mark looked stricken, but Raven couldn't stop. Years of anger and frustration were bubbling to the surface. "No one ever believes the g-guy. Maybe now they will. If I ever have to c-call the police, I have a c-court order they might listen to. But back then...if I'd started something like this, she w-would have taken Ryan. They always give the kids to the m-mother. She w-would have taken him and I never w-would have stood a ch-chance."

"I'm sorry," Mark said in such a small voice it was almost impossible to hear.

Raven swallowed. He'd started now so he might as well get it all out. "I was trying to g-get everything in place to t-take her on and win Ryan. I knew I n-needed a lawyer but...she took all the money. She controlled everything. She even insisted Ryan call her M-Mother and me R-Raymond in some kind of twisted p-power thing. She's..." Honestly there just weren't words to describe life with Maria. The thousands of humiliating little mental and emotional wounds that were every bit as crippling as the physical abuse had ever been. "That's why I started writing. To t-try and get away. Then she disappeared and it was..."

He really couldn't express how he'd felt the day he realised she had gone. That she wasn't coming home. There hadn't been enough money for food or rent. He'd been forced to bunk in with his drug-addicted brother while he scraped things back together and got the divorce through. But he'd never felt so relieved — as if a weight had finally lifted and he could breathe for the first time in years.

"Raven..."

He needed that freedom to breathe again.

"I n-need you to give me some space right now, M-Mark."

Even to his ears it sounded harsh and dismissive. He tensed, waiting for the angry words. The fight. But guilt was all that came.

Mark just swallowed and nodded slowly. Which was somehow so much worse. "If that's what you want."

Honestly, Raven had no idea if it was or not. Doubt ate at the edges of his resolve. But he couldn't back down. "I'm sorry. I just… I have to focus on Ryan. I can't th-think about anything else. I can't be what you w-want."

"I don't want you to *be* anything, Raven. I only want to help you."

"N-no, you want everything to be p-perfect and fixable. But…none of this is ever going to be p-perfect."

"I never wanted or expected perfect." Mark's voice rose and his expression turned incredulous. "I'm about as far from perfect as you can possibly get."

Raven couldn't hold back a snort. Mark was the most organised and together man he'd ever met.

"Don't!" Mark snapped.

Raven flinched at the hard bark and Mark froze. For a moment, everything stopped as they stared at one another.

Then Mark closed his eyes and took a deep breath as he ran his hand through his hair. "Sometimes…sometimes I feel so wound up and tight. I need things organised and planned or it freaks me out. And…I need to be doing something. I can't just sit back."

Mark looked so vulnerable in that moment Raven almost found himself caving in. Only the thought of what that sort of weakness could lead to, of how many times Maria had trapped him with it, held him back.

"I can't do it again, M-Mark. I can't be with someone that w-wants to control me."

"You think..." Mark blinked at him, all the life and vitality draining away from his face. "You think I'm like her? That I would ever do something like that to you?"

"I don't... I d-don't know."

Mark shook his head in disbelief. "What have I ever done to deserve that?"

Pain clawed at Raven's chest. His cracked ribs didn't even register against the agony crushing his heart right now. "I just... I c-can't think right now. I can't risk it. I never want to be that w-weak again."

"Then she's won," Mark said, his voice so rough and harsh it was barely more than a growl. Without another word, he turned and walked out.

Raven called after him but Mark didn't return. And he had no idea why it hurt so much when it was exactly what he'd asked for.

Chapter Eighteen

Raven settled into one of the seats overlooking the restaurant's front deck and watched Jaime chase the boys across the large wooden expanse. Cleared of tables and chairs by the threat of an early evening storm, the boys had quickly claimed the space as their own. Somehow, Jaime had ended up perpetually 'it' in their impromptu game of tag.

The smile that tugged at the corner of Raven's lips faded a little. He was still too sore to play chase with the boys. He flexed the fingers of his left hand. It was still awkward with the thick cast in place, but at least the pain was all but gone now. There was just the occasional dull ache, the most annoying itch on the planet about midway down his arm where he couldn't reach it driving him crazy, and ribs that protested on a regular basis—mostly because he tried to do too much.

When he'd first been released from hospital he'd tried to go back to doing everything he normally did. But reality had soon smacked him upside the head.

There were just some things he couldn't do. Roughhousing with the boys was definitely one of them. At least not for the next few weeks.

Raven adjusted the sling to settle his arm a little more comfortably against his chest. He'd found himself having to accept help from his friends on quite a number of occasions. There really hadn't been much choice. He'd never appreciated how hard it would be looking after one energetic little boy — never mind two — with his dominant hand mostly immobilised by plaster and the bruises on his torso turning some truly spectacular colours. And then there were the times his new friends just spontaneously did things for him — cooking a meal or offering to take Ryan swimming.

To be honest, it was...nice. He'd never had anyone care or look out for him when he'd been hurt before. And no one tried to overwhelm or control him — they'd just helped with the mundane, day-to-day things that needed doing. But every time someone did something for him, he would hear Mark saying he only wanted to help.

A fresh stab of guilt hit Raven as he continued to watch Jaime with the boys. He felt terrible for the way he'd treated Mark. He'd just been so angry and scared and...messed up when Maria had suddenly reappeared. He realised now he hadn't given Mark a chance. In his desperate need to prove himself — to no longer feel powerless and pathetic and finally stand up to Maria — he'd pushed Mark away.

Raven swallowed against the painful knot of emotion lodging in his throat. He'd made such a mess of everything. He hadn't wanted Mark to see him weak and vulnerable, as someone he had to prop up and protect at every turn. He wanted to be seen as an equal. Someone strong and capable. But all he'd done was drive the man away. And the trouble was, he had no idea how to fix it.

He'd hardly seen Mark in the last week and a half since coming out of hospital. Mark was apparently giving him the space he'd asked for, but...he missed him. The previous day, when Ryan had asked when Mark was going to come over and play again had been painful on so many levels. He wanted his best friend back.

And yet he couldn't seem to make himself move. He was paralysed by Mark's parting words. '*Then she's won*' echoed over and over again in his head. He couldn't help thinking Mark might be right. Maybe he was too messed up after everything that had happened.

Raven forced himself to stop thinking about it. He couldn't deal with it right now. Instead he watched Jaime chase the boys around the deck again. Flushed and breathless, she was still laughing.

Finally, she held up her hands in surrender, proclaiming the boys too fast to catch. For a moment it didn't look like the boys were going to let her go. They clung to her hands and begged for 'just one more game'. They only relented when she pleaded theatrically for a break with a great show of weakness at the knees and the possibility of needing the kiss of life. With high-pitched shrieks at the idea of getting 'girl germs', the boys instead ran to the deck rail to harass the seagulls.

Jaime grinned in triumph as she walked over and flopped down in the seat beside Raven. "Phew! I wish I had half their energy. I'm exhausted and they're still going!"

Raven smiled. "They say youth is w-wasted on the young."

Jaime raised an eyebrow at him. "I don't think either of us is old enough for that expression just yet."

Raven clamped his mouth shut. There was no way he was walking into that death trap. There were just some conversations a man was better off bowing out of. Discussions involving a woman's age were definitely one of them.

"Mmm...smart man," Jaime mumbled, lips twitching in a poorly suppressed smile as they watched the boys pretend to be seagulls now that they'd chased all the real ones off.

He was so glad they'd worked out a way for him to continue on as Wolf's sitter—with Jaime helping out a few hours each day and Brody taking some time off here and there now that the new chef had started. He loved watching Wolf and Ryan play together. But more than that, he liked seeing the friends he'd made at Sandpipers Restaurant every day. Jaime, Lark, Brody, Zak. He even counted Dave and Andy amongst his friends now. Unfortunately, it only emphasised Mark's absence all the more.

"How are you doing, honey?" Jaime asked quietly, breaking into his bleak thoughts.

Raven looked over and caught the mixture of concern and sympathy on her face. He looked away, feeling his cheeks heat. Everyone seemed to wear that look around him these days.

"I'm okay."

He'd been forced to tell them what was going on—the whole situation with Maria. It had been one of the hardest conversations he'd ever had. But he couldn't be around them—be around Wolf—and not have them know. Maria had never been violent towards anyone else, to the best of his knowledge, but he couldn't risk his friends on a first-time incident.

Fortunately, no one had seen or heard from her. He just hoped she stayed gone this time. But it was hard not to worry about when she might rear her head again. "Have you seen Mark?"

Raven started in surprise, his mind instantly jumping back to thoughts of his lover. Or were they ex-lovers now? He couldn't quite bring himself to start thinking of Mark that way.

Raven shook his head, not quite trusting his voice to offer a verbal reply.

Jaime turned her attention back to the kids. The boys ran across the deck, giggling and screeching in a game only they could comprehend. It seemed to involve imaginary enemies now and some sort of superpowers the boys possessed to defeat them. There were certainly some fairly impressive hand movements and sound effects. Suddenly, Wolf fell to the ground as an imaginary force knocked him down. Ryan was at his side in an instant, battling off whatever foe had downed his friend.

"I love watching them like this. They're so good together."

Raven managed a nod, still thinking of Mark. They'd been good together too. He felt the sudden loss of that goodness in his life keenly.

"You know, I don't think I've ever seen them have a cross word to say to one another. Have they ever had a fight?"

"N-no."

"I hope they never do. It's sad to see friends fighting. Especially when it's so obvious they care about each other."

Raven swallowed. It was no longer possible to pretend he didn't know what Jaime was talking about.

Jaime looked down at her lap, studying her nails with a look of intense concentration on her face, as if choosing her words with infinite care. "I know I don't really know what's going on between you and Mark at the moment. And I know I shouldn't interfere, but...he's hurting, and he's not the only one I'm worried about."

Raven couldn't meet her eyes when she finally turned to look at him. He opened his mouth to ask after Mark—when had she seen him last? What had he said?—but Jaime beat him to it.

"He's in the kitchen today and he doesn't look like he's slept in a week."

Raven frowned in confusion. "I th-thought today was his d-day off."

"It is. He said something about paperwork he needed to catch up on. But I saw him doing prep with the others earlier. I think he's trying to find things to keep him occupied."

There was another long silence broken only by the boys' laughter as Raven's mind worked frantically. He couldn't stand to think of Mark hurting. But he didn't want to add to it either. He wasn't sure what to do to make things right between them. Or if he even could.

"You know my mom gave me two pieces of advice when I was growing up," Jaime continued, raising her hand to tick them off on long, slender fingers. "She said never give advice and *never* give advice. Of course, I ignore her all the time, which is how I came to have all this." Raven frowned in confusion as she waved her hand nebulously. "So anyway, here's my advice, and I want you to know I say it with all the love in my heart. You need to get your head out of your ass and go to that man of yours."

Raven closed his eyes and clenched his hands. It only reminded him of his broken wrist as he came up against the restrictions of the cast. "I c-can't."

"Why not?"

"I...s-said things. Stuff I didn't really m-mean. I mean I did, but... I hurt him, Jaime. And I don't know how to m-make it right because...I don't even know what I'm doing half the t-time."

"Well, you're not alone there. Most of us don't know what we're doing. You just have to do what you can and hope for the best. And try not to hurt the people you love along the way."

"But w-what do you do when you do hurt them?"

"You say sorry."

It sounded so simple. Too simple.

"What if I keep h-hurting him? What if I can never g-get over...this and I keep hurting him? What if...what if he's b-better off without me?"

There, he'd said it.

"Don't even think it, honey. You've both looked miserable this past week. Seeing the way he is at the moment, I think he'd rather take the chance and risk getting hurt again than the way things are between you right now."

"I don't w-want to be like this, Jaime. I d-don't want to hurt him."

"I know, sweetheart. You just have to trust that the two of you can work things out."

"Do you...do you think it can? Work out, I m-mean."

"I've seen the way that man looks at you, honey. He worships the ground you walk on. I know you'll work it out. But only if you start talking to one another."

Raven took several deep breaths. None of the problems he'd been dwelling on had been solved. And perhaps they never would be. But what Jaime said made a lot of sense. In the end, the only thing he had to lose was Mark. And he didn't want that. And if Mark didn't want that either...

Was it selfish not to try? He needed to find out how Mark felt. He needed to make a move—any move—and see what happened. Working it over and over like a cow chewing cud was useless and not getting him anywhere.

"Thank you, Jaime. I think... I think, I n-needed someone to give me a shove."

Jaime reached for his hand and gave it a gentle squeeze. "You're welcome, honey. That's what friends are for."

Raven nodded. He hadn't really had much experience on that score. But he was hoping to hang on to the ones he'd found here. Hell, they were more than friends. They felt like the family he'd always wanted.

"You know, I always w-wanted a sister when I was growing up. I never knew sometimes you f-find them."

"Aww! I love you too, Raven."

Jaime wrapped her arm around him for a hug. It hurt a little as it jarred his ribs, but it was worth it.

"Thank you for b-being there for Ryan too," Raven said as the hug came to an end. "He...he hasn't had m-many good female role m-models up till now. You're...well, he couldn't have asked for a b-better one."

Jaime looked stunned. Her eyes grew suspiciously bright. "Thank you. You don't know how much that means to me, honey. Really. Thank you."

"I n-need to go find my man."

"Yeah, you really do."

Chapter Nineteen

Mark sat on the beat up old couch in the kitchen office and stared down at his abused hand. A frown firmly in place, he applied a second sticking plaster to his finger and studied the results. No blood leaked through this time, but it still might need reinforcing again later. It was a pretty deep cut—maybe even deep enough for stitches, though he was hoping to avoid them. His head ached too much to deal with the crowded waiting room at the local hospital. His headache was to blame for the clumsy accident he was currently patching up in the first place.

It was time to find some more extra strength Tylenol. Mark rooted through the first aid kit, desperately hoping someone had been thoughtful enough to include them. The stock he kept in his locker had run out earlier in the day.

When his hand wrapped around a small white bottle of acetaminophen he breathed a sigh of relief. Regular strength and generic, but better than nothing until he could replace his own.

Shaking two pills loose, Mark threw them into his mouth and swallowed them down. He'd become pretty proficient at taking tablets without water over the years. He couldn't help but notice he hadn't needed to take nearly as much Tylenol, or any pain relief for that matter, over the last few months. Not since meeting Raven.

Mark closed and rubbed his eyes. They felt gritty and dry. Not enough sleep. That was the problem. It was making him clumsy and run down, not to mention miserable. He chose to ignore the reason he hadn't been sleeping, as well as the real reason why he was miserable. He just needed to stop thinking about…things. Rehashing and second guessing what had gone wrong wasn't going to help.

A light tap at the door got his attention. He looked up, hoping for a distraction…and came face to face with—

"Raven!" Mark jumped to his feet.

His head throbbed viciously with the sudden movement. Unable to suppress a wince, Mark swallowed against the pain as his gut flip-flopped wildly with the thrill of seeing Raven for the first time in days. The combination made him feel faintly sick, which was never a good sign. If he wasn't careful he'd work himself up into a full-blown migraine.

"Are you ok-kay?" Raven asked as he continued to hesitate at the door.

"Yeah. Just got a bit of a headache," Mark mumbled, praying said head wasn't about to explode.

There was a long silence as they just looked at each other. He'd missed Raven so much. He wanted to step forward and touch him—to make sure he was real on some level perhaps. But he couldn't. He wasn't sure where they were on that score anymore—whether it would be welcomed or allowed. Even more confusing, he wasn't sure he should. Raven had hurt him badly and he wasn't quite ready to stick his neck out and risk having his head bitten off.

"What happened to your h-hand?" Raven asked.

Mark glanced down at his injured finger all but forgotten since seeing Raven.

"Frisky tomato," he quipped, turning his hand this way and that to check it had finally stopped bleeding. "It won."

The attempt at levity fell completely flat. Raven just stared at him with an inscrutable expression on his face. Mark's neck and shoulder muscles tightened painfully.

"Can I...can I c-come in?"

Mark cleared his throat. He wasn't sure why Raven was here, and they seemed to be off to a rocky start. The tension was thick and oppressive between them. But it was the closest he'd come to speaking to Raven since the night at the hospital almost two weeks ago. And they needed to talk. He couldn't stand letting things continue on the way they were now. He only had so many fingers to spare.

"Okay," Mark said. "I mean, yeah. Sure. If you want."

Well, that was smooth. *Not*. Mark cursed himself for his awkward response when Raven continued to linger at the door.

He eased back down onto the couch. When Raven stepped into the room and closed the door behind him, Mark couldn't help a nervous swallow. This was going to be an intense conversation. Mark only hoped he was up to it.

Raven sat down on the opposite end of the couch, and for a while there was just a strained silence between them.

Finally, Raven looked at him, meeting his eyes with such sorrow it made Mark's heart constrict painfully.

"I just... I w-wanted to say—" Raven took a deep breath. "I'm sorry. I was angry and m-messed up."

Mark studied Raven for a moment. The dark shadows under his eyes and fine lines of tension around his mouth added weight to the sincerity he could hear in Raven's voice.

"I shouldn't have kept pushing at you," Mark said as the second-guessing and regret lurking at the back of his mind over the way he'd ended the last conversation jumped right to the forefront. They'd both made mistakes in a truly craptastic situation. "I just didn't know what to say. I still don't."

"It w-wasn't you."

Mark heart sank when he heard the underlying 'it's not you, it's me' that seemed to be heading his way. "I just...I feel like every time I open my mouth I say the wrong thing. But... there just doesn't seem to be a right thing to say, or do or... I wasn't trying to take over."

Had any of that made sense? It had sounded coherent in his mind when he'd rehearsed over the last few days what he would say to Raven, if and when they finally spoke to one another again. But he had the feeling he'd fudged it somewhere along the line. He was so tied up in knots it was hard to know where to start unravelling the mess they were in.

Only one thing was completely clear.

"You hurt me."

"I know," Raven whispered, eyes bright with tears. "I'm so sorry, M-Mark."

Mark swallowed hard, fighting back tears himself.

Raven closed his eyes and hung his head. "I was j-just so angry and...scared. I lashed out at you and I shouldn't have. I g-got so caught up in my own p-problems and pain and...and I know I h-hurt you."

Mark couldn't take it anymore.

He shifted down the couch and took Raven's uninjured hand in his own—a single tear breaking free as all the hurt and worry of the past two weeks got mixed up with the tiny spark of hope they might actually be able to work things out.

"It's okay," Mark managed to finally croak.

But Raven shook his head furiously, squeezing his hand in a vice-like grip.

"N-no. It's n-not okay," he said, raw emotion clogging his voice. "I said...I said t-terrible things and...I d-didn't listen to you when you were telling me how you need to be doing something. I dismissed it and y-you and...that's unforgivable. I love you and I ended up hurting you in the w-worst way."

Mark couldn't seem to catch his breath. "You...you love me?"

Raven looked straight at him—raw and vulnerable and completely honest.

"Raven?"

"Yes."

"Did you just—"

"I love you." he whispered. "Please. Please g-give me another chance. Please—"

Mark closed the distance between them and sealed their lips together, cutting off whatever else Raven was about to say, losing himself in the sweet taste of the man he loved laced with the hint of salty tears and the hope of second chances. Everything else was just so much noise. Everything else could wait.

Tongues moved across one another in a timeless, unrehearsed dance that was hot and needy and so much more. Finally pulling away, Mark stared at Raven. His lover looked equal parts shocked and awestruck. Which was fine—that was exactly how Mark felt right now. And really, there was only one thing that mattered. All the turmoil, questions and stress of the past few days boiled away with four words.

"I love you, too."

Raven's breath hitched. The words were the most wonderful and terrifying he'd ever heard. All his life, he'd longed for them and what they meant—acceptance, comfort, support. The irony was, he suddenly realised the tremendous responsibility that came with them. He held Mark's heart in his hands and he was terrified he was going to break it. He didn't want to, but he couldn't help being scared he wasn't up to the task. What if he got it wrong?

A panic attack threatened. His heart rate leapt up and his breathing started to come in fast, shallow pants for air.

Then Mark's hand caressed his cheek. "Breathe, Raven. Just breathe."

As quickly as it had come, the panic attack subsided and he could think again. It was completely illogical, and Raven would never want to try and explain it, but Mark's touch had worked to bring him back from the edge. And suddenly he knew what he needed to do.

Raven fought to get the words he needed to say out. After several attempts, he finally managed to clear his throat, at least enough to be heard. "I think...I think I n-need to find someone to talk to about all this. I can't p-promise it will work out, but...I w-want to try. I'm going to g-get some help and…t-try again. I really…I really w-want us to work."

"Me too," Mark whispered.

Raven swallowed. He had to tell Mark everything. "I've tried to t-talk to people before."

"I'll be there for you whatever you decide to do. You know that, right? I promise I won't try to control it or anything. I just…I want to be there for you."

"Thank you." Raven closed his eyes and leant forward to rest his head on Mark's shoulder.

Somehow it helped make the next bit easier when he didn't have to look at Mark, but was so close and connected at the same time. The confessions seemed to be coming thick and fast now.

"The first c-counsellor I went to after Maria l-left asked me if I had a n-need to be dominated. If I didn't secretly c-crave it."

"Asshole," Mark growled.

Raven shrugged, forehead still supported by the crook of Mark's shoulder. "It made me w-wonder for a while. I started to ask myself if maybe I hung around because somewhere deep d-down I liked it…or maybe I deserved it because…I've always been attracted to m-men too. It was a p-pretty confusing t-time. You think I'm screwed up n-now? You should have seen me back then. And that really didn't h-help."

"No wonder you're leery of seeing anyone," Mark said, his voice even and calm, but Raven could feel the tension radiating out of him.

"Yeah."

"And I don't, you know," Mark said, running his hand up the nape of Raven's neck into his hair.

"Don't w-what?" Raven asked, distracted by the way Mark was touching him and how amazing it felt.

"Think you're screwed up."

Oh, that…

Raven let the words sink in for a moment.

"I know I n-need to stop telling myself that. I know you're supposed to think what you w-want to be and everything. But…it's hard to d-do when you're feeling in the bottom of the c-curve. You know?"

"Yeah. I do. Not the same, but…when things don't go according to plan or get messed up unexpectedly…it's hard not to feel like I'm wearing concrete boots and sinking fast."

Raven nodded. He'd sensed some innate vulnerability about Mark months ago, but it was only now he was coming to understand how deep it went—how much it was a part and parcel of Mark. He squirreled every word Mark shared with him away, touched beyond measure that Mark would open himself up like this. It helped and eased him. And he was determined to return the favour…somehow.

"It's not the same thing," Mark suddenly said, drawing him back to the present. "The need I have for things to be in order and organised. And my need to help. It's not the same as what Maria—"

"I know." Raven breathed through the wash of shame that overcame him. "I'm s-sorry. I was… I was an asshole."

"No." Before Raven knew what was happening, they were sharing another kiss—this one sweet and soft and filled with tender reassurance. There was an infinite patience Raven didn't feel worthy of unspoken in the caress of Mark's lips. "Okay, maybe a bit of an asshole, but you were scared."

A hush fell over them while Raven considered Mark's words. All of them.

"She was r-right, you know," he finally said. "I was holding out on her. I started saving m-money whenever or wherever I could to get away from her. It wasn't m-much. A p-pittance at first. Then I started doing t-technical writing."

Mark looked at him sadly. It was almost the same expression of sympathy and concern he'd seen on Jamie's face earlier.

"I don't w-want that. I don't want to hold out on someone I l-love. I'm sorry for...for everything that h-happened. I *was* s-scared and...you were right, I p-pushed you away."

Mark took his hand, a comfort and a promise at the same time. "I'll try to wait until I'm asked for help. It's just...it's hard to stand back sometimes. But I will try."

Raven nodded. He wasn't sure how it would all work out, but Mark saying he would try was worth a thousand empty guarantees from anyone else.

"I was so afraid," he finally managed to admit.

Mark nodded. "Yeah. Me too."

"N-no. I mean, yes...but...deep d-down I was afraid she would... I wasn't just scared for Ryan and m-me. I was scared she'd...hurt you too."

"Raven."

Mark pulled him in for a hug. The incredible thing was, despite all the turmoil and heightened emotions of the conversation, Mark was so careful that Raven hardly felt any pain from his bruised ribs. Raven soaked up the sensation of peace he found in Mark's arms, letting it soothe him until he was finally able to release some of the poison that had been lying against his heart for so long.

"Do you know when I f-finally realised we had to escape?"

Raven felt Mark shake his head where it rested against the top of his.

"She was drunk one n-night. Throwing things and yelling and...and she started on about R-Ryan. Saying how m-much of a fuck up I was. How she'd w-wanted a girl. How I couldn't even get that r-right." How could anyone not cherish Ryan just the way he was? Raven would never understand it. He didn't even try. "She would have s-started on him eventually. She's...h-hateful. I...I don't know what m-made her that way. But I c-couldn't..."

Mark nodded, still holding him and waiting patiently while Raven got his thoughts and emotions back under control.

"Maria always said I'd m-mess him up. M-make him just like m-me."

"You're a great dad!" Mark defended hotly. "Ryan is so lucky to have you. You know that, right?"

Raven let the words run around in his head for a while, testing them and checking them for a fit. He was quite shocked by what he found.

He slowly began to nod. "You know...I think I d-do. Ryan...since we m-moved here and started again, he's so much h-happier and... he smiles and p-plays with other kids now."

"You did that. You helped him become the bright, happy kid he is today."

"I just...I wish we'd m-moved sooner. M-Maybe...I d-don't know..."

"Don't, Raven. Don't beat yourself up like that. You did it when you could."

"Yeah." Raven knew Mark was right, but it didn't stop the guilt completely.

Then Mark kissed him again — a welcome distraction from his dark thoughts and regrets. Raven eagerly let himself be swept away by the tongue that gently probed at the seam of his lips for admittance, then slid inside and tasted, explored and coaxed him into playing an intimate game of chase.

A smile graced Mark's lips when they pulled away from each other some minutes later. "You were thinking too hard."

Raven was just about to reply when raised voices and the sound of a commotion in the kitchen interrupted.

Mark frowned. "What—"

Before he could finish the sentence Dave barged in, throwing the door wide without bothering to knock. His eyes were wide and he looked on the verge of panic.

"Ryan's missing."

Chapter Twenty

Mark had never moved so fast in his life. Before he knew it, he was out of the office, through the kitchen and running for the deck. And he wasn't sure how he managed it, because there was just an empty, echoing space where his vital organs should have been. It was as if a black hole had been created the moment Dave delivered the words 'Ryan's missing' and everything else but that terrifying news had been swallowed whole.

He was peripherally aware of the waiters, waitresses and barmen in the dining room calling out Ryan's name as he rushed past, but it seemed very far away somehow. If they were calling Ryan, they hadn't found him. And that was all Mark cared about — all he could focus on — finding Ryan.

He followed Raven as he called for his son in an increasingly terrified voice as they dodged tables and chairs in a mad dash through the restaurant. And all the while he prayed to see an unruly black mop of hair suddenly appear. He turned his head, frantically searching, hoping to see the familiar smile and sweet, innocent face that had stolen a huge chunk of his heart. But they made it out onto the deck without spotting even a hint of Ryan. He really was gone.

A desperate cry that chilled Mark to the bone escaped Raven as he screamed his son's name one last time then fell silent, staring around wide-eyed and terrified. But worse than the terrible sound and the expression on Raven's face was the lack of Ryan suddenly appearing. There was just a mixture of scared, sympathetic and anxious glances from those already outside on the deck looking for him.

"Oh God! Raven," Jaime sobbed as they raced forward to the small knot of people beginning to form around her. "I don't know what happened. He was right here. He was. I never left them for a second. He was right here."

"Ryan!" Mark yelled, adding his voice to the chorus of calls around him—he had to do something, even if it was something that appeared to be increasingly futile.

Mark scanned around. Zak called Ryan's name at the top of his lungs from the edge of the deck, the trace of fear underlying the thunderous bellow only increasing the horror building around them. Wolf began to cry, his little shoulders shaking violently as he buried his head in his brother's neck. Brody looked just as distressed, but was obviously trying to hold it together for Wolf's sake—his lips pulled into a thin bloodless line as he clutched his little brother tightly and murmured reassurances.

And all the time more and more of their friends spilled out onto the deck looking frightened and panicky.

"He's not up here!"

Mark's head snapped up to see Lark leaning over the balcony of the apartment above the restaurant.

Shit! He hadn't thought of that.

He needed to start thinking. Where could Ryan have gone?

Zak called Ryan's name again and several others repeated the call. The shouts radiated out from the deck, but there was still no reply. Jaime looked nearly hysterical now, tears streaming down her face as Andy tried to calm her enough to answer questions.

Think. Where could he be?

Mark swung around as Andy forced Jaime to look at him.

"Where did you see him last?" Andy asked, voice firm but gentle.

Mark ground his teeth. He should have thought to ask that. *Shit! Think!*

"He was right here. We were playing hide and seek. But I knew where he was the whole time. He always hides behind the palms over there by the rail. And then...and then we went to look and...he wasn't there."

Mark hurried over to the palms in the corner of the deck as Andy drew Jaime into his arms. "Shh, sweetheart. Shh, we'll find him."

"It's all my fault," Jaime sobbed.

Mark tried to block her out. They'd find Ryan. They would. They just had to.

The palms in the corners were thick and lush — several pots arranged together. It was the perfect spot for a child to hide. Mark stepped around behind them, scanning the area for some hint of where Ryan could be. The folding doors leading out onto the deck were pushed far enough back that Ryan could have squeezed past and hidden in the dining room without

Jaime seeing him. But he knew Ryan. There was no way he would have stayed hidden this long inside the restaurant with so many people calling out his name. And not with Raven looking and sounding on the verge of a breakdown.

The only other option was over the rail. A chill raced down Mark's spine. There was a small pad of land Ryan could have climbed out onto on the other side. Or someone could have stood on it to coax or haul him over.

Mark jumped the deck rail. He landed on the other side and immediately stepped forward to look left and right, searching for some idea of which way to go. The ground sloped away dramatically to the right, down towards the boardwalk and on further to the beach. To the left there was a narrow path along the side of the building. The beach offered the chance to get lost in the flow of people walking past. To the right was quiet and secluded with little chance of being spotted.

Someone jumped the rail behind him. Mark turned to see Jay, the newest chef in the kitchen. Several others climbed over to join them seconds later.

"I'll look down the slope," Jay said, already taking careful, shuffling steps down the bank.

Daniel, Liam and Joshua began to follow after him.

Relieved of the decision, Mark went left. "Call if you spot anything."

"Will do," Jay called back.

Mark hugged the side of the building, scanning the area intently looking for clues, a hint that Ryan might have passed by as he made his way along the wall. He heard others following. Good—the more people, the more ground they could cover.

"Check over that way." Mark pointed towards the neighbouring buildings.

Ryan's name was repeated over and over again as they fanned out in a rudimentary search pattern. He could hear Raven calling out somewhere behind him. It tore him apart. He needed to comfort and reassure his lover. He needed to find Ryan and make it all better. And all the while they called Ryan's name there was no reply.

Mark didn't want to think what that could mean. Instead, he narrowed his focus to the thick screen of bushes ahead. He suddenly realised they belonged to the gardens that surrounded the parking lot. With a little effort someone could have come from there along the side of the building. They could have come and gone virtually unseen with Ryan in tow.

Mark sprinted forward, scrambling through the thick vegetation. His clothes caught on sticks and sharp branches scratched at his arms and face, but Mark ignored them. Something told him to move faster, push harder.

Finally, he reached the other side of the garden...just in time to spot Maria shoving Ryan into a faded red sedan on the far side of the parking lot.

"Son of a—!" Mark stumbled forward, tripping on the concrete edge of the garden border in his rush to reach them. "Here!" he screamed.

It was the last breath he wasted on words. He needed to conserve every bit of air now. Behind him, he vaguely heard the sound of others crashing through the bushes, swearing and cursing and yelling for reinforcements. But the only thing he was focused on was getting to Ryan before Maria could take off with him. They'd never see Ryan again if she did, he was sure of it. He wouldn't let that happen.

In the very next second, Mark's heart leapt up into his throat as he saw Maria stumble her way around the side of the car. *Oh shit!* Did she look unsteady on her feet? Was she unwell? Or maybe drunk?

Mark poured on the speed. But even running flat out, jumping the barriers that surrounded the parking lot and the little gardens separating the rows of cars, the distance seemed to stretch out forever. Before he could reach her, she'd climbed into the driver's seat and slammed the door shut behind her.

He was close enough to see her reach for the ignition, but too far away to stop it. Mark slammed into the side of the car just as it roared to life. His lungs burned. His muscles screamed. He lunged for the door handle, but she was already moving, the reduced numbers of cars in the lot at this time of the afternoon giving her room to swing wide and lurch forward carelessly.

Mark hung on for dear life, but soon lost his footing and his grip as the car rocketed forward erratically. He grunted in pain as he hit the ground and rolled.

Before he'd even come to a complete stop, he sprang to his feet, disregarding the protest from his shoulder and knees where they'd fallen victim to the hard surface of the parking lot. With adrenaline giving him wings, he sprinted after the car.

"Ryan!"

Maria's crazy driving terrified him even as it helped slow her escape. The car swerved as Maria battled for control. It bounced wildly as it mounted the kerb and Mark saw Ryan being jostled in the back seat. But the fishtail motion and flare of brake lights gave him hope. Running as hard as he could now, Mark managed to grab the back of the car, scrabbling frantically for a handhold. The vehicle sped up and Mark knew he was in trouble.

Then Maria smashed them into a lamppost and everything went ass over head...literally. Mark was flung away at an angle, sliding across the boot of the car to end up in a low, clipped hedge at the side of the parking lot.

Without stopping to consider whether he'd done himself any damage or was even still capable of moving, Mark was up. He darted to the car, desperately fighting with the back door handle to get to Ryan. As the catch gave, he yanked open the door, pulled Ryan into his arms and quickly stepped back. There was no way he was giving Maria the opportunity to get anywhere near Ryan. Never again.

Ryan, shaken and crying, clung to him.

"It's okay. I've got you," Mark soothed, running a hand over the little boy's back while keeping a close eye on Maria. She hadn't moved in the front seat, but he didn't trust her for a second. "Did you hit your head? Are you hurt anywhere, buddy?"

Against his neck, he felt Ryan shake his head. And in the next second, Raven was there, pulling Ryan into his arms.

Heedless of casts and damaged ribs and the world at large, Raven hugged Ryan fiercely, burying his face in the little boy's dark hair with a strangled sob. Finally back in his father's arm, Ryan's tears turned to a wail. Raven checked Ryan over frantically, then, discovering he wasn't physically hurt, wrapped his arms around his son once more and began to rock back and forth. He dropped soft kisses to the top of Ryan's head between murmured reassurances.

Eyes burning with the threat of tears, Mark didn't even think about what he was doing. He just put his arms around both of them and held on tight, needing to feel them both safe and whole and protected from crazy-ass bitches.

A commotion towards the front of the car eventually caught their attention. Maria was swearing and cursing a blue streak as Dave and Zak helped her out of the vehicle and led her, equal parts supporting and restraining her, to the kerb.

Blood ran down from her forehead. Mark guessed she'd hit her head on the steering wheel in the crash and couldn't help feel a sense of satisfaction at a little justice having been served. He remembered seeing Ryan jostled around in the back seat and thanked God the little boy had somehow managed to avoid serious injury. He only hoped someone had thought to call the cops so a whole lot more justice might be handed out in the near future.

Suddenly, Raven stepped forward—Ryan still clutched in his arms—as rage poured off him in waves. "You evil bitch! You stay the hell away from us!"

"He's mine! You both are!" Maria spat, stumbling to one side, even with Dave and Zak to support her. "You can't stop me, you little fag. None of you can."

Maria tried to throw Dave and Zak off, but only succeeded in ending up flat on her ass in the gutter. Mark couldn't think of a better place for her.

"I'm n-not afraid of you," Raven said with a cold, calm anger that made Mark so damn proud he thought he might burst. "N-not anymore. N-never again. You stay the hell away from us."

In the distance, the wail of sirens could be heard. Obviously, someone *had* called the cops. All Mark wanted to do was scoop Raven and Ryan up and take them far away. But it wasn't going to happen. The police would have questions and there was no way to avoid them. Not if they wanted to see Maria get what she deserved. The rollercoaster ride of the afternoon was only just getting started.

Chapter Twenty-One

Mark paced around Raven's living room, unable to settle and too wound up to really take any of the details in. Which was a pity. This definitely wasn't how he envisioned his first visit to Raven's apartment.

After a long afternoon of answering questions, followed by both Ryan and Wolf needing some serious comfort and reassurance, then the guys insisting on feeding them, Mark was exhausted. He was ready to collapse in a heap and sleep for a week.

Several tender spots had made their presence known over the course of the last few hours. He'd come away with scrapes, bruises and a rather nasty gash to his right elbow after his run in with Maria's car and the rough asphalt of the parking lot. The muscle aches alone had him wishing for a long, hot soak in a tub. But mentally he couldn't switch off and settle. What-ifs and dark thoughts plagued him like a swarm of mosquitoes, each taking a bite out of his composure. They ate away at his peace of mind until he was running dry and ready to start climbing the walls.

Thank goodness it was actually his night off at the restaurant. He honestly didn't feel up to running a kitchen this evening. Not to mention he couldn't bear the thought of being separated from Raven and Ryan right now. Even waiting for Raven to come back from tucking Ryan into bed was killing him.

Mark turned and paced back across the length of the living room. The police had arrested Maria. Of course, there were no guarantees she would stay in jail. That was up to the courts to decide. But the fact she'd violated a restraining order, been caught red-handed kidnapping a child, crashed the getaway car and started abusing the cops that turned up to attend the scene certainly wouldn't help her case. The only saving grace was she hadn't been as drunk as Mark had initially feared. Apparently adrenaline and pressure had done a number on her driving skills and a mild concussion had messed with her coordination after the crash. Still, hopefully they wouldn't hear from her for a very long time.

But regardless of what happened in the future, Mark was unbelievably proud of the way Raven stood up to her. Raven had proven himself to be a fighter. He'd taken Maria on and won. Maybe not physically, and she might never be truly banished from their lives, but from now on, Raven would fight and win. And more importantly, the look of triumph in Raven's eyes as the police led Maria away said he knew it. That was where the real victory lay.

Unfortunately, Mark wasn't so sure he could claim a similar victory over his own demons. The crisis was over, but inside Mark's guts churned and his already sore body ached with tension. He couldn't stop thinking about how close things had come to disaster.

The muscles in his neck cramped. The room was too quiet and still. There was nothing to do. Nothing to distract and focus on but the sheer terror of Ryan having been in a car crash with a lunatic. He could have been killed.

The crash that had claimed his parents—his father in the twisted hunks of metal, his mother in the years of pain and depression that followed—came rushing to the present. Only it was Ryan and Raven he'd nearly lost. Then the shaking started and Mark simply couldn't stop. He shook so hard his teeth literally rattled. He was dimly aware of a low moan escaping, but there was nothing he could do to hold it back. Control slipping further and further away, he leant back against the closest wall, closed his eyes and bowed his head. Desperately trying to hold it all together, he clenched and unclenched his hands.

"M-Mark?"

Mark's head jerked up, sending a stabbing pain up the back of his neck and straight into the base of his skull. He swallowed and stared back at Raven, not trusting his voice to answer.

His lover looked so worried. Mark desperately wanted to do something to take that look of concern away. God knew Raven had enough on his plate right now. But he couldn't come up with anything. He just stood and stared.

Without a word, Raven walked over to him, stepped right in and very gently pulled him into a hug. Mark shuddered in the embrace.

"Shh, it's ok-kay," Raven murmured.

And the slim hold he had on his self-control shattered. He pulled Raven closer and hung on for dear life. "Don't leave me. Please. You're not allowed to die and leave me."

Raven's breath hitched. "Oh M-Mark."

His lover's arms tightened around him and it felt so good, and yet at the same time he was mortified by the words that had escaped him. They'd just tumbled out without permission. Embarrassed, distraught and so damn tight inside it felt like a giant fist was wrapped around his heart and lungs, trying to squeeze the life out of him, Mark clung to Raven. Every last word was the truth—every syllable the stark vulnerability at his core. Mark could only hang on and trust in Raven.

"You know I can't p-promise that, M-Mark." Raven stopped to take several deep breaths.

"Raven—"

"Shh." Raven raised his head to fix Mark with bright, shimmering eyes. "I can p-promise I love you. I can p-promise here and now and…as m-many days as I'm g-given."

Mark didn't have the words in that moment. And even if he did he wasn't sure he'd have been able to get them out past the painful, raw constriction of his throat. Instead he kissed Raven. Hard and desperate, Mark put everything he couldn't say into his mouth devouring Raven's.

Nothing was spared. Teeth, tongues, soft moans and the bruising pressure of their lips was everything. The rest of the world just fell away. If he could have he would have pulled Raven right into himself so they'd never have to part. Blood rushed in his ears. His heart drummed wildly, finally escaping the vice-like grip of fear that threatened to crush it.

When they eventually pulled away, something had eased and settled inside him even as a new burning desire and need had taken its place.

Raven took a step back, and Mark instantly reached for him.

But Raven just took his hand. "Come with m-me."

Caught up in the velvet-over-steel look in Raven's eyes, Mark was in no position to argue. He trailed obediently behind as Raven led him by the hand down the hallway and into what was obviously his bedroom.

It was a nice room—dark reds and creams and honey-coloured wood. Still holding his hand, Raven walked them over to a dresser and lit several candles lined up along the top. One by one the small flames began to dance and sway above their wicks. With a flick of the light switch, the room was plunged into the soft, warm glow of candlelight.

It was beautiful. But not nearly as beautiful as Raven in that moment. Inside and out, he was incredible. And he was 'it' for Mark. He knew it down to his last breath. Raven was the other half of his soul. The half he'd never realised was missing…until Raven.

They came together for another kiss, meeting in the middle as if each move was choreographed. And this time the kiss was slow and tender and filled with a gentle calm that gradually filtered in past Mark's defences.

It went on and on—wondrous and all consuming. Then, still kissing, Raven gently began to manoeuvre them towards the bed. And reality intruded.

Mark pulled out of the kiss. "Wait. Your arm and ribs. I don't want to hurt you."

"You w-won't," Raven promised, his voice low and husky and so damn sexy Mark's cock throbbed at the sound. "Just lie down with m-me."

Mark still hesitated. The thought of causing Raven any pain overrode everything, even the primitive need to make love and know they really were okay after the trauma of the afternoon and recent weeks.

"Come on. It'll be okay. I p-promise," Raven said, tugging gently on his hand.

Mark moved onto the bed, all the time watching Raven as he lay back, searching to make sure there were no doubts or second thoughts on his lover's face.

There weren't.

But as Raven crawled into the bed and wriggled into place beside him, his bottom lip still caught between his teeth.

"You're hurting?" Mark asked quickly.

"Not enough to m-make me want to stop."

Mark hesitated, studying Raven. All he saw was a sensual, determined lover staring back at him. He was so gorgeous.

Raven started to turn towards him, but stopped on a quickly indrawn breath.

"Raven—"

Raven ignored the concern and tugged at him insistently. "Kiss m-me."

Mark suddenly realised how much of an idiot he was. It would be much more comfortable for Raven with his banged up ribs and heavy cast if he lay still while letting Mark do all the work. He cursed himself for not thinking of it sooner and quickly moved to lean over Raven. He offered a light kiss to Raven's lips by way of unspoken apology.

Raven smiled and pulled him in for a more demanding kiss.

When they finally broke apart they were both breathless and Mark's cock was rock hard behind his zipper. Glancing down, he saw that Raven was in a similar predicament. Unable to help himself, Mark palmed the inviting bulge.

Raven moaned and thrust up into his hand. It was a sheer delight seeing the lust clouding his lover's eyes.

"There's one…c-condition," Raven suddenly said, and Mark froze.

"What?"

Raven's eyes cleared a little as he stared up at him. "All my d-days, freely and without hesitation, but…you have to p-promise to live them to the fullest with me. No more worrying about things you c-can't do anything about. No second-guessing each other."

It was a pretty tall order and probably completely unrealistic. But Mark could certainly get behind the spirit in which it was intended. More than anything he wanted what Raven was promising for them. And seeing the way Raven looked at him right now, he believed in it too. Together they could do anything.

He took a deep, shuddering breath and released the last of the day's tension. "Cross my heart."

Raven's soft smile turned into a wide grin. He reached down to fumble with Mark's pants. Wrong handed and at an awkward angle, Mark had to help. And while he was there he helped himself to the pleasure of freeing Raven's gorgeous cock as well.

Mark settled into a more comfortable position, then turned slightly towards Raven until he was able to reach both their cocks.

"Let me," he murmured, and Raven nodded.

One hand on Raven, one hand on his own cock, Mark began to stroke them both at the same time. Up and down, caressing the sweet spot under the crowns in unison and watching as pre-cum leaked from the slit of Raven's cock to coat and wet the mushroom-shaped head. It caught the golden light from the candles and glistened invitingly.

But as wonderful as it was to feel Raven in his hand, to be able to pleasure them together like this, it was also slightly clumsy and awkward. And he wanted more. He wanted to taste Raven. To drink him in.

He shifted until he knelt between Raven's legs and took his lover's cock into his mouth. The salty drops of pre-cum over his tongue made him moan in delight. He drew more of Raven's cock in until the tip touched the back of his throat. He couldn't quite pull off the porno swallow trick, but he put everything he had into making the sensation of his tongue and lips and the suction of his mouth as he moved up and down over Raven's cock as pleasurable as he could possibly make it.

"M-Mark!"

Oh, he wanted so much more of that desperate, needy sound. Forever.

Redoubling his efforts, he reached down and stroked his own hard shaft. He wanted to come with Raven so badly.

"Oh M-Mark! I... Oh! M-more."

Running completely on instinct, Mark reached up under Raven's soft cotton shirt and tweaked one hard, peaked nipple. And that was all it took. His mouth was flooded with the creamy, salty essence of Raven's seed. The sensation pushed him over the edge at the same time. Lightning bolts of pleasure raced up his spine. His balls pulled tight and his cock exploded, sending long splashes of cum over his hand. He moaned around Raven's cock in ecstasy.

He stroked himself through the orgasm as he continued to swallow Raven down and gently licking him clean. He finally let the softening shaft slip from between his lips right before he knew the sensation would be too much for Raven to bear.

He pulled back and looked up the length of his lover's body. Raven shuddered with an aftershock, his eyes still closed and his lips parted sensually.

"M-Mark."

Mark couldn't resist. He carefully crawled up the bed, making sure to keep his weight well away from bruised ribs and broken arm, then bent to taste the sweet look of euphoria from Raven's lips. Gently thrusting his tongue into Raven's mouth, he shared the last drops of cum still lingering there. Raven groaned in answer and thrust his tongue back, licking and exploring to find all the sweet, secret places inside Mark's mouth.

As the kiss came to an end, he realised there was a mess where he'd shot his load over Raven's leg and across the sheets. But Mark couldn't bring himself to be overly worried. He'd clean the sheets for Raven tomorrow and a hundred times over to do what they had just done again.

Retrieving several tissues from the box on the nightstand, Mark cleaned up as best he could for the moment so there wouldn't be a wet spot. But he was more interested in cuddling than fussing.

Finally, spent and blissfully exhausted, Mark crawled into place and lay down beside Raven. He pulled the blanket up from the foot of the bed to keep them both warm as they snuggled together in the afterglow.

Mark couldn't deny there had been a little pain for them. His bumps and bruises, Raven's arm and ribs. But so much pleasure and love at the same time it was worth it. Even with every twinge and ache, it would always be worth it.

"I love you," Raven whispered.

A lump formed in Mark's throat and his breath caught. The candles flickered gently and everything was perfect.

"I love you too."

Epilogue

Raven was so excited he could hardly contain it. The exhilaration building in his chest threatened to go supernova at any second. He'd done it. Finally, after years of patience and practice and plain old-fashioned persistence — going back time after time following yet another knock back — he'd sold his novel to a major publishing house.

Young adult fiction. Sixty thousand words of blood, sweat and tears. The possibility of more books in the same series. Raven's smile was so big it literally hurt his cheeks. He had to share the moment with Mark. And after that he wanted to tell all the friends he'd unexpectedly found at Sandpipers Restaurant. He wanted to shout it out loud to the world. He was giddy with the thrill of success after so much hard work.

Raven pushed through the door into the kitchen and zeroed in on Mark. His lover stood by one of the counters, concentrating on his knife strokes as he diced stalks of celery with fast, efficient movements.

As if sensing his presence as he walked towards him, Mark lifted his head and smiled.

"Hey, gorgeous," Mark said as he set down the knife and wiped his hands on a cloth. "How'd the session go?"

There was a touch of concern in his lover's eyes.

About three weeks ago, he'd finally found someone he felt he could talk to about his life with Maria. Dr Brooks was quiet and soft-spoken and seemed genuinely interested in helping him work through it all without judgement or censure. But it hadn't been easy by any stretch of the imagination. He didn't want to start talking about today's meeting right now.

"It was f-fine." He smiled and leaned in to give Mark a peck on the lips to reassure his overprotective lover.

"Really?"

Raven resisted the urge to roll his eyes. "Uh huh."

Mark searched his face. Raven could see him struggle not to press for more—to make sure he really was okay. And in the end he managed to resist.

Instead he just gave Raven a quick hug and simply said, "Good."

Raven hugged Mark back and stole another, slightly longer kiss.

"So, to what do I owe the pleasure?" Mark asked with a smile when the kiss finally came to an end. "Where are the boys?"

"Brody t-took them upstairs for a snack. I w-wanted to show you something."

Raven pulled out the letter that was the culmination of so many hopes and dreams and handed it over, waiting with breathless anticipation as Mark scanned through the text.

"Wow! That's fantastic!" Mark pulled him into another hug, a huge grin on his face. "I'm so proud of you."

The glow that had been steadily building inside Raven exploded. He hugged Mark back fiercely. He was so blessed. A year and a half ago he would never have dared dream he could find someone like Mark—someone that loved him so completely he openly shared in his joy and triumph. When he'd moved to Riversands with Ryan, all he'd wanted was a chance to start again. Now he and Ryan were safe and happy and surrounded by so many people that cared for them. It was almost too much.

Mark gave him a squeeze as they continued the embrace. "You okay?" he murmured.

"Yeah." Raven swallowed and pulled away reluctantly. He swiped at the corner of his eyes as he scanned the room, hoping no one else had noticed. Then frowned. "W-Where is everyone?"

He'd been so caught up in telling Mark his news and the rush of emotion surging through him, he hadn't realised the kitchen was unusually quiet. Normally there would be at least another chef and a kitchen hand prepping for the evening at this time of the afternoon, even mid-week, which were traditionally slower nights.

In the same moment he asked the question, Andy stepped out of the kitchen office, Zak following at his heels.

"We'll be sorry to see you go," Zak said as they stopped at the back door.

Andy held his hand out and shook Zak's. "Thanks. I mean for everything, you know. It's been—" Andy cleared his throat. "It's been a blast."

Zak hesitated for a second then drew Andy forward for a quick hug. "Don't be a stranger."

Raven stared in disbelief as Andy turned and all but ran out the back door. "What's g-going on?"

"Andy's leaving," Mark said.

"W-what? Why? W-when did this happen?"

"Just today. He came in and said he couldn't stay."

"He's l-leaving right away? But...he's not even giving any n-notice?"

Mark shook his head. "Apparently not. I don't know what's going on. I tried to talk to him. He just said he had to go." Mark looked away. "I can't imagine what they talked about in there, but he must have had a pretty damn good story. Zak wasn't happy when Andy came in and told us. Now..."

"You okay?" Raven asked. Mark liked Andy. The two not only worked well together, they'd become good friends over the last few months. They all had.

"Yeah."

Raven didn't believe it. Mark looked hurt by Andy's sudden departure without so much as a backwards glance. Sure they'd probably stay in touch, but it wouldn't be the same. The kitchen crew were close and worked long hours together. Andy's leaving like this had to sting. Raven couldn't say he didn't feel a little hurt himself.

He looked over to the door where Zak still stood, staring after Andy. A sudden thought sent a shiver of unease down his spine.

"Where's D-Dave?"

"Day off."

Raven swung back to stare at Mark. He didn't know what to say. He'd seen Jaime on his way in, but she hadn't said anything. She hadn't looked upset at all.

Maybe they knew, but Raven had a bad feeling they didn't.

"Hey," Mark said, jostling him with his hip. "He's a big boy. I'm sure he knows what he's doing."

"M-maybe." But Raven wasn't so sure.

"Don't look so worried. Things will work out."

Raven couldn't help smiling at the new, relaxed attitude Mark was increasingly embracing. He'd really started to ease up on stressing out all the time.

"I can't see Dave taking any of this lying down," Mark added.

"N-no. I just hope he's ok-kay."

"Yeah." There was a long moment of silence. Then Mark reached for him. "Come on, we should be celebrating your big news."

Raven raised an eyebrow as Mark pulled him close. The wicked gleam in his eyes was an unmistakable proposition.

"You're w-working tonight, remember," Raven pointed out, but he didn't resist Mark's insistent tugging and settled happily against his lover's hard body.

"I'm due a break."

"Really?"

"Uh huh."

"Well, you should d-definitely take it before things heat up in h-here."

"Actually, I'm kind of hoping you could help me heat things up right now."

Raven chuckled. "Your l-lines haven't improved."

"Hey, you're the writer of the family. Maybe you should write me some new ones."

Family. Raven stilled. Yeah, they were. Mark was his. And Ryan's. And they were a family.

"I... I l-like..." It was suddenly hard to get the words out. "I l-like the w-way you said that."

Mark searched his face. "Family?"

"Y-yeah."

Raven couldn't elaborate. He just couldn't find the words. But in the end he didn't have to. Mark leaned in and kissed him so thoroughly there wasn't any need to say more.

Well, maybe there was one thing.

"I love you."

"I love you, too."

Raven closed his eyes and smiled. Life just didn't get any more perfect than that.

About the Author

Jade Archer was born in 2010 after a prolonged pregnancy and labour of over 34 years! I've decided she is about 24, enjoys long walks in the country because she does not have five kids and a husband to care for, eats as much chocolate as she wants because she never has to worry about putting on weight (must be all those long walks!) and can often be found planning her next whirlwind world tour or endlessly typing away (without any interruptions) on another hot and steamy erotic romance. It might be space pirates; it might be shifters or a lonely vampire with a hunger for the girl next door, one thing is for sure, she loves variety and cannot wait to meet the next characters destined to fall in love.

Jade Archer loves to hear from readers.

You can find her contact information, website details and author profile page at http://www.total-e-bound.com.

Total-E-Bound Publishing

www.total-e-bound.com

Take a look at our exciting range of literagasmic™
erotic romance titles and discover pure quality
at Total-E-Bound.